TOMMORROW I'LL MISS YOU

Theresa Kelly

SAINT LOUIS

Our God reigns!
For Shiloh Elizabeth Houseworth—1-24-99
Welcome to God's world!

Cover Illustation by Sandy Rabinowitz.

Scripture quotations are taken from the HOLY BIBLE, NEW INTERNATIONAL VERSION®. NIV®. Copyright © 1973, 1978, 1984 by International Bible Society. Used by permission of Zondervan Publishing House. All rights reserved.

Copyright © 1999 Concordia Publishing House
3558 S. Jefferson Avenue, St. Louis, MO 63118-3968
Manufactured in the United States of America

Library of Congress Cataloging-in-Publication Data

Kelly, Theresa, 1952–
    Tomorrow I'll miss you / Theresa Kelly.
        p.   cm. — (Aloha Cove)
    Summary: Life in their newly blended family on Kwaljalein, one of the
    Marshall Islands in the Pacific, is disturbed when Tabitha's real mother
    resumes contact with her after many years.
    ISBN 0–570–05484–0
    [1. Mothers and daughters Fiction. 2. Stepfamilies Fiction. 3. Islands
    Fiction. 4. Kwajalein Island (Marshall Islands) Fiction. 5. Christian
    life Fiction.] I. Title. II. Series.
    PZ7.K2985To   1999   99–21168
    [Fic]–DC21   CIP

1 2 3 4 5 6 7 8 9 10   08 07 06 05 04 03 02 01 00 99

"How can next week be Halloween already?" Cass said in wonder as she set the table for supper. "I guess it's true that time flies when you're having fun."

Her stepsister, Tabitha, made a face at her from across the table. "It flies even when you're not," she said darkly. "I'm definitely not having any fun in my physics class, but the semester is zooming by anyway. Midterms are coming up, and I'm still struggling to maintain a C in the class. I'd hoped by now to have it up to a B, but I'm running out of time."

"Maybe if you and Micah would do something constructive on your dates, like have him tutor you," Cass said lightly, "you might have an A+. That's what he got when he took the class last year." She shook her head in mock disappointment. "Instead, you choose to spend all your time gazing into each other's eyes and whispering gooey stuff."

While Mom laughed from across the room, Tabitha pretended to be insulted. "How do you know what we do on our dates?" she said. "What do you do, sneak around and spy on us?"

"Yup, Logan and I need all the help we can get," Cass retorted good-naturedly, referring to her boyfriend. "You and Micah are our role models. We really look up to y'all when it comes to dating tips."

"You girls had better change the subject before your Dad gets home," Mom said good-naturedly as she stirred the beef stew she had made for dinner. "I don't have a problem with the fact that you're dating. But he's a father, and he doesn't like to think about it, much less hear you discuss it. If he had his way, neither of you would start dating until you were 35. At least," she added with a laugh.

"I'm glad we have one rational parent." Tabitha shared an amused look with Cass. "Imagine what a nightmare my life would have been if Dad hadn't married you," she continued, addressing Mom. "I'd probably be stuck in a tower by now, watching life pass me by like some modern-day Rapunzel." She gave a delicate shudder. "A fate worse than death."

"Well, good thing I came along and saved you." Mom replaced the lid on the pot of stew and grinned over her shoulder at Tabitha. "Although to be honest, that was the last thing on my mind when I married your Dad this past summer."

"No kidding," Tabitha drawled. "And all along I thought you married him to get me."

"Hey!" protested Cass. "Why would she need you when she already has me?"

"I need both of you in my life," Mom declared quickly, ending the argument Cass and Tabitha had waged since their parents had gotten married in July. "God knew that, which is why He brought Steve and me together when he and Tabitha came back to Tennessee for his twentieth high school reunion. The Lord's timing is always perfect. He knew we were ready to be a family. Think of what we all got as a result of the marriage. I acquired another daughter, as well as the world's most perfect husband. You girls now have each other. And Steve has a harem of females who dote on him."

Cass snorted. "I wonder what he'd have to say about that. Except for you, there's not a lot of doting that goes on around here. Tabitha and I just give him a hard time."

"That's our job," Tabitha said firmly. "What else are kids for?"

"And sometimes he brings it on himself. Like worrying about us dating and how we're doing in school and what will happen when we go back to the mainland for college. At least he doesn't have to worry about us driving since there aren't any privately owned vehicles on the island. I haven't heard of any fatal bike crashes since moving here."

"Yeah, what's the worst that can happen on a bike?" Tabitha laughed. "We wind up with a few bumps and bruises. Dad doesn't know how easy he has it. This is the perfect place to raise teenagers. There's absolutely nothing we can get into around here."

Cass frowned. She wasn't sure, but she thought she detected a note of dissatisfaction under the laughter in Tabitha's voice. But how could Tabitha be tired of living on Kwajalein? She always said she loved it here—and it had never seemed to bother her before that there really wasn't much happening on this tiny island in the middle of the Pacific Ocean.

Before she could ask Tabitha, Dad arrived. Whistling a cheerful, if off-key, tune, he strolled into the kitchen from the back porch. He immediately went to Mom and swept her into his arms for a kiss. Cass and Tabitha groaned.

"Yuck! I don't think people your age should be acting like this. I mean, honestly—you're almost forty, Dad," Tabitha said.

Dad just shrugged. "So sue me. I can't help it if I'm madly in love with my wife. Oh," he added with a twinkle in his eyes, "and I'm pretty crazy about you girls too."

"Gee, thanks," Cass said sarcastically. "I don't know

about Tabitha, but I really feel special now."

Dad walked around the counter to playfully tap her nose. "You know you have a special place in my heart."

It was true. Cass did know it. Having lost her father in a car crash when she was two, she'd been learning all about the joys of having a dad since her mother's marriage to Steve Spencer. Sometimes it amazed her that she'd managed to live fourteen years without one. Steve brought so much happiness and security to her life—she could no longer imagine what life would be like without him.

Tabitha edged close to Dad, slipped her arm through his, and pouted up at him. "What about me? Do I have a special place too?"

Dad dropped a kiss on her forehead. "You, my dear, took up residence the first moment I laid eyes on your little, scrunched-up, red face in the delivery room."

"Oh, Dad." Tabitha gave an impatient flounce. "You've always said I was a cute baby."

"You were the most beautiful baby I'd ever seen." Dad paused, flashed her a wicked smile, and added, "Red, scrunched-up face and all."

Cass smiled to herself at Tabitha's disgruntled expression. Her stepsister had a tendency to be somewhat vain when it came to her blond, good looks, and she obviously didn't like Dad's less-than-flattering description of her as an infant.

Cass and Tabitha quickly finished setting the table and they all sat down to dinner. As usual, they held hands while Dad asked the blessing.

"Father, we thank You for this food and for the hands that prepared it. Bless it to our nourishment and us to Your service. In Jesus' name, amen."

"Amen," echoed the others.

"So what did my family do today?" Dad asked as Mom served the stew.

Cass listened while Mom described her morning of volunteering at the high school library and her afternoon of preparing the lesson for the Sunday night youth group she and Dad led. She couldn't help reminiscing about their life back in Tennessee before the huge changes marrying Steve had brought about.

As a single mother, Mom had little time for the extras. She did her best to work around her job and attend Cass' school and sports activities, but she wasn't always successful. Fortunately, Cass' grandparents, who lived in the same town, were able to fill in for her when she couldn't make it, but it wasn't the same as far as Cass was concerned. She was glad that Mom had the time now to volunteer, but she couldn't help being a little resentful it had happened during her junior year in high school. It would have meant so much more when she was younger.

Still, Cass continued to muse as she savored Mom's beef stew, *I can't complain too much. We hardly ever had suppers like this back when she worked.*

After Mom finished giving a rundown of the events of her day, Dad turned to Tabitha. "What about you, sweetie? What new and exciting things happened to you today?"

Tabitha shrugged. "Like anything new and exciting ever happens to me."

Cass shot her a curious look. *Something is definitely not right,* she thought. *That's the second time she's hinted that she's not happy.*

Dad didn't seem to notice anything wrong. "Come on, you must have something to talk about. Did anything unusual happen in one of your classes? Did you and your friends do something interesting after school?"

Tabitha made a face. "School was boring, as usual. Micah and I spent a couple of hours at the library this afternoon. He needed to do research for a history paper, and I had to look up some magazine articles for current events."

She broke off a piece of biscuit and popped it into her mouth before adding as an afterthought, "I also stopped by and picked up the mail. There was another letter from my mother."

Cass almost dropped her spoon.

Dad's face tightened with displeasure, but his voice was nonchalant. "That's the third time you've heard from her since last month, isn't it?"

Tabitha frowned. "You know it is. You're the one keeping track of how many times she's written."

Dad took a moment before responding. "So what did she have to say?"

"The usual." Tabitha took a spoonful of stew.

"Which is?"

"She'd like me to write more often and send pictures. She told me about what she and the kids have been up to." Tabitha waved a breezy hand, but Cass didn't buy it. She knew the letters from Tabitha's real mother always upset her. "Yada, yada. Like I said, the usual. You can read it if you'd like. I'm not keeping anything from you."

"I didn't mean to imply you were."

Cass caught the glance Dad sent Mom and decided to come to his rescue. "Are you going to write back to her?"

"I don't know." Tabitha stared down at her bowl of stew.

"Well, do you like hearing from her?" Cass asked.

Tabitha still didn't look up. "I guess. The problem is, I don't know what to write back. I don't have that much to tell her. She does all this neat stuff, like weaving and painting. What do I do? I go to school, come home, hang out with my friends, go to sleep, get up, and do it all over again. Big whoop. Like she wants to read about that week after week."

Cass' stomach sank. So it was her mother, Beth, reappearing in her life that was making Tabitha unhappy with her so-called boring life on Kwaj.

"Have you written to her about the youth group?" Mom asked quietly.

Tabitha shot her an "are you kidding?" look. "I don't think my mother would be interested in hearing about what a church group is up to. You've read her letters. She's into New Age stuff. You know—crystals and all that. She says traditional religion is a bunch of garbage."

Cass frowned. "How come she's allowed to write whatever she wants to about what she believes, but you're not?"

Mom smiled slightly. "Cass has a point."

The defiant thrust of Tabitha's chin clearly said she didn't want to talk about it. "She's never said I can't write about my beliefs," she replied stiffly. "I just choose not to."

"But you and your mother are supposed to be finding out about each other. How can you leave out something as important to you as your faith?"

Tabitha glared at her. "What's it to you what I do and don't write about?"

Cass met and held her gaze without flinching. "You're my sister. I care about you. I guess I figure that gives me the right to ask questions."

"You're my *step*sister." Tilting her head back, Tabitha stared down her nose at Cass. "I have a real sister, remember? My mother's baby girl, Sunshine. There's also my brother, Peace. Don't forget him. They're my real siblings."

Too stunned to say anything, Cass could only gape at Tabitha.

"Tabitha Joi," Dad said quickly in a low, quiet, and terrifying voice, "that was totally uncalled-for. Apologize to Cass. Right now."

"Why?" challenged Tabitha. "What I said is true. She's not my sister. Okay, technically, Sunshine is my half-sister, but at least we're related. Cass and I aren't."

"Tabitha—" Dad began.

"It's okay," Cass broke in. She didn't want Tabitha getting in trouble on her account. "I know what Tabitha meant. She's right. I am just her stepsister." Try as she might, she couldn't keep from sounding hurt.

Tabitha had the grace to look ashamed. "Maybe I shouldn't have put it like that," she conceded. "You know how I feel about you. But I guess I don't like you assuming you're allowed to pry into my private life just because our parents are married."

"Don't worry. It won't happen again." Cass stared down at her stew, hoping to hide the tears she felt coming.

"Tabitha, what is the matter with you?" Dad said, his tone only somewhat less scary. "You've been in a bad mood ever since we sat down to eat."

"I'm fine," Tabitha snapped. "Excuse me for being human. Everybody has an off day every now and then."

"Yes, but yours seem to coincide with hearing from your mother." He paused. "Perhaps it's time I exercise my parental rights and forbid you to communicate with her anymore."

Cass glanced up in shock. Tabitha's face had gone white. "You can't do that!" In her agitation, Tabitha balled up her napkin and tossed it on the table. "She's my mother. You can't keep us from writing to each other."

"I can—and I will—if I decide it's in your best interest to do so," Dad coolly informed her. "It's my job to look out for you."

Tabitha turned to Mom. "You won't let him stop me from writing to her, will you?"

Mom shifted uneasily in her chair. "Sweetie, you're going to have to trust your Dad and me to look out for you," she replied slowly. "We'll pray about the situation and we'll continue to talk to you about it. I'm sure we'll eventually come up with a solution that everyone can live with."

"Does it bother you that my mother has started writing to me?" Tabitha stared challengingly at Mom.

Cass looked back down at her soup, unable to stand the pain in Mom's eyes.

"I'm not entirely comfortable with it."

"Oh. Why not?"

"Well, quite honestly I'm suspicious of her motives. There's something fishy about the timing."

"I know," Tabitha said, and Cass looked up in surprise. "I keep asking myself why now. Why is she suddenly interested in me after all these years?"

"Would you like to talk about it?" Mom asked softly.

Tabitha shook her head. "No. I need more time to figure out how I feel about the possibility of having her in my life. Then maybe I'll be able to talk about it."

"Don't you think discussing the situation with us might help you make up your mind?" suggested Dad.

Again, Tabitha shook her head. "You're pretty biased when it comes to my mother." The glance she sent Mom was apologetic. "Both of you are. I figure Dad's told you his side of the story, so you probably don't like her very much either."

Mom gave a slight nod. "Even so, I'd do my best to listen to what you have to say and respond fairly."

"I know you would." Tabitha emphasized the you, then glared at Dad. "I'm not so sure Dad could, though. Admit it—you've been mad at Beth ever since the divorce."

"Of course I have, with good reason." He pushed aside his bowl of stew. "I don't want you to forget what she did."

"I won't. I don't think any child could forget being abandoned." There was a bleakness in Tabitha's tone and face that tore at Cass' heart. "But that doesn't mean I can't forgive her, does it?"

"Of course not," Mom said quickly.

"As long as Beth admits that walking out on you was wrong," Dad added. "You can't forgive someone who refuses to acknowledge their guilt."

"When Jesus was hanging on the cross, He forgave the people who put Him there, and I don't remember them asking Him for forgiveness," Tabitha said quickly.

Dad paused, then gave a short laugh. "You're right. Maybe Beth doesn't have to apologize, but I'd feel a lot better about things if she'd finally take responsibility for her actions. To my knowledge, she hasn't addressed the issue in any of the letters she's sent."

"No, she hasn't." Tabitha retrieved her napkin and began smoothing it out. "It bothers me that she hasn't mentioned it, but I don't want to be the one to bring it up." She shifted suddenly. "Can I be excused? I'm not really hungry anymore, and I don't want to talk about this."

Cass caught the hesitant look Mom and Dad gave each other before Mom finally nodded. "Sure. Let us know if you need anything later."

Tabitha started to say something to her as she left the table, but Cass just looked away.

CHAPTER 2

Awhile later, Tabitha approached Cass' closed door and knocked hesitantly.

"Yes?" came the wary response from inside.

"It's me. Can I come in?"

There was a long pause, then Cass called gruffly, "Fine."

Tabitha found her stepsister lying on the bed with her arms folded beneath her head, staring at the ceiling. When Cass didn't acknowledge her presence, Tabitha walked to the desk chair and sat down.

"What are you doing?"

Snorting, Cass drawled, "What does it look like?"

"Thinking?"

"Ding-ding! Right answer. Johnny, tell our lovely contestant what she's won."

Tabitha ignored the sarcasm. "What are you thinking about?"

Cass glanced away from the ceiling long enough to shoot her a baleful look. "How to bump you off and dispose of the body without getting caught."

"You want some help?"

Cass narrowed her eyes. "What are you saying?"

"That I deserve to be tarred and feathered for what I said

to you before." Tabitha sighed. "I don't know what's wrong with me. I've never been this crabby for this long. I know I hurt your feelings, and I feel awful about it."

Rolling onto her side, Cass propped her head up on her hand. "You have been pretty touchy."

Tabitha looked out the window at the lingering early evening sunshine. "Would you like to go for a walk? I want to talk, but not here." She stirred restlessly. "Lately, I feel like the walls are closing in on me. Even Kwaj is starting to seem too small."

She knew that would get Cass' attention. Tabitha loved the island, and for her to say anything even remotely negative about it meant something was seriously wrong.

Cass sat up and reached for her sandals. "Okay, but you better tell me what's going on."

After Tabitha told their parents they were going out for a while, they left by the back door. Crossing the lawn, they clambered over the rocks onto the beach that stretched about a mile and a half in each direction.

"Which way?" asked Cass.

Tabitha immediately pointed left. "We're less likely to run into anybody if we head toward the school."

They walked in silence for a few minutes. The tide was out, leaving the waves to break about fifty yards from the shore.

"It's so peaceful out here," murmured Cass. "I wonder what it'll be like when I get back to civilization someday, with all the different sights and sounds. Here there's no hustle and bustle. No cars honking or dogs barking, no birds chirping or construction sounds."

Tabitha looked at her curiously. "Do you miss it?"

"Civilization you mean?" Tabitha nodded, and Cass shrugged. "Not as much as I did when I first got here."

Tabitha didn't respond. She dropped her head and scuffed the toes of her sandals into the sand as she walked.

"I've been wondering what I've missed by living here practically all my life."

Cass turned to her in amazement. "You have? You? The person who's spent the past four months trying to convince me Kwajalein is heaven on earth?"

"Me." Tabitha gave her a wry smile. "I can hardly believe it either. It's all part of this strange mood I've found myself in since—"

"The fall formal," Cass said suddenly, "four weeks ago last Saturday."

Tabitha just stared at her, startled. "How do you know it started then?"

"That's the day you got the first letter from your mother," Cass said. "You haven't been yourself ever since."

"So you blame my mother too?" Tabitha frowned.

"If you're going to jump down my throat before this conversation even gets started, we might as well forget it. I thought you said you wanted to talk, not argue."

Tabitha suddenly felt very hollow. "You're right. I don't know why I automatically leap to Beth's defense every time someone says something that sounds the least bit critical."

"I'm glad you brought it up because I don't get it either. I mean, honestly—the woman walked out on you." Cass looked out at the ocean. "Why you feel you owe her one shred of consideration is completely beyond me."

Tabitha couldn't help laughing. "You don't take very kindly to somebody you care about being treated badly."

"No I don't. But really—what gives with you and your mother?" Cass' attitude was more puzzled than accusing. "Why don't you just tell her to get lost?"

"Because—" Tabitha spread her arms in a helpless gesture as she attempted to convey how she felt, "she's my mother."

"You could have fooled me," scoffed Cass. "We've talked about this before. Real mothers don't abandon their children, especially while they're still babies. They also don't have anything to do with them for twelve years then expect to pick up where they left off. Personally, I think Beth has a lot of nerve."

"Half the time, so do I." Tabitha slipped her hands into her shorts pockets and shrugged dejectedly. "The rest of the time, I find myself imagining what it would be like to spend some time with her, getting to know her and her two kids."

"In any of these fantasies, do you ever imagine having a conversation in which she explains to you why she left you and your father all those years ago?"

"Of course."

"Does any of it make sense?" It was clear from Cass' tone that she doubted it.

"Well … no," Tabitha was forced to admit. "Just because I can't come up with a logical explanation doesn't mean she didn't have a perfectly good reason for doing what she did," she added, trying to sound convincing when she wasn't fully convinced herself.

"Uh-huh. Sure." Cass shot her an exasperated look. "How understanding of you to excuse your mother's totally outrageous behavior."

"Hmm. Let's hear what you really think," Tabitha said sarcastically.

"Well, I don't have a lot of respect for people who abandon their children," drawled Cass. "Call me old-fashioned, but I think parents should stick around while their kids are growing up. Like your Dad did."

Tabitha brushed back several strands of hair the wind had blown across her face and anchored them behind an ear. "Way to kick a person when she's down." She gave Cass a wry smile. "I agree with you. It's just—" She sighed sadly. "I'm so confused. I know I should tell my mother to take a hike, but for some reason I can't."

"You want me to do it for you? I'll write her a letter, and

you can sign it."

"Don't tempt me. I'm so anxious to get this thing settled, I might take you up on it." Tabitha sighed. "No, I realize this is something I have to take care of myself. Unfortunately, I can't do that until I figure out how I want to handle it."

"Don't worry. You'll know what to do when the time comes." Cass bumped shoulders with her in a gesture of affection. "I have faith in you."

Tabitha looked at her in surprise. "You do? Why?"

"Because I've learned once you get past stressing about things, you're usually very sensible. Plus," Cass went on, "Mom, Dad, and I are praying for you. You'll make the right decision."

Touched, Tabitha smiled. "Thanks. I'll keep that in mind whenever I start agonizing over what to do."

They reached the rocky portion of the beach and opted to turn back instead of climbing over the boulders that blocked their path. Their conversation on the return trip was on lighter and much more interesting topics—Micah and Logan—so by the time they returned home and went off to do homework, Tabitha felt much better.

CHAPTER 3

The weekend arrived in a swirl of wind-driven rain. Cass had learned that nothing was quite as wet as a tropical storm, and she dressed accordingly Saturday morning to go over to her friend, Rianne Thayer's, house. Regardless of her poncho, however, she still felt like a drowned rat by the time she arrived.

"Get in here," Rianne laughingly urged from the front porch as Cass leaned her bike against a tree and made a mad dash across the lawn.

Reaching shelter, Cass pushed the poncho hood back from her face and shook herself. Her bangs were plastered to her forehead, but her auburn ponytail had stayed dry enough to bounce around her shoulders.

"Wow! Maybe I just should've swam over here." She withdrew a plastic bag containing her sandals from beneath her poncho. "I've learned something since moving here." She triumphantly held up the bag before opening it and letting the sandals drop to the porch floor. "Don't wear your sandals in the rain. Store them someplace dry until you get to where you're going then put them on." Slipping damp feet into them, she wiggled her toes. "Ah! That beats wet leather any day."

Rianne laughed. "I'm proud of you for learning such an essential lesson so quickly. It takes some people years to figure out how to keep their sandals dry during the rainy season."

"Go ahead, make fun of me." Cass waved a dismissive hand. "The more survival tips I pick up, the easier it makes life on this rock."

"Uh-oh." Leading the way into the house, Rianne glanced over her shoulder. "Are you in one of your 'I hate Kwaj' moods?"

"Not really." Cass waved hello to Rianne's younger brother, Robby, who was playing video games in the living room. "You won't believe it, but Tabitha's the one who's been badmouthing the island the past few days."

"No way!" Rianne paused on the stairs on her way up to her room. "What gives?"

Now that she'd started the conversation, Cass belatedly realized she probably shouldn't discuss it. "Uh ... I'm not sure. Maybe you should ask her."

Rianne shot her a knowing look. "You're not supposed to talk about it, huh?"

"Actually, I don't know if I am or not." Cass followed Rianne into her room. "So let's talk about something else. How are you and Josh doing?"

The sudden droop of Rianne's lips told Cass that all wasn't well. "Basically he's driving me nuts." She flopped down onto her bed. "One day everything's terrific then the next day it's like I don't even exist. Other than a couple of weeks around the time of the fall formal when he was really attentive, that's the way it's been. I'm about ready to end it."

Tossing her poncho over the back of Rianne's desk chair, Cass sank cross-legged to the floor. "I'm sorry. Y'all were so cute together at the formal. I figured you'd be together for a while. But if it's not working—" she stopped and shrugged, "it's not working. Time to move on to greener pastures."

"That's easy for you to say," grumbled Rianne. "You and Logan are getting along great."

Cass shrugged and lowered her face to hide the smile she knew always came with mention of Logan. "We're doing okay."

"Okay?" Rianne snorted. "You're in the running for couple of the year."

"No, that would be Tabitha and Micah. They're so disgustingly sweet together they make my teeth ache." Cass smiled as she pictured her stepsister and her boyfriend. "Actually, after all these years, they deserve to be happy. It's cute the way they secretly had a crush on each other but never wanted to admit it."

Rianne snapped her fingers. "Speaking of crushes, Randy told me he might ask one of the girls in his class to go to the movies next weekend."

"No kidding? Who?" demanded Cass.

"Stacy Jamieson. She's about your height—short brown hair and brown eyes. She hangs around with Holly Edwards and Anne Mott."

Cass nodded. "I know who you're talking about. I've seen her around. She seems really nice."

"She is. She and Randy are taking American History together, and the teacher teamed them up to do some project. She was over here three nights last week so they could work on it." Rianne smiled down at Cass. "Stacy reminds me of you. It doesn't seem to matter that Randy's in a wheelchair. She accepts him the way he is."

"Good," declared Cass. "She should. It's about time Randy started letting other people know what a catch he is."

"He couldn't have done it without you." Rianne's voice was thick with emotion. "When you accepted his invitation to the formal, you boosted his self-confidence a thousand percent. I think he finally realized, chair or no chair, he still has a lot to offer a girl."

Uncomfortable with Rianne's praise, Cass tried to deflect it. "Don't forget he's an incredibly good-looking guy with a dynamite personality. Fortunately for the female population on the island, he decided to quit hiding and go out there and break some hearts."

Rianne wagged a scolding finger at her. "I know what you're doing and I'm not going to let you get away with it. If it weren't for you treating Randy like a normal guy from the first moment you met him, he'd never have gotten up the courage to ask you to the dance. From there, it looks like he's going to branch out to asking other girls for dates."

"Are you saying I've created a monster?" teased Cass. "What happens if Randy turns into another Alex?"

Rianne groaned at the mention of a guy in their class famous for his romantic conquests. "Don't even joke around about something like that. If Randy ever showed any signs of turning into Alex Johnson, I'd have to disown him. Otherwise, I'd be too embarrassed to ever go out in public again."

"Don't worry," Cass assured her. "I honestly don't think Randy's capable of being as—what's the right word?—despicable as Alex. He has too much class."

"That's a relief." She giggled. "It's funny. I've never thought of my brother as classy before. Annoying, sure. Irritating, definitely. But classy? No way."

"Sometimes it helps to get someone else's point of view. It's hard to be objective when it comes to your own family." She hesitated, shifting her position to buy some time. "That reminds me of something I want to run past you. I got a letter from my friend, Janette, back in Tennessee."

"Great. I know you've been anxious to hear from her." When Cass didn't say anything, Rianne's expression turned uncertain. "It is great, right?"

"That's the thing." Cass leaned back on her hands and gazed up at her friend. "I hate to sound like I'm whining, but she hardly ever writes anymore, and when she does, it's about nothing."

"What do you mean? How can she write about nothing?"

"Well, maybe it's not about nothing," Cass said. "It's just that it's all about her and what she's doing. For example, I wrote to her about the formal. I even sent pictures. But in the letter that came from her a few days ago, she didn't respond to anything I wrote. She mentioned in passing that she'd gotten my letter, but that was it. Then she went on to tell me about a bunch of parties she'd been to and how she was asked to join one of the social clubs at school. She never used to go to parties. She said she didn't like the drinking she heard went on. And both of us swore we'd never join a social club because of the stupid initiation stuff and the fact that they were for snobs."

"Sounds like she's gone through some changes since the last time you saw her," Rianne said quietly.

"Some changes?" scoffed Cass. "Try a whole truckload of them. I feel like I hardly know her anymore." She didn't bother trying to hide her misery. "I never thought this would happen."

"I remember when we first moved here and my best friend back home and I vowed we wouldn't let time or distance come between us. We promised each other we'd pick up right where we left off the minute I got back." Rianne smiled crookedly. "We lasted about as long as you and Janette."

"It's so sad. I don't understand why two people like Jan and me, who've been friends forever, can't maintain a friendship, despite being thousands of miles apart." Cass felt like crying, but settled for a mournful sigh. "I wish there were some way I could go home, just for a little while, so Jan and I could talk. I know if we did, everything would be back to normal in no time."

"How about calling her?" suggested Rianne.

Cass made a face. "I've done that, and it's not the same. We never used to have a problem finding things to talk about, but now there are these long, awkward silences while we try to think of something to say. I hate it."

Sliding off the bed, Rianne sat on the floor, propping her back against the wall. Her brown eyes thoughtful, she studied Cass for several seconds. "I have a confession to make," she finally admitted. "There's a part of me—a part I'm not very proud of—that's sort of glad you and Janette aren't as friendly anymore. I like knowing you tell me things you don't tell her. I consider you my best friend, and I guess I hoped you'd start thinking the same about me."

Cass swallowed, emotion suddenly threatening to overwhelm her. "Actually, I'm closer to you than I am to just about anybody."

"Even Tabitha?" Rianne asked softly.

Cass hesitated. "I don't know how to explain it. It's different with Tabitha. Living in the same house, we have things in common that we don't share with anybody else. But then there's stuff I wouldn't dream of talking about with her and I'm pretty sure she feels the same way. I know she tells Kira things she doesn't tell me and I do the same with you. We've gotten closer than I ever imagined we would, but we still get testy with each other."

Rianne laughed. "When I first met you, I didn't have much hope that you two would ever get along. I'm impressed you haven't killed each other."

"It was touch-and-go there for awhile," Cass said, grinning as she remembered how much she and Tabitha disliked each other in the beginning. "Somehow we managed to hang in there until we got to the point where we actually enjoy each other's company."

"What Pastor Thompson said in last Sunday's sermon is

true then. God does work miracles," Rianne said. Before Cass could comment on her sarcastic tone, she went on, "Anyway, to get back to the situation with Janette, what are you planning to do about it?"

Cass' good mood evaporated and her disgruntled expression returned. "I don't know. I guess I should accept the fact we've both moved on in our lives, but I don't want to. I want to beat the odds and come up with some way to maintain our friendship, in spite of the separation. After all, I'll be going back to the mainland for college, and that's only two years away. Janette and I always planned to go to the same college and room together."

"You're the most determined person I know. If you want to hold onto your friendship, then you'll find a way to do it." Rianne gave her an impish look. "Just because I failed, along with everyone else I've ever known who was in the same boat, doesn't mean you won't succeed. Who knows? Maybe you'll wind up being the one in a million."

"Gee, thanks for the encouragement," drawled Cass. "I hope you don't plan on going into counseling as a career. Your patients would leave even more depressed than when they arrived."

"So I'm a realist." Rianne shrugged. "Sue me. I just call 'em like I see 'em."

"You make me want to go home and call Janette just to prove you're wrong." Cass' laugh came out more as a sigh. "But I'm afraid it would be another dead-end conversation, and I'd have to come crawling back here and admit you were right."

"It hardly seems worth the trip then." Rianne glanced at the window where the rain continued to lash at the glass. "Especially in this weather. Let's go downstairs and see what Randy's up to. You can tease him about Stacy and watch him turn all red."

Cass didn't make any move to get up, and neither did

Rianne. "You think he likes her in a different way than he likes me?" She wasn't sure how she felt about the possibility. She secretly enjoyed thinking she was special to Randy.

Rianne nodded enthusiastically. "There's no doubt about it. Randy practiced flirting with you, but he's serious about it with Stacy. Whenever he talks on the phone with her, he goes off someplace so he can be alone. With you, it doesn't matter if people listen in. He stays where he is."

"Oh." Although she didn't appreciate Rianne sharing this bit of information, Cass would've died rather than let her friend know. "Do you think Stacy's genuinely interested in him?"

Again, Rianne responded with a vigorous nod. "You should see her when she's around him. She gets all dreamy-eyed, and she hangs on his every word." She grinned. "Sort of like the way you act around Logan."

That got Cass' attention. "You're crazy," she protested. "I'm definitely not the hang-on-a-boy's-every-word type."

"Talk about being out of touch with your behavior," teased Rianne. "Maybe I should videotape you when you're with Logan so you can see how you really act."

Folding her arms, Cass glared at her. "You'd better be prepared to borrow your parents' video camera because seeing it with my own two eyes is the only way I'll ever believe you."

Pushing off from the floor, Rianne stood up and, laughing, held out her hand to Cass to help her up. "You're such a grouch sometimes. I don't know why I love you so much."

Cass reluctantly allowed herself to be pulled to her feet. "And you're such a pain I can't imagine why I put up with you."

"We're a match made in heaven." Rianne headed for the door. "Before we go bug Randy, let's get something to eat. It's been two whole hours since I had breakfast and I'm starving."

CHAPTER 4

At the Spencer house, Tabitha and her friend, Kira Alexander, had taken over the porch. With the rain drumming on the roof and the gray light filtering through the windows, Tabitha could almost convince herself it was a chilly fall day back on the mainland.

"I don't know why Cass misses autumn back home so much if this is what it's like," Tabitha said darkly. "Give me sunshine any day."

"Same here." Kira ran her fingers through her short cap of dark curls. "I feel like going into hibernation when it gets like this."

"How are we supposed to come up with a devotion for tomorrow night's meeting when it's so gloomy?" Tabitha propped her feet on the coffee table and stared out at the window. "We're supposed to prepare something uplifting. There's nothing uplifting happening. The weather's pathetic. School's a drag. Life basically stinks."

Kira grinned mischievously. "How can you say that when you and my brother are involved in the romance of the century?"

Tabitha's expression softened at the mention of Micah. "Okay, you've got me there. But I don't think Dad and

Mom would approve of a devotion written about Micah. I may find him inspiring, but he's hardly what they had in mind when they gave us this assignment."

"True." Kira reached for her Bible on the coffee table and set it on her lap. "There has to be something in here we can use. I have a concordance in the back. Give me some topics, and I'll see what I can find."

Drumming her fingers on the arm of her chair, Tabitha did her best to think of a subject. She kept drawing a blank until she finally threw her hands up in exasperation. "I'm not in the mood for this. Let's work on it later."

"Sorry, no can do. We've been putting it off for two weeks, and now it's crunch time. Come on, concentrate. We don't want to embarrass ourselves tomorrow night."

"How come it's my responsibility to come up with an idea?" Tabitha asked. "This is supposed to be a joint effort. You think of something."

Kira frowned, but her voice told Tabitha she was trying to be reasonable. "Okay. Let's see. Peer pressure. School. Parents." She snapped her fingers. "That's it. Let's do something about relating to parents. I'll bet the Bible has a lot to say about that."

Tabitha's stomach clenched. *Let's not*, she thought. *That's the last thing I feel like getting up and talking about.*

Aloud, she hedged, "I don't know. It doesn't seem like a good devotional topic to me. Maybe we should do something on grace or … uh …" She wracked her brain for another possibility. "What about sin? That's always a popular subject."

Kira arched an eyebrow at her. "Grace? Sin?" she echoed. "What do you think we are? Theological experts? Let's stick with something we know about and that other kids are interested in. Everybody has parent problems."

Tabitha glared at her. "I don't want to do a devotion about parents," she insisted stubbornly.

"Too bad." Kira was already flipping through the concordance. "Here we go—parents. Oh, good. There are—" she quickly counted, "twelve references."

"Hello?" Tabitha waved to get Kira's attention. "Didn't you hear me? I said I don't want to talk about parents."

"I heard you. I'm ignoring you." Keeping one finger in the concordance, Kira turned to the first Scripture verse. "This is from Proverbs. It says, 'Children's children are a crown to the aged, and parents are the pride of their children.' " She glanced up at Tabitha. "What do you think?"

Refusing to respond, Tabitha continued to glare at her.

"You're right. I'm not that crazy about it either. I'll look up the next one." She turned back to the concordance.

Tabitha noisily cleared her throat. "How come you're not listening to me?" she demanded when Kira glanced her way.

"Because nobody died and left you boss," Kira shot back. "First, you tell me to come up with an idea. Then when I do, you say you don't like it, and I'm supposed to think of something else. What makes you think you get to call all the shots?"

Tabitha felt her cheeks flush. "The fact that I'm a self-centered jerk who doesn't deserve to live?"

"Close enough." Kira smiled wryly. "Now that we have that settled, what do you say we work together on this devotion? I'll look up the Scriptures, and you decide which one we'll use."

"I can't talk you out of doing the devotion about parents?"

Kira's expression was adamant. "Nope. I really feel it's what we're supposed to talk about." She stared at Tabitha with a penetrating gaze. "You don't want to because of the situation with your mother, right?"

Tabitha shifted her attention from the window to a thread dangling from the hem of her shirt. "I'll feel like a hypocrite talking about parental relationships when

28

mine are so messed up."

"You're really starting to bug me," Kira testily informed her. "I'll admit you didn't have the easiest summer, but things have finally settled down. Are you enjoying life, though? No. You're getting all worked up about your mother and letting it affect things between you and your parents. What's the point? Do you like being upset?"

Stung by Kira's criticism, Tabitha bristled. "Of course not! You're acting like it's my fault I have this situation with my mother hanging over my head. I didn't ask her to start writing to me."

"Yes, but you could put an end to it," Kira replied quietly. "You could tell her to crawl back under the rock where she's been hiding all these years."

Tabitha gasped in shock. "That's a terrible thing to say! Don't forget you're talking about my mother. I'd never say something like that about your mother."

"That's because she doesn't deserve it. She acts like a mother." Some of the harshness left Kira's voice. "What I'm trying to say is, remember who's stood by you and raised you. Think about how Cass' Mom has stepped in and been more of a mother to you in four months than your own mother's been in twelve years. Don't let your birth mother poison your relationship with the people who've loved and supported you all along, not just when they felt like it."

Tabitha's face tightened with suspicion. "Have you been talking to Cass?"

"Not about this. Why?"

"Because I feel like the two of you are ganging up on me," Tabitha said darkly. "I wish you'd both back off and let me decide on my own how I'm going to handle things with my mother. I don't like being pushed into a corner."

"Okay." Kira raised her hands in surrender. "I won't pressure you. I just hope you make the right decision," she added under her breath.

29

"I heard that," snapped Tabitha. "Honestly, I don't know why you and Cass aren't best friends. The two of you are exactly alike. You're both pigheaded."

Kira grinned. "Thank you. I admire Cass' stubbornness so I'll take that as a compliment."

Throwing her hands up in the air, Tabitha growled her exasperation. "You're impossible. Can't you even tell when you've been insulted?"

"Sure, but I'm trying to practice turning the other cheek. You remember the devotion Dan and Justin did last week at the meeting, don't you?" Kira held up her Bible and gave it an enticing shake. "Which brings me back to why I'm here. Are we going to do this devotion or not?"

"What if I said not?" challenged Tabitha.

"I'd go find your parents and tell them you're not cooperating." Kira smirked. "Ever since I've known you, everybody's parents and all the teachers have always made a big deal out of how eager to please you are. You don't want to ruin your reputation, do you?"

Tabitha sniffed and glared at her. "Maybe it's time I started standing up for myself more. Maybe I'm tired of people taking me for granted. It might be nice to be known as undependable and irresponsible for a change."

Kira frowned. "What's up with you? Really, Tabitha—what's going on?"

Tabitha shifted restlessly in her seat. "Maybe all the stuff that happened this summer is finally catching up with me." She attempted a light laugh and a casual wave. "Forget what I said. I'm not planning on changing a single one of the many wonderful things you know and love about me." She made a comic face to show she was teasing. "I'll go on being good old reliable Tabitha till death do us part. Now," she gestured toward the Bible, "let's get this show on the road. I'm supposed to go to an early movie with your brother, and I need time to get all spiffed up."

Kira stared at her for a moment, and Tabitha knew she was trying to decide what to believe. Tabitha gave her another smile, slightly more heartfelt. Kira sighed. "Fine." She opened to the concordance and located the next Scripture listing. "Let's see what Matthew has to say on the subject."

While Kira flipped through the Bible, locating different verses, Tabitha alternated between staring out the window and pretending to pay attention. She'd deal with it only when she had to. After all, now that her mother was back in the picture, she had more parents than the average person needed.

CHAPTER 5

"Nobody move! I'll get it!"

When the bell rang for the fifth time in as many minutes, Cass jumped up from the couch to run to the door. She flung it open to reveal a trio of costumed children shouting, "Trick or treat!" and jockeying for position to be the first one to be rewarded with candy. Cass picked up the bowl Mom had placed next to the door and grinned.

"Let me think," she teased. "Should the ladybug be first? Or how about the football player? Or maybe Cinderella?"

"Me! Me!" the children squealed, waving their hands.

Cass retrieved three candy bars from the bowl. "Ladies first. Here you go." She dropped one into Cinderella's bag, followed by the ladybug, then the football player.

"Thank you!" the children exclaimed before turning and scurrying next door to the Simpsons' house.

When Cass closed the door, she found Dad smiling at her from the couch. "I do believe you enjoy that as much as the kids do."

"More," she said. She settled back into the recliner. "I hope I was that cute when I was little."

"I'll ask your Mom, but I'm sure you were since you're pretty cute now." Affecting an air of nonchalance, Dad turned the newspaper to the next page. "I wish I'd been around when you were little. I would have liked being your Dad all along, instead of showing up so late in the game."

Cass felt herself blush. "That would've been nice," she said shyly. "There were times I felt left out because I didn't have a father. When I was in third grade, I started telling people my father was an astronaut and that was why he was never around. My teacher called Mom, and she had a long talk with me about the situation." She laughed at the memory. "I think she was concerned I'd lost touch with reality. I remember telling her I knew my father was dead, but that I liked the astronaut story better. It was more exciting, and it got me a lot of attention. That's when she lectured me about telling the truth, even when I thought it was boring."

Dad smiled and shook his head in admiration. "That sounds like your mother. She's the most honest person I've ever met. It's one of the things I love about her."

"Oh, Dad." Cass made a wry face at him. "You love everything about her. Admit it, you worship the ground she walks on."

"Worship may be too strong a term," Dad protested with a grin. "Let's say I greatly esteem it. And my prayer is that some day you and Tabitha will meet young men who love you as much as I love your Mom."

Cass gave him a mischievous look. "Maybe we already have."

Groaning, Dad disappeared behind the newspaper. "That's not funny. It'll be at least twenty years before I'll even consider letting you girls marry."

"I heard that." Tabitha appeared at the end of the hallway, having come from her room. "I believe Cass and I might have something to say on the subject."

"That's right," Cass agreed. "Like something along the lines of 'fat chance.' "

"Donna," Dad called to Mom in the kitchen. "Could

you come here? The girls are ganging up on me."

"Sorry, pal, you're on your own," Mom called back. "I've been listening to your conversation, and you're going to have to dig yourself out of this particular hole on your own."

"Gee, and after I said such nice things about you," Dad said sourly, grinning at Cass.

While they laughed, the doorbell rang. Cass moved to get up and answer it, but Tabitha beat her to the door.

"My turn," she said. "You've been hogging all the fun and it's not fair."

The voices Cass heard greeting Tabitha when she opened the door weren't young, childish ones. They were deep and rumbled with laugher.

"Happy Halloween! We're Kwaj's official treat inspectors. We'll need to sample about half your candy to make sure it's fit for human consumption."

"Get in here, you goofs." Giggling, Tabitha pulled Micah and Logan into the house. "Have you no shame?" she pretended to scold. "Trying to steal candy meant for the kids. What a lowlife thing to do."

"We're sorry." Although Micah hung his head, he didn't sound the least bit repentant. "But no one will give us anything. We were desperate."

"How could they turn you down with those great masks?" Tabitha covered her mouth and acted embarrassed. "Oops, you're not wearing any."

"Ha-ha," drawled Micah. "You're quite the comedian."

"Hello, boys," Mom called from the kitchen. "You're just in time for supper. Would you like to join us? We're having spaghetti."

Logan acted like he was deep in thought. "Hmm. When was the last time I turned down a free meal?" His face lit up. "That would be never. I don't know about Micah, but I'm staying. Let me call my mother and tell her. She'll be thrilled. Her nickname for me is the bottomless pit."

"Uh, honey," Dad said quickly, "maybe you should rethink your invite. The rest of us would like to eat tonight."

Cass shot him a sour look. "Don't single Logan out. I've seen Micah eat and it's not a pretty sight."

"Who says I'm even staying for supper?" Micah asked.

"Is he?" Cass asked Tabitha.

She nodded. "Absolutely."

"Hey!" Micah protested. "Don't I have a say in this?"

"If you're going to let a woman into your life," Dad advised with mock weariness, "you'd better get used to her calling the shots. The sooner you accept that fact, the easier your life will be."

"You should listen to him." Mom emerged from the kitchen with a loaf of garlic bread to set on the table. "He knows what he's talking about. After all, he lives with three females."

"That's right." Dad smiled fondly at Mom. "Some guys have all the luck."

After supper, Cass and Logan opted to go for a walk. Instead of heading out back to the beach, they chose to stay on the street. Cass was curious to see if there were any Halloween stragglers. They ran across a few, but most of the children were already in for the night.

Taking Cass' hand, Logan entwined his fingers with hers. A shiver tingled up Cass' spine, despite the balmy evening.

"Are you glad Micah and I decided to surprise you and Tabitha?"

Cass gave him a flirtatious look. "What do you think?"

A smug smiled played across Logan's lips. "I'm thinking yes. You looked pretty happy to see me, if I do say so myself."

Elbowing him in the ribs, Cass teased softly,

"Egomaniac. I don't know why I put up with you."

"Because I'm cute?" guessed Logan.

"No, that's not it." Cass giggled at his yelp of protest. "Okay, maybe that has a teeny bit to do with it." She smiled up at him, liking the way the moonlight silvered his red hair. "Mostly, it's because you're about the nicest guy I've ever met."

"About the nicest?" echoed Logan, and Cass could hear a tinge of seriousness in his joking tone. "Who else is in the running?"

Cass shrugged, smiling. "Dad, of course. And my grandfather and uncle back home." She paused for dramatic effect, knowing what she'd say next would annoy Logan. "I can't leave out Randy. He's pretty special."

"Randy!" Logan was outraged. "What's he still doing in the picture? I thought he and Stacy Jamieson are going out."

"No! Really?" Cass injected as much dismay into her voice as she could muster. "I haven't heard about that."

She didn't do a very good acting job because the face Logan turned to her was suspicious. "You're pulling my leg, aren't you?"

"Me?" Cass pressed her hand to her chest, smiling innocently. "Now why would I do something like that?"

"Because you have a sick sense of humor," grumbled Logan. "Plus, you like seeing me squirm."

"Guilty on both counts." Cass wanted to look contrite, but couldn't stop grinning. "If you weren't so much fun to tease, I wouldn't do it."

Logan snorted. "Sure, blame the victim."

Cass briefly rested her head on his shoulder. "Will saying I'm sorry help make it up to you?"

Logan hesitated. "It might."

"Okay." Cass straightened with a laugh. "I was just wondering."

"You …" Pulling her close, Logan draped his arm around her shoulders. "What am I going to do with you?"

"I don't know." Cass slipped her arm around his waist. "Thank your lucky stars I'm your girlfriend?"

"I'll go you one better," murmured Logan. "Every night, when I count my blessings, I'll make sure I mention you several times."

Cass' smile gleamed in the moonlight. "My mother was right. You are good. Where did you learn to talk like that?"

"I could lie and tell you it comes naturally." Logan took her hand again. "But the truth is, I used to watch Oprah every afternoon when I lived in Pennsylvania. She taught me everything I know."

Cass gave a shout of laughter. "Yeah, right. I can't picture you sitting through an entire Oprah Winfrey show. You're too much of a … a … guy."

Logan laughed. "Thanks. I do believe that's the nicest thing you've ever said to me."

Cass hit him lightly on the arm. "Well, since that's pretty pathetic, I guess I'll just have to think of something better."

CHAPTER 6

After Cass and Logan left, Tabitha and Micah wandered out back to sit on the rocks behind the house. The tide was in, which meant they were soon covered with a fine layer of sea spray. Sighing impatiently, Tabitha pushed damp blonde curls away from her face.

"Why does it always have to be so wet around here?"

Mistaking her irritation for amusement, Micah teased, "In case you haven't noticed, we live on an island. We're surrounded by about a gazillion gallons of water. Some of it's bound to get on us."

"Well, I'm tired of it," Tabitha said darkly. She lifted the hair off her neck and fanned herself. "Just for once, I'd like to live someplace dry and cool."

"I see," Micah said after a slight pause. "Someplace like—oh, I don't know, I'm going to take a wild guess here—Oregon, maybe?"

Annoyed by his tone, Tabitha scowled. "What's wrong with Oregon?"

"Nothing." Micah moved closer so his shoulder brushed Tabitha's. "Except for the fact it's too far away. I kind of like having you around where I can see you every day."

Tabitha liked the sound of that, but she didn't see any

reason to let Micah know. "Are you forgetting you're going to be leaving for college in nine months? While you're living it up on the mainland, I'll be stuck here for another year."

"Going off to college hardly ever leaves my mind." His expression unreadable, Micah stared down at the swirling, foaming water. "You might find it exciting to think about getting out of here, but it scares me to death."

Tabitha, about to launch into another discussion of her mother, immediately forgot what she planned to say. *Micah—her Micah—was scared?* She was so startled she was speechless.

After a long pause, Micah turned to her with a teasing smile. "Cat got your tongue?"

Tabitha punched his arm. "It's not funny. You surprised me. I've never known you to be scared of anyone or anything."

"Sure you have." Micah's dark eyes met and held Tabitha's gaze. "Remember how terrified I was of asking you out?"

Tabitha dismissed his question with a wave. "What does that have to do with this situation?"

Taking her hand, Micah began playing with her fingers, gently bending them back and forth. "I've spent just about my whole life on Kwaj. We moved here when I was five, and I've gone all the way through school here." He sighed, glancing over his shoulder at the palm trees swaying in the breeze. "We kid around about it being a tropical paradise, but in a way it really is. It's small. It's safe. Even though I'm half black, I've never encountered any prejudice. Face it, Kwaj is just about perfect."

He paused, and Tabitha waited for him to continue. When he didn't, she nudged him. "Then what's the problem?"

"It's not—" Micah paused to search for the right word,

"—real. The real world is big and definitely not safe. It's full of people who won't give me the time of day—just because of my color." His breathing grew shallower, the longer he talked. "I barely know how to drive. I have my license, but it's a joke. I can count on two hands the number of times I've been behind the wheel of a car, and I'm not ashamed to admit it made me nervous as all get out when I was. How am I supposed to get around a college town when just the thought of driving makes me break out in a sweat?"

Before Tabitha could answer, he went on, "And another thing, I know I'm going to spend the first six months I'm in school getting lost on a daily basis since I've never had to find my way around on my own. Do you have any idea how humiliating it's going to be?"

Releasing Tabitha's hand, Micah dropped his head into both of his. A rush of sympathy surged through Tabitha, and she rubbed his back.

"You'll do fine," she said softly. "You'll see. Everything will work out great."

Micah shook his head, staring out at the ocean. "What if it doesn't?" he whispered. "What if ... I ... I can't cut it in the real world?"

Even though her heart was sinking, Tabitha said firmly, "That's the silliest thing I've ever heard. You're smart. You're talented. You have a terrific personality. You can do anything you set your mind to."

Micah glanced at her, a faint smile twitching at the corners of his mouth. "What is this? A pep talk?"

"I don't care what you call it as long as it gets you to quit thinking so negatively," Tabitha declared. "Somebody has to show you how ridiculous you're being. Since I'm the only other person here, I guess it's up to me."

He laughed. "You've been around Cass too long. She's rubbing off on you. You're a lot feistier than you used to be."

"Does that mean you'd like to borrow some backbone?" Tabitha asked sarcastically.

"Wow!" Micah held up his hands as if to ward off an attack. "What are you so riled up about?"

To her surprise, Tabitha suddenly realized she was on the verge of tears. "For somebody so intelligent, you can be really stupid sometimes. I happen to think you're wonderful, and I don't like anyone saying you're not, including you. You're going to go to college, and you're going to have the time of your life because you're going to do everything just right. And I'm ... I'm ..." Emotion threatened to choke off the rest of her words, but she doggedly finished, "Going to miss you so much, I want to cry every time I think about it."

"Gee, does this mean you care?" Micah asked lightly after a slight pause.

Tabitha almost slugged him. "You are such a jerk. If you don't know by now how much I care, we might as well call this relationship off because, as far as I'm concerned, it's hopeless."

Even though she resisted him at first, Micah succeeded in gathering her close. "I'm sorry. Of course I know you care. I didn't know what to say so I made a stupid joke. Forgive me?" He gave her his most imploring expression.

"Oh, all right," Tabitha grudgingly agreed. Deciding she liked it just fine where she was, she made no attempt to move. "How did we get on the subject of you leaving for college anyway? I know I would never bring it up."

"We were talking about Oregon, then I got us sidetracked onto college. Do you feel up to talking about your mother and Oregon?"

Tabitha snorted. "Are you kidding? One emotional breakdown a night is my limit. I'll take a raincheck on discussing my mother. It's not like the situation's going anywhere—it's just going to sit there as a lump of dread in my stomach."

"Okay, we'll talk about her some other time. One question, though." When Tabitha didn't object, Micah proceeded, "Are there any new developments?"

Puzzled by his question, Tabitha frowned. "Like what?"

Micah shrugged, bouncing her head where she rested it on his shoulder. "I don't know. Another letter? More pictures?" He hesitated. "Maybe a videotape or a phone call?"

Tabitha abruptly sat up and pivoted so she could look him in the eyes. "You think she's going to send a tape or call next?" She couldn't decide if the possibility was more intriguing or frightening.

"Uh … the thought has occurred to me," he hedged. "But I'm probably way off base. Pretend I didn't say anything."

"Oh, right," Tabitha scoffed. "Plant an idea like that in my head then tell me to forget it."

"Then at least promise me you won't tell your parents I mentioned it. I don't want them to think it's something I hope happens."

Seeing how anxious he looked, Tabitha nodded. "Your secret's safe with me. My lips are sealed."

Micah continued to appear troubled. "I'm not asking you to keep secrets from your folks."

Tabitha butted her shoulder against his. "Lighten up. It was a joke. I can't come up with a single reason why my parents and I would even discuss what you think my mother might do."

"Okay." Reassured, Micah settled back down.

He and Tabitha sat in silence for several seconds, enjoying the evening. As the wind picked up, it sent clouds scudding across the sky, blotting out the moon and stars.

"Looks like we're in for another storm," Micah said.

Sighing, Tabitha nodded. "Tomorrow's November first

so we're right in the thick of the rainy season. I guess we'll all start growing webbed feet before long."

"I thought you didn't mind the rainy season." Micah leaned back to peer down into her face, squinting in the darkness. "It gets old after a while, but in the beginning, it's a nice change of pace from sunshine all the time."

Tabitha's face tightened with dissatisfaction. "Yeah, well, I'm rethinking a lot of things. Maybe I'm finally growing up. I don't know." With an impatient shake, she stood up, brushing off her shorts as she did. "I'd better head in. I still have trig homework."

"I take it that's my cue to leave." Rising, Micah took her hand, and they turned toward the house. "Being the gentleman that I am, I'll see you to the door."

Tabitha laughed up at him. "You're not being a gentleman. You just want to talk Mom out of another piece of cake."

Micah hung his head, his expression sheepish. "How come you know me so well?"

"Because I'm a girl. Like Mom says, we just know things." Her high spirits restored, Tabitha swung Micah's hand as they walked. "God may have made men bigger and stronger, but He gave us women's intuition. I'll take that over muscles any day."

"Why do I get the feeling guys got the short end of the stick in this deal?" grumped Micah.

"Maybe—" Tabitha danced ahead of him then turned so she was walking backwards, "because you did." She stuck her tongue out at him.

Micah growled and lunged for her, but she took off running. She reached the lanai two steps ahead of Micah, skidding to a halt when she discovered Logan and Cass in the swing. Micah bumped into her then grabbed her to keep her from falling. He peered around Tabitha to see why she'd halted so abruptly.

"Hi, you guys," he said.

Cass arched an amused eyebrow at him. "Practicing for the fifty-yard dash?"

"Practicing your wrestling moves?" Tabitha retorted sweetly.

Laughing, they all headed into the house.

CHAPTER 7

Two days later Tabitha unexpectedly dropped in at the radio station to see Dad. She waited until he was finished broadcasting the hourly news before bursting into the studio, waving a letter and grinning from ear-to-ear.

"What's been one of your major objections about my mother writing to me?" she asked the second she came through the door.

Dad leaned back in his chair and gazed at her from under lowered brows. "Hello to you too."

"Oh, yeah. Hi." Tabitha perched on the edge of the desk. Her grin grew even wider. "Now answer my question."

"I have so many objections, it's impossible to single out one."

Tabitha ignored his cold tone. "Come on. Think. You know what bugs you the most about her writing."

"I'm not in the mood to play games," snapped Dad. "Either tell me what you came here to tell me or it can wait until I get home. I'm too busy to engage in a game of twenty questions."

Stung, Tabitha considered walking out, but the letter she'd just gotten was too important. Swallowing her pride, she said stiffly, "Fine, I'll tell you. The thing you keep harping on is Beth not accepting any responsibility for walking out on me. You don't like the fact that she's never said she's sorry. Ta-da!" She flourished the letter. "I think you'll be as happy as I am to see what she has to say."

Dad reached for the letter Tabitha held out to him as if touching something from his ex-wife was the last thing he wanted to do. Tabitha watched him intently as he read it from beginning to end, and then reread several sections. When he was finished, he handed the letter back to her without comment.

"Well?" she prompted as the silence lengthened.

"It's a start," he said tersely.

With the current song ending, Dad held up a finger for quiet. He then introduced the next several selections before turning off the microphone.

"Is that all you're going to say?" persisted Tabitha the moment he pressed the off switch. "Aren't you glad she's finally admitting what she did was wrong?"

"If she honestly believes she was," Dad responded cautiously, "then I'm happy she's owning up to her responsibility. However, neither of us can say for sure yet whether this is a ploy on her part. Only time will tell if she's sincere."

"She said she was sorry," Tabitha pointed out. "What more do you expect her to do?"

"For starters, I'd like her to go into more detail about why she's sorry." Dad gestured for the letter, and Tabitha gave it to him. "All she writes here is that she's sorry she missed out on your childhood, that the children she has now make her realize how enjoyable mothering can be." With a grimace of distaste, he dropped the letter onto the desk. "It's all about her and what she lost. There's no mention of the pain she caused you, let alone me."

"Is that what this is about?" demanded Tabitha. "You want her to apologize to you?"

Dad emitted an impatient snort. "Come on. You know me better than that. My only concern is for you."

Tabitha frowned. "Well, then explain something to me. Since you supposedly care only about me, if I'm satisfied with what Beth wrote, why aren't you?"

Dad took a deep breath. "It's understandable that you'd be more forgiving of Beth's past behavior. After all, she's your mother, and it's natural you'd want to give her the benefit of the doubt." Dad hesitated, then continued carefully, "I, on the other hand, have a right to remain suspicious of your mother's motives for reestablishing contact with you. Until I know what it is she wants out of this, I'm not about to let down my guard." His voice and expression hardened as he continued, "She's not going to hurt you again, not if I can help it."

"You can think what you want." Standing up, Tabitha retrieved the letter from the desk and stuffed into the back pocket of her shorts. "I believe she's truly sorry for what she did and that she wants to make it up to me somehow. I'm sorry you're choosing to still carry a grudge, but I've decided to give her a second chance."

Dad's head snapped up, and he looked alarmed. "What does that mean?"

Tabitha stiffened at his tone. "When I write back to her, I'm going to ask her to call. I think it's time we actually talked."

"I don't think that's wise."

Tabitha glared down her nose at him. "Are you forbidding me to ask her to call?"

"I'd like to," Dad confessed. "But, no, I'm not. You're sixteen, and ultimately you have to make your own decisions concerning your mother. Donna and I will continue to advise you, but it's up to you."

"Oh." Having prepared herself for battle, Tabitha was both relieved and disappointed that arguing wouldn't be necessary. "Well … I appreciate you being so understanding."

Dad's smile was weary. "Like I always say, that's what dads are for."

Her mission accomplished, Tabitha began edging toward the door. "I guess I should let you get back to work." She jerked a thumb over her shoulder. "Plus, I left the rest of the mail in my bike basket. There were a couple of letters for Cass, so I ought to get them home to her."

"Tell Mom I'll see her in about an hour." Dad started to fiddle with the equipment. "Thanks for stopping by. It reminded me of the good old days."

Tabitha reached the door and paused. For some reason, she found herself having to blink away tears. "I'll try to remember to come by more often. I … I love you, Dad."

"I love you too," he replied, and Tabitha turned away quickly before he could see she was crying.

CHAPTER 8

Cass was thrilled when Tabitha returned and delivered a letter from her grandparents and one from Janette. She read her grandparents' letter out loud so Mom could hear all the news too. After that, she headed to her room to savor Janette's letter in private. Sinking cross-legged onto the bed, she eagerly tore into the envelope.

Dear Cass,

Hey, girl! Don't drop dead of a heart attack, but it's really me writing back. I bet you were starting to think I'd been carried off by a pack of wolves or something, huh? Anyway, loved your letter and the pix. You are so tan! And your hair's almost blonde now. Cool!! All that sunshine will do that to you, I guess. Tabitha still looks like a stuck-up snob. How can you stand living with her? I showed Logan's picture to everyone. We all think he's cute, but not as cute as the guy in the wheelchair. Too bad about the chair. If it weren't for that, he'd be PERFECT.

Now that I have all the nice stuff out of the way, it's time to get to the real reason I'm writing. You moaned and groaned in your letter about feeling left out of what's going on around here. Excuse me for saying this, but WHAT DID YOU EXPECT? You live a million miles away, and it's not like you're pining away for us here. All you ever talk about in your letters is what you're doing, who you're dating, what's going on at school, your youth group. On and on and on. Then I'm supposed to believe you miss Tennessee and, even more importantly, me? Puh-leeze! If anyone should feel left out, it should be me. You're off having all these exciting adventures, and I'm stuck here in boring, old Jonesborough, doing the same stuff I've always done with the same people I've always done it with. Maybe we'd be more connected if I felt like I still mattered to you. But no. All I ever hear about are Rianne and Kira and Tabitha and the guys you hang out with. It makes me wonder where I fit in and if you even need me anymore. It's just a suggestion, but have you thought about staying home a little more often and writing to me? Okay, that's enough lecturing. You hear more than your fair share of that from your mother. I just wanted to get a few things off my chest.

I'll write longer next time. There's a party at Erin Harris' house (you remember her—she's a cheerleader, really tall and thin with long brown hair, used to date Zack Miller), and I've got to get ready. Think about what I said. I really hope we can stay friends.

Jan

When she finished, Cass carefully folded the letter and slipped it back into the envelope. Her cheeks burned from what Janette had written. Cass had seen herself as the innocent victim in their deteriorating friendship. It never occurred to her that she might share some of the responsibility.

Lying back on her bed, Cass stared at the ceiling. *Is Janette right?* she wondered. *Am I to blame for the way things are between us? Did I make it sound like I was so happy with my new friends that she wasn't important to me anymore?*

Too restless to stay still for very long, Cass rolled over and stood up. Wandering about the room, she stopped at the window to peer outside for a while. She moved to the desk where she picked up and set back down pencils, paper clips, and a handful of change she didn't remember leaving there.

"What was I supposed to do?" she whispered. "Hole up in the house and act like a hermit? I tried that when I first got here, but it got so lonely I thought I'd die. Mom's always talking about having the right balance in your life. Maybe I can figure out a way to balance my friendship with Janette with the situation here."

The more she thought about it, the more Cass liked the idea. It wasn't a matter of giving up one or the other. All she had to do was devise a plan that kept her from being too involved with Kwaj's social life while, at the same time, it didn't leave her entirely stranded. Pleased to have a goal, she stayed in her room working out an acceptable strategy until Mom called her to supper.

They were halfway through the meal before Cass realized no one was talking. She'd been so preoccupied with her own thoughts that she hadn't noticed the silence. She glanced curiously around the table and asked, "What's going on? Why is everybody so quiet?"

Tabitha ignored the question and kept eating. Dad shrugged. Only Mom bothered to reply. "It seems we all have a lot on our minds this evening." She sent Cass a teasing grin. "You haven't been your usual chatterbox self either."

Since she didn't care to go into detail about what she was thinking, Cass nodded and changed the subject. "Mom, when you were on the phone earlier, were you talking to somebody about having our things from home delivered?"

Mom's face lit up. "That's right. I forgot to mention it. Someone called from the dock and said the barge carrying our household items has finally arrived. They'll be bringing them over some time tomorrow. Aren't you excited? I know how much you've looked forward to seeing your old furniture again."

Cass wasn't sure how she felt. It was true she'd missed having her own things around, but now that they were here, it was more evidence that she was staying. Knowing that Mom was waiting for a response, she produced a wan smile and said, "I hope everything survived the trip. I don't want them unloading a pile of sticks."

Mom laughed. "I asked what kind of shape our things were in, and they assured me the crate didn't have any damage, which means the items inside should be fine."

"Good." Not wanting to arouse Mom's suspicions, Cass injected more enthusiasm into her voice. "Actually, it's great. Do I need to take my clothes out of the dresser tonight or can that wait until tomorrow?"

"I can take care of it tomorrow after you leave for school." Mom beamed with pleasure. "Just think, by the time you get home from school, your bedroom furniture should be in place."

Cass couldn't hide her frown. "That will be so weird— sort of like transporting my Tennessee room eight thousand miles to the middle of the Pacific."

For the first time, Mom looked uncertain. "Do you want your old things set up in your room or would you rather keep the furniture that was already here?"

Cass hesitated. "Put in my furniture," she finally said. "Wow, tomorrow night I'll be sleeping in my bed for the first time in four months. You packed my quilt and the afghan Mamaw knitted, didn't you?" When Mom nodded, she grinned. "Okay, now I'm getting excited. I'll have all my stuff back."

"Should we throw a party to celebrate?"

Cass gaped at Tabitha, taken aback by her heavy sarcasm. It was obvious she wasn't joking, and Cass couldn't imagine why the arrival of her furniture would annoy her stepsister. She took a deep, calming breath, however, and opted not to retaliate.

"That won't be necessary," she blithely assured Tabitha. "I'm sure my things will be tired out from the journey."

Tabitha made a face. "That's just plain stupid," she said darkly.

"No more stupid than your party suggestion." Cass' sugary sweet smile masked her mounting irritation.

Cass saw Dad and Mom exchange uneasy glances.

"What all did you have sent?" Dad hastily asked Cass. "It's been so long, I can't remember."

Cass shifted her attention from Tabitha to Dad. "Let's see. My bed, dresser, desk, nightstand, stereo, the hope chest Papaw built me for my sixteenth birthday." She frowned, trying to recall what else she and Mom had decided to send four months earlier. "The quilt and afghan I already mentioned, my clock radio, a bunch of books and pictures."

As she listed the items, Cass' spirits lifted. By tomorrow, she'd be surrounded by momentos of home.

That should help me remember Janette and everybody, she decided. *It'll make it easier to balance my life here with the one I left behind.*

Aloud, she concluded, "I think that about does it. Can you think of anything else, Mom?"

She shook her head. "Other than what I sent, no."

Tabitha sighed nosily. "Hello? What's this obsession with what'll be delivered tomorrow? It's just stuff. Why do you care so much?"

"Your personal belongings are important to you, aren't they?" Mom replied calmly. "Wouldn't you miss them if you had to do without them for a while?"

"Nope," Tabitha said immediately. "Like I said, it's just stuff. Relationships are all that really matter in life."

Cass snorted. "Spoken like somebody who's never had to do without her *stuff*." She sneered the word, earning herself a frown from Mom.

"Look, girls," Mom said, glancing between the two of them, "this discussion is going nowhere. If you continue in this vein, someone's going to wind up upset. I think we can all agree there's nothing more important than the people in our lives."

"I thought God was supposed to be number one." Tabitha's tone and expression oozed innocence, but Cass could read the challenge in her gaze.

"You're right," Mom conceded calmly. "I stand corrected. After God, people should take precedence over everything else. Now," she continued, "let's talk about something else. Tomorrow's Friday. What plans do you girls have?"

"The school is putting on a pizza and movie night." Spearing a potato, Tabitha nibbled at it. "I assume that's what I'll be doing." She glanced at Cass. "What about you?"

"I don't think I'll go." She felt rather than saw Mom's start of surprise. "I thought I might do something different and spend a Friday night at home." She summoned up a smile. "You know, give Mom and Dad a thrill." *And give my friends back home some of my time,* she added silently.

"Are you and Logan on the outs?" Tabitha demanded immediately. "You seemed fine at school. Did something happen after you got home?"

"Nothing happened. Logan and I are great. In fact, we couldn't be better." Cass mentally kicked herself for saying anything. She knew Tabitha would keep after her until she gave her a satisfactory explanation. "It occurred to me the other day that I hardly spend any time at home anymore. It won't kill me to stay in every now and then on the weekend."

The look Tabitha gave her was totally bewildered. "That's so weird. Why would you want to stay here when you could be someplace else?"

"Thanks," drawled Dad. "I guess that lets Mom and me know what you think about our company."

Tabitha's cheeks reddened. "You know what I mean. It's just not … not …" she hesitated, "normal that a teenager would willingly pass up a night out with her friends to be with her folks."

"So I'm abnormal." Cass shrugged. "Oh, well."

She wracked her brain for something else to talk about in order to take the spotlight off her. Since she realized it wouldn't stand up to much scrutiny, she wasn't about to disclose her decision to spend less time with her Kwaj friends. She had no doubt Mom would feel like she had to talk her out of it. Before Cass could change the subject, however, the phone rang. Dad answered it.

"Cass, it's for you." He didn't look happy as he handed her the phone. "Your friends aren't supposed to call at supper time."

"I know." Cass accepted the receiver with an apologetic look. "I won't be long," she assured him, getting up and walking into the living room.

When she returned to her seat, she explained, "That was Rianne. She wanted to know if I'd like to come over for a while after supper."

"Is your homework done?" Mom asked automatically.

"Yes, but I told her no." As three pairs of surprised eyes turned her way, Cass grimaced at her family. "I didn't feel like going anywhere, okay? Honestly, can't a person stay home once in a while without everyone making a federal case out of it?"

"No one said anything," Mom pointed out in the reasonable tone Cass heartily disliked, particularly when she had to admit to herself she was being unreasonable. "It appears you're the one making a big deal about this."

Cass shot Tabitha an exasperated look. "Would you please do something to bug them and take the heat off me? I feel like I've been on the hot seat ever since we sat down to eat."

Tabitha glared at her. "Right, and get myself in trouble?"

"Well, I'd say you've both been acting rather peculiar lately," Mom said before Cass could respond.

Tabitha turned her glare to Mom. "What do mean? What have I said or done out of the ordinary?"

Mom passed a weary hand across her eyes. "I'm sorry I said anything. I don't feel like going into it right now."

"You're the one who brought it up," persisted Tabitha. "You can't make a comment like that then say you don't want to talk about it. It's not fair."

"Let it go, Tabitha," Dad said.

"You always take her side," Tabitha grumbled.

Dad shrugged. "Do you remember the wedding?" he asked Tabitha, his lips twitching. "I promised to love, honor, and cherish Donna. Nobody made me promise a thing when you were born. I've been making it up as I go along."

Tabitha sniffed her disdain at his attempt at humor. "Maybe you should have read a couple of books along the way. You might have done a better job."

Dad raised his eyebrows. "Actually, I think I've done quite well, considering my lack of training. And support," he added with a meaningful glance.

Instead of responding, Tabitha glared down at her plate.

Cass looked back and forth between Mom and Dad. "Is there something up with you two? You seem kind of on edge lately."

Dad laughed. "Most likely it's the stress of dealing with a couple of teenage daughters catching up with us. Mom and I could use a break. As a matter of fact," he crumpled his napkin and tossed it on his plate, "that sounds like a great idea, if I do say so myself. Donna, how would you like to stroll on over to the Yokwe Yuk for coffee and dessert?"

Following his example, Mom threw down her napkin. "That sounds wonderful. I can't think of anything nicer than spending an hour or so alone with my husband." She stood, then smiled at Cass and Tabitha. "Except for coming home to you two—and a clean kitchen."

Cass smiled at Mom, then rolled her eyes at Tabitha.

Dad joined Mom at the door. "We should be back no later than eight."

"Good." Cass helped herself to another piece of meat loaf. "We'll make sure the party's over by seven-thirty, just in case."

Dad just laughed. "Good idea. Have fun."

They left, and Cass and Tabitha grinned at each other.

"They're so cute." Tabitha sighed, and the sound was a mixture of sadness and pleasure. "You know, when I think about us—our family, I mean—sometimes I really wonder why I want to have anything to do with my mother."

"I know what you mean. Right now, I'm asking myself why I still care about what's happening back in Jonesborough."

"When all is said and done, though—" Tabitha propped her chin on her hand and gazed at Cass, "we do care. Does that mean there's something wrong with us?"

Cass' laugh lacked mirth. "Probably. Why can't we forget all the other stuff and be content with what we have?"

"Good question. I mean, I don't want to ruin what I have here, but I also don't want to miss this chance with Beth."

Cass thought about that for a couple of seconds, then said, "My advice is to follow your heart—and pray. A lot," she added solemnly.

"Whatever's going on with you and your friends back home, the same applies to you." Tabitha paused. "Do you think life ever gets any easier?"

"I hope so," replied Cass. "I really hope so."

CHAPTER 9

"Cassandra Aileen Devane, what in the world is wrong with you? You are the most stubborn, pigheaded person it's ever been my rotten luck to know."

Cass, who'd jumped at Tabitha's roar of displeasure, looked up from where she was sprawled on the couch reading.

"Wow," she said with a mixture of irritation and alarm. "Since you're the one storming in here, calling me names, maybe you're the one with the problem."

"Not me, buddy. Uh-uh." Tabitha adamantly shook her head. "I'm not the one who told Kira she couldn't go to her slumber party this Thursday. Why did you change your mind?"

Setting aside her book, Cass rolled up to a sitting position. She clasped her arms around her knees and gazed at Tabitha. She no longer felt alarmed, merely annoyed. "Why is it any of your business whether or not I go to Kira's party?"

"Kira planned the sleepover for the four of us. You know that. She's been talking about it for weeks. Since we don't have school on Friday, she figured Thursday would be the perfect time for it. As of a couple of days ago, you were going. Now all of a sudden you're not. What gives?"

Cass examined her fingernails. It hadn't occurred to her that Tabitha would care one way or the other about her being at Kira's party.

"Well?" Tabitha prompted when Cass remained silent.

"I'm thinking," Cass snapped.

"What's there to think about?" countered Tabitha. "I asked you a question. You give me a truthful answer. It's simple. Unless—" her eyes narrowed, "you're planning on lying to me."

"I don't lie," Cass said quickly. She thought about starting an argument to distract Tabitha, but realized the ploy would provide only a short-term delay. Sooner or later, her stepsister would demand an answer so she might as well get it over with. "I'm not going to Kira's party because I don't want to. There, are you happy now?"

"How can I be happy when you're not going to be part of the fun?" Tabitha sounded more confused than angry. "I thought you were looking forward to the sleepover."

"I was," Cass grudgingly admitted.

"So what changed?"

Cass chewed on her thumbnail and shrugged.

"Look—" Grinning, Tabitha plopped down onto the sofa before she continued, "you might as well 'fess up. You know me. I'm going to keep bugging you until you do. Why don't you save us both a lot of time and trouble and tell me what I want to know?"

Reluctantly, Cass smiled. "You can be pretty persistent when you want to be."

"It's one of my charms." Tabitha leaned back against the cushion, giving the impression that she had all the time in the world. "Does your change of mind about the party have anything to do with the letter you got from Janette last Friday?"

Cass raised startled eyes to her stepsister. "What makes

you think it might?"

Tabitha shrugged. "Because I can put two and two together. At lunch on Friday you were right in there discussing movies and what kind of snacks we should get for the party. Fast forward to Monday, and you tell Kira during Spanish class today that you're not going. So I have to ask myself what happened between then and now, and the only thing I can come up with is Janette's letter. Am I wrong?"

As much as Cass would have liked to shoot down her theory, she couldn't. "No, you're not wrong." She sighed heavily. "But I don't want to talk about it."

"Tough." Tabitha fixed her with a steely stare. "I let you get away with not seeing Logan this weekend. I didn't say anything when you didn't go bowling with the rest of us after youth group last night. But now you've gone too far. You're not going to ruin Kira's party by not showing up."

Cass' snort was a small, sad sound. "You'll still have a good time without me."

"No, we won't," insisted Tabitha. She hesitated, then added quietly, "Even more importantly, I won't."

Cass studied her for several seconds before finally deciding she was serious. "I appreciate that." She flashed an impish smile. "I'm still not going, but I appreciate it."

"Okay."

Tabitha's too-quick agreement made Cass suspicious. Sure her stepsister was up to something, Cass warily waited for her to continue.

Crossing her arms, Tabitha regarded Cass with a stubborn gaze. "If you don't go, I don't either."

"Oh, come on. You don't mean that."

"Ha! Try me." For someone Cass secretly thought of as a pushover, Tabitha sometimes surprised her. "We'll stay here together and have our own slumber party."

Cass couldn't tell if she was serious. "You're joking, right?"

"Nope." Tabitha settled into the corner of the couch and tucked her legs beneath her. "If staying home is good enough for you, it's good enough for me too."

"Knock it off," Cass ordered irritably. She suspected Tabitha was mocking her. "You're being stupid, and you know it."

"How come it's fine and dandy for you to stay home, but it's stupid when I want to?" Tabitha challenged.

Cass didn't have an answer and that annoyed her. "It's just different, that's all," she finally muttered.

Tabitha shook her head in disdain. "You're pathetic. You used to be able to fight way better than this."

"Maybe I don't want to fight." Cass hoped that acting superior might get Tabitha to back off.

"Since when?" jeered Tabitha. "Look." She held up her hand to forestall the protest forming on Cass' lips. "This is getting us nowhere. Just tell me why you don't want to go to Kira's party, and I'll leave you alone."

"All right, fine," Cass grudgingly agreed. "You were right about Jan's letter upsetting me. She gave me a hard time for whining about our friendship not being what it used to be. She said it's my fault because I'm so caught up with my friends here that it's all I ever write about. She doesn't want to hear about what I'm doing with everyone here. So I thought …" Her voice trailed off. Suddenly she was uncomfortable voicing what she knew was an illogical decision.

Tabitha finished her sentence for her. "You thought if you stopped spending so much time with us, that would somehow magically improve things with your friends back home."

Cass ducked her head in embarrassment, letting her hair swing forward to cover her burning cheeks. "It sounds silly when you say it out loud like that."

"You're right. It does." Tabitha glared at her. "The question now is, what are you going to do about it?"

"I … uh …" Cass frowned. "I don't know!" she finally blurted. "I'm so confused. I hate the thought of losing Janette's friendship after all these years. But I … I …" She took a deep breath and admitted, "I don't want to be lonely either." She turned imploring eyes to her stepsister. "What do you think I should do?"

"I think the first thing you should do is write to Janette and tell her to get off your case," Tabitha said immediately. "You're the one who moved and had to start over. She got to stay where she is and go on with her life. She doesn't seem to understand the difference between your situations. It seems as far as she's concerned, you're supposed to do nothing except wait to hear from her about her exciting life."

"Yeah." Cass frowned as the truth of Tabitha's statements began to sink in. "I felt guilty after reading her last letter, like I've done something wrong because I didn't curl up and die after we moved here." She raised troubled eyes to Tabitha. "That's not right, is it?"

"It's so not right, it makes me gag," Tabitha declared forcefully. "But it explains why you suddenly found yourself too busy to hang out with the rest of us."

Cass sighed. "Sometimes I'm too stupid to live."

"True." Although her tone was solemn, Tabitha's eyes danced. "But lucky for you, you're also quite likable. I'm sure everyone will agree to give you a second chance."

Cass' eyebrows drew together in a scowl. "You talked about me with the others?"

"Of course," Tabitha breezily assured her. "And I was elected to be the one to straighten you out. Everybody pretty much figured out what was going on. Kira was all for writing a letter to Janette, telling her off. Rianne and I voted that I should at least try talking to you before we let Kira take such drastic action. She's going to be disappointed that you listened to what I had to say. She was really looking forward to writing the letter."

"Wow—talk about a close call. I'd have never been able to explain Kira's letter to Janette. Our friendship would've been history, for sure." Leaning back into the corner of the couch, she gazed thoughtfully at Tabitha. "Did you mean what you said before about not having fun at Kira's sleep over if I wasn't there?"

"Absolutely." Tabitha gave a single, emphatic nod. "We may have our ups and downs, but you're still one of my favorite people to have around."

"Only one of them?" Cass couldn't resist teasing.

"Hey!" Tabitha wagged a warning finger at her. "Don't push it. After the way things started out between us, it's amazing we're even on speaking terms, let alone friends."

"We really did get off to a bad start." Cass' smile held a hint of mischief. "But look at us now. We can say anything to each other without worrying the other one might take it wrong."

Tabitha rolled her eyes at the ceiling. "Why do I have the feeling you're about to unload something on me?"

"Maybe because you know me so well?" Cass suggested. "Because we're as close as sisters? Because ..."

"Save the baloney for Mom and Dad," Tabitha broke in. She folded her arms protectively across her chest, as if bracing for some unpleasantness. "Just say what you have to say, and let's get this over with."

"Okay, here goes." Cass took a deep breath and said in a rush, "Don't mess up the family by getting any more involved than you already are with your mother. We've got a good thing going, but I'm scared something will go wrong if Beth stays in the picture. There." She sighed with equal parts relief and apprehension. "I said it." She watched Tabitha out of the corner of her eye, anxiously awaiting her reaction.

Tabitha slowly stood up, her movements carefully controlled. Her face and tone were icy as she glared down at Cass and declared, "My relationship with my mother is none of your business, and I'd appreciate it if you didn't bring it up again. Whatever decisions I make about her will be based on what's best for her and me. You have nothing to say about it. Neither do Mom and Dad."

Taken aback by her response, Cass protested, "But—"

Tabitha held up a hand to cut her off. "But nothing. Those are the rules and they're not negotiable. I've told Dad and Mom, and now I'm telling you."

"But that's not fair." Cass wasn't about to let her have the last word. "What you decide won't just affect you and your mother. It'll affect all of us, so we should be allowed to give you our opinions."

Tabitha assumed a pitying expression that didn't strike Cass as entirely sincere. "Face it. You're clueless when it comes to my situation with my mother. Your father's dead. You don't have to relate to him anymore or decide how to fit him into your life. My mother, on the other hand, is very much alive, which means you don't have any right to tell me what to do since you have no idea what I'm going through."

Cass was stunned by the cruelty of her words. *She actually threw my father's death up in my face*, she fumed, her eyes narrowing into angry slits.

"Boy, you'll sink to any depth to make your point, won't you?" As Cass stood up, her obvious fury caused Tabitha to take a hasty step backward. Cass laughed, but the sound was mocking rather than humorous. "Don't worry. I'm not going to hit you, even though you deserve it. Funny thing, though, I suddenly find the atmosphere in here is making me sick. I'm going out for some fresh air. Maybe that will get the bad taste out of my mouth."

"What are you going to do?" Tabitha sneered. "Hightail

it over to the lagoon so you can barge in on Mom and Dad's picnic and whine to them that I was mean to you?"

Cass refused to dignify her question with an answer. She did, however, pose a query of her own. "Seeing as how your loyalty seems to be shifting more and more to Beth, don't you think it's about time you quit calling my mother *Mom*? Am I being picky or don't you agree it's a tad bit hypocritical on your part?"

Before Tabitha could think of a comeback, Cass retrieved her sandals from beside the couch and sauntered to the door. She left the house without another word since the earsplitting slam of the door behind her said everything she felt.

CHAPTER 10

The moment Cass was gone, Tabitha sank down onto the coffee table and covered her face with her hands. *Why did I say that about her father?* she berated herself. *That was totally uncalled for and just plain nasty. What's the matter with me?*

Raising her head, she stared bleakly out the front window. Cass was marching across the lawn with her back ramrod straight and her head held high. Tabitha experienced a sudden urge to jump up, fling open the door, and yell, "Wait! I'm sorry. Please come back so we can talk this out." But she remained where she was and watched Cass until she disappeared down the street.

The last thing Tabitha wanted at the moment was to be alone with her thoughts. Too restless to sit still, she got up and wandered out to the kitchen. Since Mom and Dad were having a romantic picnic at the lagoon to celebrate their four-month anniversary, Mom had left cold fried chicken, fruit salad, and cole slaw for the girls' supper. Opening the refrigerator, Tabitha briefly considered helping herself to some before rejecting the possibility and shutting the door. The thought of food was enough to turn her stomach. Besides, until she sorted things out with

Cass, she didn't feel right about eating.

"As Cass likes to say," she muttered, returning to the living room, "I'm lower than a snake's belly. Anyone as low as I am doesn't deserve to eat. I deserve to suffer. And to suffer without complaining about it," she added when her stomach growled.

When fifteen minutes passed and Cass didn't return, Tabitha decided to go in search of her. On her way out back to fetch her bike, Tabitha paused in the kitchen long enough to pack several pieces of chicken, a container of coleslaw, and six peanut butter cookies. If all went well in her conversation with Cass, it might be nice to celebrate with a meal.

After twenty minutes of riding, Tabitha finally discovered Cass walking the track at the high school. She stopped her bike and watched for several seconds before making her presence known.

Although she couldn't be sure from this distance, Tabitha thought Cass looked like she'd been crying. Of course, that could be chalked up to the fact that her stepsister was sweating profusely. Tabitha didn't know how many laps she'd made around the track, but in this heat, just a couple were enough to leave a person dripping with perspiration. Tabitha decided it was time to rescue Cass before she melted away completely.

Parking her bike, she started across the schoolyard. From Cass' quick glance in her direction, Tabitha knew her stepsister realized she was there, but Cass declined to acknowledge her. Instead, she tilted her chin to an even more defiant angle and increased her pace until she was almost jogging. Tabitha intercepted her on the far curve.

"Would you mind stopping before I have a heart attack?" she panted, clutching her side. "I need to talk to you, but I can't do that and breathe at the same time. I'm not in shape like you are."

Ignoring her, Cass didn't slacken her speed until she'd gone about ten yards beyond Tabitha. Coming to an abrupt halt, she spun on her heels, propped her fists on her hips, and glowered at her stepsister. Being this close, Tabitha concluded Cass had been crying, which made her feel like the dirt under a snake's belly.

"Well?" Cass demanded when Tabitha merely stared at her without speaking. "What was so all-fired important that you came looking for me? Do you want to gloat even more about my father's death?"

Tabitha winced. Even though she accepted the fact that she deserved Cass' scorn, it was still hard to hear the bitterness in her stepsister's voice. "No. I came to say I'm sorry." Encouraged that Cass didn't sneer in disdain, she moved a few steps closer. "I shouldn't have said what I did about your father. I'm sure he was a wonderful man and that you miss him a lot."

Cass stared at her for a few moments before speaking. "Not really," she finally said, shrugging. "I was so young when he died that I don't remember anything about him. You can't miss what you never actually had."

"Still, I shouldn't have been so—oh, I don't know— cold when I mentioned his death." Tabitha kept walking until she stopped directly in front of Cass. "We've both lost parents. In different ways, sure, but the end result is the same."

"No it's not." Cass avoided Tabitha's eyes by gazing over her shoulder at the ocean. "I can't ever get my father back, but your mother's working like crazy to reconnect with you. I guess—" Her voice trailed off, and she cleared her throat before continuing, "I guess that makes me kind of sad and a little … jealous. I thought about it while I was walking, and maybe that's one of the reasons why I don't want you to work things out with your mother." She finally looked Tabitha in the eyes. "Because I can't with my father, and it doesn't seem fair."

Amazed at her honesty, Tabitha didn't know what to say. Instead of trying to think of something, she impulsively reached over and gave Cass a quick, hard hug. When she released her, she glanced up at the sky and wrinkled her nose.

"How about we get out of the sun?" She gestured toward her bike. "I brought supper. Do you feel like eating?"

Cass nodded. "Now that you mention it, I am a little hungry."

The girls started toward the bike and Tabitha elbowed Cass in the side. "All that exercise on an empty stomach will do that to you. How many times did you go around the track?"

"I stopped counting after the third lap." Using the hem of her shirt, Cass mopped her face. "Wow! I'm burning up. Did you bring anything to drink?"

Tabitha groaned. "I'm sorry. I didn't even think of it. I can run home and get us something, though."

"It's okay." Cass dismissed her offer with an airy wave. "I think I might have … yup, I do." Fishing in her pocket, she produced two quarters. "We can get a Coke out of the machine by the cafeteria."

While Tabitha retrieved the food from the bike, Cass ran to the soda machine and bought a soft drink. They met up on the side of the building facing the water.

"I thought we'd eat here," suggested Tabitha. "It's in the shade, and you can't beat the view."

"Fine with me." Cass sank cross-legged to the sidewalk and leaned against the sun-warmed cinder blocks. Popping the top on the can of Coke, she took a long swallow before looking over at Tabitha who'd sat down beside her. "What did you bring to eat?"

Tabitha showed her instead of telling her, taking the items out of the bag one-by-one. As Cass grabbed a drumstick, Tabitha sank her teeth into a breast piece.

"Mmmm," she said. "Mom sure is a great cook." When she noticed Cass' sidelong glance, she observed tartly, "And yes, I'm going to keep on calling her Mom. Whatever happens with Beth, Mom will always be Mom to me. With the way she loved me right from the start, she deserves the title."

"You won't get an argument from me." Cass dug a plastic spoon into the bowl of Cole slaw and ate straight from the container.

They ate in silence for a few moments. When the quiet threatened to become uncomfortable, Tabitha cleared her throat and Cass turned to her with an expectant look.

"I'm going to tell you something I haven't told Dad and Mom yet so you have to promise me you won't breathe a word until I've talked to them. Okay?" Tabitha's blue eyes sought and held Cass' hazel gaze.

Cass set down the spoon. "Mum's the word."

"As you know, Beth called me the other day." At Cass' encouraging nod, Tabitha continued, "It was weird talking to her at first. We're still pretty much strangers to each other. Plus, it was hard to think of things to talk about when what I really wanted to do was ask her why she left me and why she wants me back now. But I'm too scared to bring those subjects up yet. Anyway, during the conversation, she asked me if I would consider spending Christmas with her and the kids."

Cass choked on the sip of soda she'd taken. After a fit of coughing and with her eyes watering, she finally managed to sputter, "What did you tell her?"

"That I needed to think about it. Then after that, I'd have to talk it over with Dad and Mom." The face Tabitha turned to Cass was troubled. "Do you think I did the right thing?"

"I wish you'd given her a flat-out no and let it go at that.

But I understand why you didn't." Cass drew up one leg and rested her wrist on her knee. The partially eaten drumstick dangled from her hand. "I know I've asked you this before, but have you prayed about what you're supposed to do?"

Tabitha frowned. "I've tried praying and I guess I'll keep trying. But I don't think I'm doing it right because I don't get any clear-cut answers. Sometimes I think one thing after praying, sometimes I think another. I pray for God's will to be done in the situation, but—" she spread her hands in a gesture of helplessness, "—how am I supposed to know what His will is when I can't hear Him responding? I'm sure you hear Him all the time since you've been praying so long and you're probably good at it, but I never heard a word He might say to me. It's frustrating."

Cass laughed. "Welcome to the club. I've been saying for years that I wish we were each issued our own personal chalkboard when we were born for God to write messages on every day. That way, when we got up in the morning, we could check it for instructions about what to do, plus He could write out His answers to our prayers. Don't you think it would make life so much easier? It would take all the frustration out of the process."

Bypassing the cole slaw, Tabitha rummaged in the bag for a cookie. "Have you told Mom about your idea?"

"Uh-huh." Cass made a face. "She said we already have a set of directions to follow—the Bible—and, according to her, God doesn't get any clearer when it comes to how He wants us to live."

Tabitha exchanged an exasperated glance with her. "Parents can be so dense sometimes. Or at least they pretend to be."

Cass gnawed the last shreds of meat off the drumstick then, setting it aside, reached for another. "Actually, to be fair to Mom, she did admit she struggles with knowing God's will too. She said a chalkboard would be helpful, but it would do away with the need to have faith, since everything would be spelled out in black and white."

"And that would be a bad thing?" drawled Tabitha, making it clear she didn't think so.

Cass laughed. "I guess God wants there to be a little more to our faith than just getting up every morning and reading some to-do list He left for us the night before."

"I guess." Tabitha twisted her mouth with a touch of bitterness. "Of course, it's easy for Him. He knows everything. The best we can do is stumble around in the dark and hope we don't fall in any holes."

"It's not quite that bad," disagreed Cass. "There are the Ten Commandments and Jesus' example to follow—and Jesus' grace and forgiveness when we don't. I don't know. Praying usually helps me see things more clearly, even if God doesn't do anything as dramatic as shout the answer I'm looking for or write it across the sky."

"But Jesus never had to deal with a situation like the one with my mother," Tabitha reminded Cass. "How can I follow His example when what I'm experiencing never happened to Him?"

"Hmm." Cass rested her head against the wall and appeared to be deep in thought. "I don't know if this is the right answer, but whatever the circumstances, Jesus always did what was loving and pleasing to God." Cass frowned. "So I guess what you need to do is figure out what would be loving and pleasing to God in this situation."

Tabitha frowned and she slumped against the wall. "But how do I know for sure what will please Him?"

"I have no idea." Shaking her head, Cass smiled wryly. "Sometimes I think it'd be easier if I weren't a Christian. Then I wouldn't have to worry about trying to do things God's way. I could just make up my own mind about things, and that would be that."

"Except you'd probably decide wrong and wind up in a

bigger mess than before," remarked Tabitha.

"Tell me about it. That's happened more times than I care to count. I don't do too well when I try to go it alone." Cass picked up the bowl of cole slaw. "Prayer may not be the clearest of methods, but it's better than the alternative."

"Amen to that," Tabitha agreed fervently. "Now let's talk about something else. There's really nothing else to say on the subject of spending Christmas with my mother until I talk to Mom and Dad."

CHAPTER 11

On their way home, Cass and Tabitha met their parents about a block from the house.

"Looks like great minds think along the same paths," Dad greeted them. "Did you decide to go on a picnic too?"

"We didn't exactly plan it that way," Cass replied honestly. "It's just how it wound up. Don't try to figure it out," she said when Mom appeared confused. "Let's just say life is complicated sometimes and leave it at that."

Once they were inside the house, Tabitha asked if she could talk privately with them. Cass sent her a questioning look, and Tabitha nodded slightly to let her know she'd be telling them about Beth's invitation to spend Christmas with her.

"Y'all go on," Cass urged, taking the picnic basket from Dad and the bag of food from Tabitha. "I'll take care of these things."

While Tabitha and their parents disappeared into her room, Cass took her time in the kitchen. She left the radio off so she could hear any snatches of conversation that might float down the hall. After several minutes passed without an explosion, she was relieved that Mom and, particularly, Dad had obviously taken the news well. Still, she wished someone would raise their voice so she could get a hint about what was going on.

When she couldn't think of any more excuses to linger in the kitchen, Cass reluctantly folded the dish towel on the counter and headed out back to sit on the rocks. A crescent moon hovered just above the horizon and played peekaboo with the clouds. Cass guessed it would be raining in the morning. Behind her, palm fronds clacked in the breeze, and she realized how familiar the sound had become.

If I were home, she mused, *I'd be hearing cars and people and maybe some mountain music coming from one of the craft shops downtown. There'd be the smell of woodsmoke in the air from neighborhood fireplaces.* She sniffed and identified the mingled aromas of the ocean and nearby hibiscus flowers. *Definitely not Tennessee smells. But that's okay,* she realized with a sense of surprise. *I never thought I'd like anywhere as much as I like home, but Kwaj comes awfully close.*

Although Cass expected someone to come looking for her, an hour passed and nobody showed up. That struck her as odd, so she crept back into the house, sure she'd find her family engaged in verbal combat. Except for the low murmur of voices coming from Tabitha's bedroom, all was quiet.

Baffled, Cass propped her fists on her hips and wondered what to do next. Calling someone was out of the question since people could start emerging from the bedroom at any moment. She wanted to make sure all parties concerned realized she was available to talk. Taking a walk wasn't an option because she wanted to stick close to the action, and she was tired of sitting on the rocks. That left getting ready for bed, which Cass proceeded to do, making as much noise as possible so everyone knew she was there.

Ten minutes later she found herself lying in bed, staring up at the ceiling as she strained to eavesdrop on the next room. She couldn't understand any of what was being said, however, and flipped over onto her stomach with an irritated sigh. A glance at the clock told her it was only 9:10.

"What a pathetic life I live," Cass muttered to herself. "In bed before 9:30. Oh, well." She molded the pillow to her satisfaction and pulled the quilt up around her ears. "At least I finally have my own bed and things from home."

It wasn't much comfort, but it was the best she could do under the circumstances. Despite her plan to stay awake until Tabitha's discussion with their parents ended, Cass was asleep within a half-hour.

Cass' first thought when she awoke the next morning was that she should never consider going into police work. One stakeout, and she'd be fired for falling asleep on the job. Disgusted with herself for being such a slacker, she pushed back the covers and jumped out of bed. She met Mom in the hall.

"Good morning, sweetie." Smiling, Mom smoothed Cass' sleep-tousled hair. "How do pancakes sound for breakfast?"

"Uh ... fine." Cass glanced at Tabitha's door, which remained shut. "What's with Tabitha? She's usually up by now."

A brief shadow passed across Mom's face. "We told her she could sleep in this morning. The conversation got rather emotional at times last night, and Dad and I thought she'd appreciate a break. She might head on to school later this morning, but it depends on how she feels."

"Oh." Cass darted another glance in the direction of Tabitha's bedroom. "Did it get bad last night? Was she really upset?"

A slight smile curved Mom's lips. "It was tense at times. But all in all, I'd say it went well, especially considering the subject we discussed. Both Tabitha and her father have very strong feelings when it comes to Beth. I did my best to keep the conversation on track, but sometimes it veered off into very painful areas. They aired feelings they've kept buried all these years, which was good. Still," she wearily passed a hand over her eyes, "it's not fun to dredge up the past. People tend to say things they later regret."

Cass didn't like the sound of that. "Did Dad and Tabitha say things they regretted?"

Mom nodded. "Yes, but they apologized and everything ended on a positive note."

Then why do you look so worried? wondered Cass. Aloud, she asked, "Did y'all reach a decision about whether or not Tabitha's going to Oregon for Christmas?"

Mom hesitated. "I'd be more comfortable if you talked to Tabitha and let her answer whatever questions you have about the situation."

"But she's asleep," protested Cass. "At least tell me what's going to happen at Christmas. I can't go to school without knowing that."

Mom sighed. "It's obvious you're anxious. Tabitha said she told you about her mother's invitation last night."

Cass made a hurry-up motion with her hands. "Come on," she urged. "Forget the build up. Is she spending Christmas with her mother? Yes or no?"

"No." Mom smiled when Cass sighed in relief. "We told Tabitha in no uncertain terms that we'll be celebrating our first Christmas as a family together. No one's going anywhere."

"Good," Cass said, then frowned. "How did she take it though? Was she upset?"

"I'll let her fill you in on all the details." Mom started for the kitchen, paused, and looked back at Cass. "And don't go stomping around, slamming doors, and clearing your throat a hundred times to wake her up. Honestly, it sounded like a herd of elephants out here last night while we were talking to Tabitha."

Cass grinned. "I wanted to make sure y'all knew I was here. You know, in case anybody wanted to talk to me."

"From the racket you made, half the island knew where you were," Mom good-naturedly retorted. "Okay, I'm off to make breakfast now. Just think, you have the bathroom to yourself this morning. No arguing with Tabitha over who's taking too long or whose turn it is."

Throughout the morning at school, Cass kept an anxious eye out for Tabitha, but her stepsister never showed. When she met up with Kira in Spanish class, Kira questioned her about Tabitha's absence, but all Cass gave her was a vague response about Tabitha being tired.

Cass barely had time to sit down and open her lunch bag before Kira questioned her again.

"All right, what's going on? And don't—" she fixed Cass with a warning stare, "—give me some song-and-dance about Tabitha needing a break. She was fine yesterday. In fact, she was looking forward to school today because we were supposed to go to the library during history period and research a paper for class."

Cass squirmed when she realized Rianne was also awaiting her reply. "I'm not sure I'm allowed to talk about what's going on," she mumbled. To forestall having to provide a more detailed answer, she crammed half her sandwich into her mouth.

Her action didn't discourage Kira in the slightest from following up with another question. "Does it have anything to do with Tabitha's mother asking her to fly to Oregon for Christmas?"

Rianne's mouth dropped open in shock while Cass scowled at Kira. Hastily chewing and swallowing, she scolded, "What if Tabitha hadn't mentioned her mother's invitation to me?"

Kira waved aside her concern. "She told me the day before yesterday that she was going to talk to you about it. I assumed she had by now and obviously I was right. Anyway, to get back to my question. Is the reason she's absent because of Beth in some way?"

Cass glanced warily at Rianne. "I guess it'll all come out sooner or later," she grumbled, turning her attention back to Kira. "Tabitha and our parents had a long talk last night. I don't know anything that was said, except for the fact that they told her she wasn't allowed to go to Oregon over Christmas. Mom didn't tell me how she took the news, but I can't imagine she was happy about it." Hesitating, she added softly, "Personally, I'm thrilled. When she told me about the possibility yesterday, I couldn't believe she'd given the trip a second thought."

"Same here." Kira's hearty agreement surprised Cass. "I can't understand what the deal is with her and her mother. Why she hasn't told the woman to get lost is beyond me."

Before Cass could comment, Rianne raised her hand. "I'm kind of in the dark here. I know about Tabitha's mother all of a sudden showing back up in her life. But what's this about her wanting Tabitha to visit her—and at Christmas, of all times?"

Taking turns, Cass and Kira filled her in on what they knew. Since Tabitha had shared more information with Kira, Cass found out Beth had offered to pay for Tabitha's plane ticket and wanted her to spend her entire ten-day vacation in Oregon.

Cass startled her friends by slapping the table. "You're her best friend. Can't you talk to her?" she demanded of Kira. "She doesn't seem to want to listen to me, but maybe you can talk some sense into her."

"Believe me, I've tried." Kira shook her head in disgust. "It's like she has this huge blind spot when it comes to her mother. She keeps insisting she has to give her a chance, that maybe she really has changed. I can't explain why, but I don't think she has. There's something about Beth's sudden interest in Tabitha that gives me the creeps. I've tried telling Tabitha that, but she doesn't want to hear it. She's convinced she should give her mother the benefit of the doubt."

"Maybe she should," Rianne said softly. Although she flinched when Cass glared at her, she didn't back down. "We don't know what God's plans are in this. We all have our opinion of what they are and what we'd like Tabitha to do. But I think the bottom line is Tabitha has to be respectful toward Beth because she is, after all, her mother. I think we all need to trust that because God cares so much about her, He will lead her where she needs to go."

"But what if it's away from Kwaj?" Kira said in a small voice. "Do you honestly think God might be leading her to eventually move in with her mother?"

"I … I don't know." Rianne's confidence faltered. "I don't want to think that, but I guess anything's possible."

"No." Cass' quiet, but steely, tone caused the others to turn to her. "I refuse to believe God would bring us together as a family only to have Tabitha leave after such a short time. It doesn't make any sense."

"God doesn't always make sense, at least not to our way of thinking," Rianne said gently.

As a sick feeling crept into her stomach, Cass pushed aside her lunch. "Has Tabitha said anything to you about wanting to live with her mother?" she asked Kira.

Kira shook her head, although her face had taken on a haunted expression. "No. So far all she's talked about is visiting her. But it's like the situation is escalating. In the beginning, she was just happy to get a letter every now and then from Beth. Then she started saying she'd like to talk to her. Now she wants to see her." By turns, Kira gazed at the two faces solemnly staring at her. "I'm scared to think what's next."

Moaning, Cass buried her face in her hands. Beside her, Rianne patted her back in an effort to comfort her.

"Why can't life ever be simple?" Cass raised her head.

"It's a constant struggle. As soon as you get one thing set-tled, something else pops up. Tabitha and I went through our parents getting married and learning how to get along. She finally worked things out with Micah and I did the same with Logan. Now this. I used to wish for a more excit-ing life. Now all I want is for it to be boring."

"What was it your mother said a couple of meetings ago?" Rianne frowned, trying to recall her exact words. "Something like, don't pray for an easy life. Pray for the strength to meet the challenges God sends your way."

Cass glowered at her. "You're starting to get on my nerves. Would you please let me moan and groan awhile without being so reasonable? I don't want advice or catchy little sayings. I just want to vent a little, and I'd appreciate your cooperation. When I throw myself a pity party, I expect you to show up and participate."

"Oh, okay," Rianne said, and Cass could tell she was try-ing not to laugh. "I didn't know the rules. Go ahead and whine away to your heart's content. I won't say a word." She assumed an expression of mock concern. "Unless, of course, I'm supposed to respond in some way. This is all new to me."

Cass refused to respond to Rianne's teasing, although she felt a good deal of the tension starting to drain away. "How did you put up with such a goody-two-shoes all those years before I got here?"

"Mostly we ignored her. Ow!" Kira yelled suddenly. "Don't kick me." She glared at Rianne, then turned back to Cass. "Plus, we flipped coins. The loser had to spend time with her." She grinned and before Rianne could respond added, "Now let's talk about something fun, like my party. Have you thought of any good movies we could rent?"

CHAPTER 12

After school had let out, and Cass had run in and run out to go snorkeling with Logan, Tabitha was surprised to hear the doorbell ring. Since Mom was out on the lanai, Tabitha went to answer it. She shrieked and nearly slammed the door in Micah's face when she discovered him standing on the step.

Why, oh why, didn't I at least bother to fix my hair? she lamented.

"Uh …" Micah hesitated. "Did I come at a bad time? You don't seem too happy to see me."

"I'm sorry." Tabitha raked her fingers through her curls in a fruitless attempt to restore some order. She didn't even want to think about what she looked like in her wrinkled shorts and faded T-shirt. "I wasn't expecting you." She stepped aside. "Come on in. Mom's out back, repainting a knickknack shelf that got banged up on the trip from Tennessee."

Micah followed her into the living room and handed her a candy bar and magazine. "I thought you might need something to cheer you up."

Tabitha's features softened with appreciation. "You're so sweet. Thank you." She placed the magazine on the coffee table, but held onto the candy bar. "I'll read that later. Would you like to split this with me?"

Micah shook his head. "That's okay. I brought it for you."

"Then it's mine and I can do whatever I want with it." Tabitha's eyes danced with mischief. "And what I want to do is share it with you. Would you like a glass of milk to go with your half?"

Micah conceded defeat with a smile. "Fine, you win. Milk and half a candy bar sounds good." He blocked Tabitha's way when she started for the kitchen. "At least let me do that much for you. Sit down and I'll be right back."

While Micah poured their milk, Tabitha carefully divided the candy into two equal pieces. She waited until Micah sat down on the other end of the couch before giving him his share.

"I take it you haven't been sick with an upset stomach," Micah remarked as he watched Tabitha devour her piece in a matter of seconds.

She smiled, slightly embarrassed. "I kind of inhaled that, huh?"

"That's putting it mildly." Micah held out his half to her. "Are you sure you wouldn't like my piece too?"

"What, and be greedy as well as a hog?" Tabitha said with mock indignation. "I have my pride, you know." Dropping the pose, she urged him, "You eat it. It's not like Mom starved me all day. She's one of those mothers who believes food is the answer to just about all of life's problems."

"So what was wrong today?" Micah took a bite of candy and leaned back against the sofa arm to await Tabitha's reply. After a heavy silence he added, "If you don't feel like talking about it, that's fine. I understand."

"Don't worry," she said quickly in response to his embarrassed look, "It's nothing personal. I just … well … I wasn't actually sick or anything. Mom let me stay home from school because I … uh … we had a … a difficult discussion last night, and I was pretty beat this morning."

"Oh. Are you in some kind of trouble?"

"Not really. Dad's upset with me, but it's on account of my mother." Tabitha checked the kitchen to make sure Mom hadn't come in before continuing, "I told them about her asking me to go to Oregon for Christmas."

Micah emitted a long, low whistle. "I'll bet that went over like a lead balloon."

Tabitha's answering laugh was droll. "That's putting it mildly. Anyway, to make a long story short, they told me I wasn't allowed to spend Christmas with her."

Micah hesitated. "Are you mad at them for that?"

Torn between nodding and shaking her head, Tabitha settled for a shrug. "I was at first, but mostly because of the way Dad put it. He got all huffy and said stuff like, 'who does my mother think she is' and 'what kind of game is she playing.' Actually, I wonder the same thing about her and what's going on, but I didn't like hearing him say it. I felt like I had to defend her. Then that got Dad going even more, and it turned into a big hassle for a while before Mom settled things down again."

"You did have a rough night," agreed Micah. His brow knitted in a frown. "Okay, so you're not all that mad at your folks for their decision. But are you sad you won't be going to see your mother?"

Tabitha, who'd spent most of the day contemplating that question, still didn't have a definite answer. "There's a part of me that was looking forward to spending time with her and getting to know her. It would really help if I could ask her about the past and why she did the things she did. I guess I could on the phone, but I think it would be better to do it in person. But," she went on, "I realized today how relieved I am that I'm not going to see her. I'm not ready for it. She's still a stranger, and the thought of spending almost two weeks with somebody I hardly know was kind of scary. Even though I acted like I wanted to go in front of Mom and Dad, deep down, I was glad when they said no. The only problem is ..." Her voice trailed off, and she stared over Micah's shoulder, chewing on her bottom lip.

"Is what?" he prompted when the silence lengthened to several seconds.

"What if my not going makes Beth so mad she cuts me off again?" Tabitha asked in a rush.

There! she thought. *It's finally out in the open.* She hadn't been able to voice her fear to anyone until now, and saying it out loud was like having a crushing weight lifted off her shoulders.

Micah scooted across the cushions and took Tabitha's hand, sandwiching it between his. "You're one of the strongest people I know. If that happens, you'll deal with it. Plus, it'll tell you a lot about the kind of person she is and what her motivation was for contacting you."

Tabitha nodded slowly. "That's true. Besides, I've done fine without her all these years. If she decides to pull another disappearing act, I'm sure I'll be disappointed for a while but I'll get over it. Who needs somebody like that in their life anyway?"

Micah grinned. "That's the spirit. Like I said, you're one tough cookie."

Tabitha felt herself truly relax for the first time since her conversation the night before with her parents. "So whatever happens, it's going to be okay." She briefly rested her head on Micah's shoulder. "Thank you. I needed to talk to someone about this. I thought it would be Cass, but she's off snorkeling with Logan." Straightening, she smiled at Micah. "I'm glad you turned out to be the one I confided in."

Brushing a stray curl off her cheek, Micah murmured, "I'm glad, too. You're very special to me. When you hurt, I hurt."

Tabitha's breath caught in her throat. "That's probably the nicest thing anyone's ever said to me."

"Oh, yeah?" Micah's pleased grin stretched from ear to ear. "In that case, you ain't heard nothing yet. I plan to shower you with so much sweet talk, your head will spin."

"Ooh, goody." Tabitha clapped. "When are you going to start?"

Micah grinned. "That would be ... as soon as I finish my candy bar." He popped the rest into his mouth.

Tabitha punched his arm. "Men! All you ever think about is your stomachs."

"That's not true," Micah argued then glanced behind him at the kitchen. "Hey, do you think your Mom would mind if I fixed myself a sandwich?"

Throwing her hands up in the air, Tabitha declared, "I rest my case."

Micah stood up and extended his hand to help Tabitha off the couch. She followed him to the kitchen, thinking, *I might not have my mother anymore once I tell her I'm not coming, but I have a great family, terrific friends, and*—she smiled at Micah's back—*the absolutely best boyfriend in the whole world. Mother or no mother, I am very blessed.*

Chapter 13

"I love this time of year." Hugging herself, Cass twirled twice then stopped to grin at Tabitha. They were at the bowling alley, waiting for Logan and Micah to join them. "It's just one holiday after another. Only two weeks until Thanksgiving. Yum. Wait until you taste Mom's turkey."

"Cut it out," Tabitha ordered irritably. "You're off the perkiness meter and it's embarrassing me."

"Party pooper." Cass stuck her tongue out at her. "You're just mad because you know Logan and I are going to beat you and Micah at bowling tonight."

"You know I don't care about winning the way you do," Tabitha coolly informed her. "If I'm crabby, it's because you're getting on my nerves by being so annoyingly cheerful."

Cass shrugged. "I can't help it if I'm naturally upbeat. I consider it my solemn duty to spread joy and happiness wherever I go."

Tabitha pretended to gag. "Puh-leeze. You spread something all right, but it's not joy and happiness." She lifted her feet as if slogging through thick mud. "In fact, it's getting pretty deep in here."

Cass laughed. "How rude! If I weren't such a good-natured person, I'd be highly insulted."

"Just my luck you're so good-natured," grumbled Tabitha. "I meant to insult you."

"I know." Cass lightly pinched Tabitha's cheek, chuckling when Tabitha brushed her hand away. "I'm sorry I'm being so uncooperative."

"Like that's anything new."

"I am predictable, aren't I? I'm going to have to work on being more wild and crazy."

Micah and Logan appeared before Tabitha could respond. She greeted the boys with a tight smile.

Logan elbowed Micah in the ribs. "Doesn't look like your girlfriend's too happy to see you," he teased.

"Aw, I'm not worried." Micah sidled up next to Tabitha and slipped an arm around her waist. "She may not show it, but inside she's turning cartwheels."

Tabitha laughed. Batting her lashes at Micah, she cooed, "Nobody knows me like you do. That's why I chose you out of the dozens of guys who were after me."

Micah made a face. "Gee, now I feel special."

Logan mopped his brow in mock relief. "I'm glad you don't talk to me like that," he said to Cass.

She rounded on him, pretending to be upset. "What are you saying? That no other boys are interested in me?"

"Yes … uh … I mean, no," Logan sputtered.

Cass' face lit up. "You know guys who'd like to date me?" She pretended to hold a notebook and pencil. "Names. I want names."

Grinning, Micah jostled Logan. "Makes what Tabitha said to me seem pretty tame, doesn't it?"

"Drop dead," growled Logan, although the corners of his mouth twitched with amusement.

They moved to the desk, where they were assigned a lane and given shoes. Tabitha held hers at arm's length as they headed to their lane.

"These—" she gave the shoes a shake, "—are the main reason why I could never be a professional bowler. You'd think somebody could design a pair of shoes that didn't make bowlers look like complete dorks."

"The shoes are part of the charm of the sport," protested Cass. "That and the shirts. I knew some people on bowling leagues back home. The shirts are made out of this shiny material, and you can get your name embroidered over the right pocket. They're adorable."

As Cass expected, Tabitha shot her a "you've got to be kidding" look. "I used to think you had very little fashion sense. Now I realize you don't have any at all. Zero, zip, nada."

"We've known each other five months, and you just figured that out?" Cass shook her head in amazement. "You're even slower than I thought you were."

Tabitha laughed, so Cass figured the shadow that passed over Tabitha's face was her imagination. "I like to give people the benefit of the doubt. I kept hoping you had some shred of taste."

"Hey, good one," Micah said, laughing. "Score one for the feisty blonde."

Tabitha executed a demure curtsy before going off in search of a bowling ball. Micah soon followed, leaving Cass and Logan by themselves.

Leaning close to Cass, Logan joked, "Ah, alone at last."

"Yup, throw in a few candles, and this could be quite the romantic setting." Mimicking Tabitha's flirtatious display, Cass fanned her lashes at him. "You sure know how to show a girl a good time."

Logan puffed out his chest. "Nothing's too good for you."

"I appreciate that." With a wry glance around the noisy alley, Cass added, "I think."

They both laughed and finished tying their shoes and

went in search of their own bowling balls. As they hunted for the right ones, Logan suddenly nudged Cass.

"Look at Tabitha." He pointed to where she was sitting alone at the lane, waiting for the others. "She usually works so hard at being up. But she doesn't know we're watching her right now, and she's as down as I've ever seen her. This thing with her mother has really gotten to her, huh?"

Cass' expression was grim as she secretly studied her stepsister. "Yes it has and I'd love to give Beth a piece of my mind. The least she could do is let Tabitha know it's okay she's not going up there for Christmas, even if she has to lie. Tabitha's scared she's never going to hear from her again. Personally, I think it'd be the best thing that could happen to her, but she's thoroughly depressed at the possibility."

"Is there anything Micah and I can do to help?" Logan asked.

Cass smiled at him, filled with gratitude. "Just keep doing what you've been doing. Be her friend. Include her in whatever's going on. That way maybe she'll remember her place is here with us, not in Oregon with her sorry excuse of a mother."

Logan smiled. "No problem there."

As expected, Cass and Logan handily won all three games. Their next stop was the Ten-Ten, where they bought chips and colas to snack on while they sat on the beach and talked.

Gazing at the phosphorescence shimmering on the ocean, Cass remarked, "I've almost gotten used to the fact that the temperature will be in the eighties on Thanksgiving Day. Mom's even brought up the possibility of going swimming that afternoon just so we can tell everybody back home we did it."

"In that case, you'd better hope it doesn't rain." Crossing his legs Indian-style, Micah propped his bag of chips in his lap. "Actually, though, it wouldn't make much difference if it did. It's not like we have to worry about thunder and lightning around here."

"Plus, the rain is so warm it's like standing under a shower," Tabitha added.

Cass turned to Logan. "You're from Pennsylvania, so you're used to it being cold at Thanksgiving. Do you miss being home for the holidays?"

Logan stiffened the way he always did when anyone brought up Pennsylvania. "No," he replied flatly. For a moment, it seemed as if he wouldn't say any more then he added, "You know I don't ever think about where I came from. All that matters to me is what's happening here and now. I don't care about the past or the future. I just live for today."

As usual, Cass wondered what it was about his past that Logan was hiding. She knew better than to ask, because no matter how hard she tried, she couldn't get him to open up to her.

"Christians can't just live for today," she argued. "We're always supposed to be looking ahead to heaven. Like Paul wrote in one of his letters, we have to keep our eyes on the prize as we run the race."

Digging a small shell out of the sand, Logan tossed it at Cass. "You know that's not what I meant. Of course I think about heaven." His voice lost its teasing quality. "I just don't think about Pennsylvania. Or what's going to happen when I leave here to go to college," he added softly.

Suddenly, they all grew quiet. This wasn't exactly Cass' favorite topic, and she knew the others felt the same.

Micah noisily cleared his throat, breaking the mood. "Okay guys, we have a choice. We can either sit here and make ourselves miserable thinking about what's going to happen almost a year down the road, or we can make the most of what we have."

"Which is?" Cass muttered, not quite ready to quit moping.

Micah spread his arms in an expansive gesture. "Each other. Right now. This place. It hardly gets better than this."

Cass snorted. "You sound like a sappy greeting card."

"Hey!" Tabitha huffed indignantly. "That's my boyfriend you're insulting, and I won't have it."

Micah flashed her an appreciative smile. "Thanks for sticking up for me."

Tabitha reached over to pat his arm. "Any time. No one's going to badmouth you while I'm around." She paused, then laughed. "That's my job."

"Way to ruin a tender moment," Micah said darkly, but then laughed as well.

They stayed on the beach and talked until Logan checked his watch and announced it was 10:30. Since Cass and Tabitha had an 11:00 curfew, Tabitha and Micah stood and brushed the sand from their shorts.

"I guess Tabitha and I will get going." Micah reached for her hand and Tabitha slipped it into his. "We'll meet you guys back at the house."

Logan and Cass waited a few minutes while the other couple located their bikes and took off. Sitting next to Logan, Cass' emotions were a mixture of happiness and expectancy. The chant, *Will this be the night?* repeated itself over and over in her head. They had yet to kiss, and each time they were together Cass kept hoping it would finally happen.

"I had fun tonight," Logan broke the comfortable silence that had descended between them.

"Me too." Cass heaved a contented sigh. "I like double-dating, especially with Tabitha and Micah. They're a great couple."

Logan scooted closer to Cass so that their arms brushed.

"Are we a great couple?"

"We—" Cass turned to him with a soft laugh, "—are an outstanding couple."

The laughter died in her throat when she realized that Logan's face was just inches from hers. Her breathing immediately kicked into overdrive. She tried to look away, but Logan's unblinking stare kept her eyes riveted to his.

"May I kiss you?" His whispered request was as gentle as the breeze that caressed them.

Unable to speak, Cass merely nodded. As if in slow motion, Logan's face moved closer and closer until, at the last second, Cass remembered to close her eyes. The feel of his lips against hers lasted only a moment, but it was enough to send her pulse racing and to set off a flurry of fireworks in her head.

"Thank you." Taking Cass' hand, Logan laced his fingers through hers. "I've been wanting to do that for a long time."

Without thinking, Cass blurted, "Not as much as I've been wanting you to." At Logan's yelp of surprised laughter, she blushed with embarrassment. "Oops. I guess I'm not supposed to admit that."

"You don't ever have to hold back when you're around me. You can always say whatever's on your mind," Logan said softly. "Besides," he added, grinning, "it's nice to know you've been thinking about kissing me." He puffed out his chest in a mock display of vanity. "I can't tell you what it does for my ego to know you daydream about me."

Snorting, Cass rolled her eyes. "Like your ego needs any more building up. I think guys are born feeling good about themselves."

"Hah," scoffed Logan. "That just shows how little you really know about the male of the species. We're actually very insecure, which is why we thrive on compliments. Would you like to help me feel less insecure by letting me know what you think of my kissing ability?"

With effort, Cass managed to control the smile tugging at the corners of her mouth. "I don't know if I can. I don't have anything to compare it with."

Logan's jaw dropped in astonishment. "That was your first kiss?"

"If you don't count the ones I got playing spin the bottle in middle school." Cass shrugged, not the least bit uncomfortable with her admission. "Yes, it was."

"Wow." Logan beamed at her. "That's terrific."

Cass no longer bothered to hide her amusement. "Why does that make you so happy?"

"Because," Logan explained, his face and tone earnest, "I heard a friend's sister talking with her friends once, and they all agreed that girls always remember the boys who gave them their first kiss."

Touched, Cass squeezed Logan's hand. "You like the thought of me remembering you?" she asked softly.

"I don't want you to ever forget me," Logan murmured in response.

"Don't worry," Cass assured him. "One thing you're not is forgettable." Before things could get too sappy, she suggested, "Let's head on. That way, we can take our time and not race back to the house."

When they reached their bikes, they decided to walk instead of ride. As they wheeled them toward the road, Logan glanced at Cass, his expression mischievous.

"You want to see if we can find Micah and Tabitha?"

"You mean to spy on them?" When Logan nodded, Cass acted shocked. "What a totally juvenile suggestion." She couldn't hold back her grin. "I love it. Unfortunately, it would be wrong. Besides, we wouldn't want them spying on us."

Logan laughed. "Until tonight, they wouldn't have wanted to bother." He gave Cass a curious look. "Are you going to tell Tabitha that we kissed?"

Cass' nod was immediate and definite. "Of course. That's one of the perks of having a sister. She's right there to share something as wonderful as tonight with. I don't have to wait until tomorrow to call her, like I will with Rianne."

Logan's eyebrows shot up in alarm. "You're going to tell Rianne too?"

Cass grinned at his obvious discomfort. "Face it, the news is going to be all over the island by tomorrow night. Kwaj has a very active grapevine."

Logan frowned. "Does that mean everyone knew we hadn't kissed yet?"

"Yup." She reached out and lightly hit his arm. "Everyone was taking bets as to when you'd finally kiss me."

"Oh, man." Logan groaned. "I wish you hadn't told me that. Come Monday, I won't be able to look any of the girls in the eye. They probably think I'm some kind of a throwback to the last century."

"No way," Cass asserted. "They all think it's sweet. They're sick to death of every date turning into a wrestling match. As far as most of my friends are concerned, I'm the luckiest girl on Kwaj to be dating you."

"Wow." Logan stood a little straighter. "So I'm considered a catch."

Cass smiled to herself. "I just hope you don't let it go to your head and wind up dumping me because of all the other girls out there dying to date you."

Logan just looked at her in a way that made breathing difficult. "You don't have anything to worry about."

In an effort to lighten the mood, she gave him a stern look. "Good. I wouldn't be very happy about losing you to some other girl who wouldn't appreciate you as much as I do."

"It's not going to happen," Logan reassured her again. "The only way you're going to get rid of me is if you tell me to take a hike. And even then," he added with a laugh, "I'd probably still hang around, hoping you'll change your mind."

When they reached the house, they found Micah and Tabitha already there, talking quietly on the lanai. Cass just grinned at her when Tabitha raised a questioning eyebrow. The moment the boys left, Tabitha rounded on Cass.

"You look like you're about to burst. Did 'it' finally happen?"

Savoring Tabitha's curiosity, Cass decided to tease her a bit. "I guess that depends on what it is you're referring to."

Tabitha took her by the arms and playfully shook her. "Don't play games with me, missy. You know what I'm talking about. Did Logan kiss you?"

"He—" Cass drew out the word to prolong the suspense. "Did." Once she said the words, she found it impossible to contain her excitement. "It was wonderful! If I'd known kissing was this much fun, I'd have started years ago."

Tabitha laughed. "But aren't you glad you waited for someone as special as Logan to come along to give you your first one?"

Cass nodded enthusiastically. "I'm more than glad. I'm ecstatic. Like Logan said, I'll always remember him because he was the first."

Linking arms with Cass, Tabitha began leading her toward the back door. "I won't forget it, either. Sisters are supposed to remember stuff like this for each other."

Cass shot her an amused glance. "Where did you get that? Out of the sister handbook?"

Tabitha refused to take the bait. "I made it up," she admitted cheerfully. "But it sounds good, don't you think?"

"It sounds perfect." Unable to squeeze through the door together, Cass slipped her arm out of Tabitha's and motioned for her to go first. "Being able to come home and tell you about it made the experience even more special."

"So you're not sad Janette isn't around to talk to?" Tabitha asked over her shoulder.

"Not in the least," Cass answered without hesitation. She poked Tabitha in the back. "And aren't you happy you're here, instead of off somewhere with your mother, missing out on all the fun?"

Tabitha halted and spun around to glower at her. "Don't ruin things by bringing up the situation with Beth. Let's just leave it that I'm honored to be the first one you told about Logan kissing you."

"Okay, fine." Cass bit back the rest of what she wanted to say and nodded toward the kitchen. "We'd better get inside before Mom and Dad send out a search party."

CHAPTER 14

The next morning, Cass woke up to an empty house. Tabitha had left a note saying she had gone off on a bike ride, and Mom and Dad left a note that a shipment of turkeys had come in from Honolulu, so they were off to buy Thanksgiving dinner. She enjoyed the chance to play the stereo as loud as she wanted and wander aimlessly from room to room until Dad and Mom returned. As they came through the front door, she jumped off the couch and ran to turn down the music.

"Nice song. We could hear it halfway down the block," Dad complained good-naturedly. "We were hoping it wasn't coming from our house, but alas, we were wrong."

Cass grinned. "Yeah, but just think—if they'd invented stereos back when you were a teenager, you'd have listened with the volume all the way up too."

"Did you hear that?" Dad turned to Mom. "She thinks we were born before record players and hi-fi's."

"Record players? Hi-fi's?" Cass gazed impishly at Dad. "You know, I think I remember seeing those items in an antique shop in Jonesborough. They were really expensive because they were so-o-o old."

Mom and Cass laughed as Dad pretended to be hurt and

staggered out of the room, then they followed him into the kitchen. Once there, Cass hoisted herself onto the counter and accepted the brownie Dad offered her.

"I thought y'all were going shopping for Thanksgiving. Were they already out of turkeys by the time you got there?"

"Nope," Dad answered around a mouthful of brownie. "Your Mom got us a fifteen-pounder. There'll be enough left over for sandwiches and soup." He licked his lips in anticipation. "In fact, we wound up buying so much stuff we couldn't carry it. The taxi's going to deliver everything."

"We are going to have cranberry sauce and sweet potatoes, aren't we?" Cass asked.

"Of course." Mom broke off a piece of Dad's brownie. "It wouldn't be Thanksgiving without cranberries and sweet potatoes."

"Wait until you taste Mom's sweet potato casserole," Cass told Dad. "You'll think you've died and gone to heaven."

Coming up behind Mom, Dad wrapped his arms around her waist. "Just being married to her makes me feel that way."

Mom reached up to pat his cheek. "Aren't you sweet?"

"Exactly when will you be getting over this honeymoon phase?" Cass complained sarcastically. "It's been more than four months, and you still act like a couple of newlyweds."

"Technically, couples are considered newlyweds for the first year of marriage." Mom moved out of Dad's embrace and stepped to the refrigerator.

"Yeah, but isn't that just for young people? It's cute to be young and in love. At your age though—" Cass shuddered. "It might be better if you got over the lovebird stage as quickly as possible."

"Just for that," Dad retrieved a foil-wrapped brownie from the cookie jar and held it just out of Cass' reach, "no more brownies for you. Right, Donna?"

"Absolutely," she concurred.

"Hey!" Cass protested. "Isn't blood supposed to be thicker than water?"

"Not when it comes to old-age jokes," Mom retorted. She linked arms with Dad. "We oldtimers have to stick together."

Before Cass could think of a comeback, the doorbell rang, signaling the arrival of the groceries. She helped Mom and Dad carry the bags from the front door to the kitchen, but opted out of putting away their contents.

"Since Tabitha isn't back from her bike ride yet," she said, "I'm going to head over to the pool and see who's there to hang out with. Tell her come on over when she shows up, okay?"

Busy with maneuvering the turkey into the refrigerator, Mom only paused long enough to nod. Dad lifted a hand in farewell as Cass left the kitchen.

Once at the pool, Cass promptly forgot about Tabitha. Dennis McCrory, a guy from her class, was there as well as two girls she knew from Spanish class. It was after twelve before she even thought to ask about the time.

Goodness. She frowned and glanced in the direction of the house, although she couldn't see it over the fence. *I can't believe Tabitha hasn't returned yet. Maybe I should go home and find out what's happened to her.*

Bidding her friends a hasty goodbye, Cass gathered her belongings, slipped on her sandals, and headed out the gate. Instead of going in the front door of the house, she detoured around back to see if Tabitha's bike was in its usual place on the lanai. It was, which made her not showing up at the pool puzzling. Normally, Tabitha was glad to join Cass when she went swimming. Curious to find out what was going on, Cass hurried into the house. Dad was the first person she encountered.

"Where's Tabitha?"

Dad looked up from the peanut butter and jelly sandwich he was making. "In her room, I think. Why?"

"Did you tell her I wanted her to come to the pool when she got back?"

"Yes, but she decided to call her mother first." He frowned. "After they talked, she went off to her room."

Cass was suddenly filled with dread. "Why did she call Beth? Did she get tired of waiting to hear from her? I know it's been bugging her that Beth hasn't contacted her."

Dad turned and leaned back against the counter to look at Cass as he spoke. "I guess you don't know that Tabitha's mother called while the two of you were out last night. Since a Christmas visit is out, she wanted to know if I objected to Tabitha going up there during winter break."

Cass' stomach lurched. She'd thought the matter had been settled when Tabitha rejected Beth's Christmas invitation. Now it had reared its ugly head again.

"I hope you told her you absolutely, positively object," she declared heatedly.

"Actually, I said it's Tabitha's decision." Dad hung his head, as if regretting his response. "Your Mom and I talked to Tabitha after you went to bed last night and told her it's her call. We'll support her, whatever she decides."

"Are you nuts?" Cass exclaimed. "She might decide to go."

"She already has." Dad's sigh was heavy with regret. "That's why she called her mother, to let her know she's flying up to Oregon in January."

Several seconds passed before Cass could speak. Anger and fear clogged her throat, choking off the words she wanted to hurl at Dad. After a few deep breaths, she finally found her voice.

"You cannot let her do this," she ordered, speaking slowly and distinctly. "She'll be making the biggest mistake of her life."

"Your mom and I discussed it, and it's a risk we're willing to take." Dad passed a weary hand over his eyes. "We're trusting God to work His will in the situation."

"But what if His will is for Tabitha to stay in Oregon with Beth?" It pained Cass to speak the possibility out loud.

Dad's expression was haunted as he shifted his gaze to stare out the window. "Then we accept it," he replied so softly Cass had to strain to hear him. "Mom and I believe God is in control, and we have to be willing to go along with His plan, no matter what. You know, like Jesus went ahead with His plan to die on the cross. Sometimes things look like they're wrong—when really, it's the only way it can happen."

Cass refused to subscribe to this theory and vehemently shook her head. "Uh-uh. I don't believe God brought us together as a family only to break us up." Squaring her shoulders, she announced, "And I'm going to tell Tabitha that. Somebody around here has to talk straight to her. If you and Mom won't put your foot down, I will."

With that, Cass marched past Dad, through the living room, and down the hall to Tabitha's room. She flung open the door without knocking, startling her stepsister who was sprawled on her bed.

"Excuse me?" Tabitha arched a questioning eyebrow at Cass. "I don't remember giving you permission to come in."

"That's because I didn't ask." Shoving aside Tabitha's legs, Cass plopped down on the bed.

"Hey!" Tabitha yelped. "Your suit's still wet. Get off."

Cass ignored her. "Not until we talk. What's this about you going to Oregon in January? Have you lost your mind?"

"Gee, don't hold back," drawled Tabitha. "Tell me what you really think about the idea."

"This is no laughing matter," Cass scolded. "We're dealing with your future here, and what affects you affects the rest of us. Has it occurred to you that you might not come back if you go through with this stupid trip?"

Tabitha's eyes flickered away from Cass. "I'll come back," she muttered.

"Yeah? Says who?" challenged Cass. "It seems to me you're playing with fire if you visit your mother. What if she lays a humongous guilt trip on you about your Dad having you all these years and now it's her turn? Have you thought about that? What if you fall in love with your little brother and sister and can't stand the thought of leaving them? Don't you realize the disastrous consequences the trip could have?"

Tabitha raised up to a sitting position and glared at her. "For your information, I have thought it through. That's all I did while I was out riding this morning. I wanted so badly to stop and talk with Kira and Micah, but I knew I had to make up my own mind. I eventually wound up at the lagoon and was sitting on the beach when I realized seeing Beth is something I have to do. Whatever it means to me and to the family, I have to go up there. I won't be able to lay things to rest until I do."

"I hate this!" Cass' hands clenched into fists in her lap. "What about me? What happens to me if you decide being with Beth is the right thing to do? How am I supposed to live here without you?"

For the first time, Tabitha's face crumpled. "I don't know," she whispered. "I wish I could tell you it'll be all right, but I can't." She shook her head, her expression miserable. "I'm sorry."

Realizing Tabitha's confusion matched her own, Cass let up on her attack. "Maybe it'll all work out somehow." She neither looked nor sounded convinced it would, but she felt honor bound to try being hopeful. "Dad said he believes God is in charge and that He won't let anything happen against His will." Unsure where she stood on the subject, she glanced at Tabitha. "Do you believe that?"

Tabitha shrugged. "I'm not sure what I believe anymore. Besides, you've been a Christian longer than I have. You're the one who's supposed to have all the answers."

"Hah!" scoffed Cass. "I'm as clueless as you are when it comes to something like this. I know what I should believe, but there's a part of me that wants me to be in charge, not God. It's hard to turn control over to Him and say 'Your will be done.' What if things don't turn out the way I want them to?"

"You deal with it?" suggested Tabitha. "Of course, that's easier said than done. Plus in my case, I don't know exactly what I want to happen. I go back and forth between wanting things to work out with my mother and wanting the visit to be a bust so I can come back here with a clear conscience, knowing I tried."

A ghost of a smile curved Cass' lips. "You're one mixed-up chick," she teased.

"Tell me about it." Tabitha relaxed against the headboard. "I figure I'm going to be doing a whole lot of praying between now and when I leave for Oregon."

"Same here." Cass stood up slowly.

"What will you be praying for?" Tabitha asked as Cass moved to the door.

Her hand on the knob, Cass stopped and bowed her head a moment. When she spoke, her voice was low and intense, "That you'll come back to us once your visit with Beth is over and that our family will pick up where we left off."

"Oh." Tabitha stopped and when she turned toward the window, Cass decided she wasn't going to say more so she left the room.

CHAPTER 15

The next day in church, Cass found herself praying more fervently than she ever had. Seated between Mom and Tabitha, she paid little attention to Pastor Thompson's sermon as she silently begged God over and over to somehow prevent the trip to Oregon. When the service ended, Cass was surprised to find she was exhausted.

This praying without ceasing is harder than I realized, she thought as she accompanied her parents and Tabitha to the bike rack outside the chapel.

"Who's up for lunch at the Yuk?" Dad retrieved Mom's bike before going back for his own.

Tabitha hesitated. "Uh ... could I check with Micah and see if he's planning on us doing something?"

"In other words, you'll go with us if you don't get a better offer?" Dad laughed. "I'm kidding. Go on. Ask Micah what the plans are, if any."

"Logan's standing over there," Cass said as Tabitha hurried off. "Do you mind if I go talk to him before I give you an answer?"

Logan had a history test to study for, as well as math homework. After he and Cass talked for a few minutes, he reluctantly climbed on his bike and took off for home. Cass returned to Mom and Dad, filled with discontent.

"Looks like I'm going to lunch with y'all," she said darkly.

"Gee, try to contain your enthusiasm." Mom patted Cass' back in sympathy. "I know we're not your first choice, but we'll do our best to show you a good time."

"Don't try to cheer me up." Cass accepted the bike Dad wheeled over to her. "I want to be in a bad mood, and I'd appreciate it if you'd let me."

Dad executed a courtly bow. "Your wish is our command. Since we aim to please, we promise we won't do anything that might accidentally make you happy. How's that?"

Although she wanted to smile, Cass outwardly refused to respond to Dad's teasing. She busied herself with mounting her bike and modestly arranging her skirt. *No need to let him think he's funny*, she thought sourly.

As hard as she tried, Cass couldn't maintain her sour mood in the face of Dad's determined effort to lift her spirits. By the time the trio arrived at the restaurant, Cass was laughing along with Mom at Dad's story about his latest mishap at the radio station. They entered the Yokwe Yuk on a burst of laughter as Dad finished his tale of mixing up the tapes he was supposed to be playing.

"And they actually pay you?" Cass asked.

"Hard to believe, huh?" Dad retorted good-naturedly. "Lucky for me, there aren't that many people willing to relocate to the middle of the Pacific Ocean in order to work in radio. The competition's virtually nil."

"Now, Steve," chided Mom, "you're very good at what you do."

"Such loyalty." Dad slipped an arm around her shoulders and pulled her to his side. "I'm a lucky man."

"Hello?" Cass said loudly. "We're out in public, you know. Look, here comes the hostess. Don't embarrass me by acting like a couple of lovesick teenagers."

Mom sent her a teasing look. "Are you saying this is how you and Logan act?"

Before Cass could sputter a response, the hostess arrived to direct them to a table. She trailed after her parents, scowling.

Cass waited until the meal was half over before she brought up a topic she wanted to discuss with them.

"Was the sermon good this morning?" she asked by way of introduction.

Mom's brows drew together in a puzzled frown. "You should know. You were there."

"I wasn't listening," Cass blithely confessed. "I was too busy praying about the situation with Tabitha and her mother."

"The sermon was excellent. I'm sorry you missed it. However," Mom continued, "I'm pleased you're taking the need to pray for Tabitha seriously. She needs all the prayers she can get as she prepares to visit Beth."

"Oh, she won't be going." Cass dipped a French fry in ketchup and popped it into her mouth. "That's my prayer, that something will happen to cancel the trip."

Mom's expression grew concerned. "Sweetie, I know you mean well but I'm not sure that's the way you should be praying. It's all right to state your preference to God, but you need to realize what happens is ultimately in His hands."

Cass shook her head. "Nope. I spent an hour looking through the Bible last night, and there are a lot of passages about believing what you pray for so it'll happen. You just have to have faith, and I do. I believe with all my heart that God isn't going to allow Tabitha to go to Oregon because, if she goes, it'll ruin everything."

Mom pushed aside her plate and folded her arms along the edge of the table. "Wiser people than I have tried to explain the connection between faith and answered prayer," she said with a slight frown, "but the bottom line is God makes the final decisions, sometimes for reasons we can't ever understand here on earth. We have to trust that He always has our best interests at heart."

Cass scowled. "I don't like that plan," she said darkly. "Why can't God be nice and do what we ask Him?"

"Because then the world would be in an even bigger mess than it already is. Think of some of the things you've prayed for that later turned out to be bad ideas." Mom paused. "For example, Dad and I wouldn't be married if you'd gotten your way. Last year, you wanted more than anything to be allowed to go skiing with that group from your class, which would have resulted in you being in the car accident that put several of the kids in the hospital. Then there was—"

Cass held up her hand. "Okay, I get the picture. Only God knows the future and what's best for us." Her expression turned wistful. "So where does that leave us poor human beings? Are we doomed to stumble around, trying to figure out His will? It seems so hopeless."

"Not at all," Dad jumped in. "Romans 8:28 says 'And we know that in all things God works for the good of those who love Him, who have been called according to His purpose.' God works for our good in all things. Not some. Not even most. All. That's a powerful promise, and it's one I'm hanging onto concerning Tabitha and her mother."

Chewing on another fry, Cass thought about Dad's words. "It's a good verse," she conceded. "But it doesn't guarantee anything."

"Well, the verse itself doesn't guarantee anything," Mom said. "But the promise guarantees everything. The God who worked the ultimate good in sending Christ to die for your sins guarantees that He will continue to work good in your life."

"Yeah, but—"

Mom cut her off. "But what you were saying is that it doesn't guarantee that things will turn out the way you want them to."

Cass sighed. "Is it wrong to want things to go a certain way?"

"Of course it's not wrong." Mom pulled her plate back in front of her and picked up her fork. "As long as you remember God has the final word."

"This faith thing was a lot easier when I was younger." Cass smiled wanly at her parents. "It makes me sort of wish I didn't have to grow up."

She picked up her hamburger, trying to ignore the lump of dread in her stomach that seemed to be growing bigger by the day.

CHAPTER 16

"What are you going to do while Tabitha's in Oregon with her mother?"

It was the day after Thanksgiving and Cass was at the Thayer house, feasting on leftover turkey with Rianne and Randy. She looked up from her sandwich at Rianne.

"I'm going to go crazy, that's what I'm going to do," Cass declared, earning herself a reproachful look from Randy.

"That's taking a negative view of things," he observed.

Cass flashed him an impatient glance. "Think about it. Tabitha will be gone the two weeks we're off from school, which means I'll be home alone with our parents. Talk about exciting. I'll feel like a fifth wheel since I'll be the one thing keeping them from having the house to themselves."

"You can spend the night here as often as you want," Rianne offered. "And I'm sure Kira would love to host a couple of sleepovers. She's not going to like Tabitha being gone any more than you will."

"You see how many people she's going to affect with this trip?" Cass said darkly. "I wish I could talk some sense into her and make her see how selfish she's being."

"I wouldn't call her selfish," Rianne replied. "But I do

wish somebody could talk her out of going. But then, if Micah couldn't do it, no one can."

Cass propped her elbow on the table and leaned her chin on her fist. "I wonder how hard he tried, though. Whenever anyone brings up the trip, he usually says Tabitha should do whatever she thinks is right. I'll bet if he flat-out told her to stay here, she would."

"Probably, but it wouldn't be right if he did that, and I'm glad he knows it." Rianne studied her sandwhich. "I think Micah's handling the situation quite admirably, even though I have it on the highest authority that his heart is breaking because Tabitha will be gone during his last winter break."

"What authority?" Out of the corner of her eye, Cass caught Randy smothering a smile, and she rounded on him. "It's you, right? Micah's talked to you."

His eyes dancing, Randy held a finger to his lips. "Sorry. I'm not allowed to say. I've been sworn to hold whatever's been told me in the strictest confidence."

"Don't give me that," ordered Cass. Sweeping an arm in Rianne's direction, she pointed out, "You already spilled the beans to your sister."

"Hmm. It appears you have a point." Dropping the secrecy act, Randy continued, "Micah never came right out and told Logan and me we couldn't repeat what he told us. The truth is, he's totally bummed about Tabitha leaving. He had a lot of plans for the break. He'd even been talking to his mother about the possibility of her, Kira, and him flying up to Hono for a few days and having Tabitha come along."

Cass' jaw dropped at the thought. "No joke. Wow. Does Tabitha know about this?"

Randy shook his head. "Before Micah got around to saying anything to her, the thing with her mother came up. He didn't want to make the decision about whether to go or not any harder for her so he didn't mention it."

"I really wish he had. There's no way Tabitha would've turned down the chance to spend time in Hawaii with Micah and Kira."

"Yeah, well, that's water under the bridge," Rianne said briskly. "No use crying over spilled milk."

Cass made a face at her. "Aren't you full of snappy little sayings today?"

Rianne just shrugged. "What's the point of talking about what might have been? The reality is, Tabitha's heading off to Oregon in six weeks and there's not a single thing any of us can do about it."

"Way to sum things up in a nutshell," grumbled Cass. She shot Randy an exasperated look. "Is she always this blunt?"

Although he nodded, his expression was affectionate. "Always. As far as she's concerned, the world would be a much better place if people would just accept things the way they are and get on with their lives, instead of whining about what might have been."

"Don't talk about me as if I weren't here," Rianne jumped in. "I'm perfectly capable of defending myself."

"I wasn't defending you." Randy gave her his most charming smile. "I was explaining you. I've been in enough arguments with you over the years to know you don't need any help in holding your own."

Rianne nodded with satisfaction. "Good. I'm glad you realize how capable I am."

Cass watched the exchange between them, thinking this was one of the things she would miss while Tabitha was gone. She and her stepsister had gotten quite good at bantering with each other. What if she got rusty during Tabitha's absence? Would they have to start from scratch once Tabitha returned?

If she returns. The thought appeared, unbidden, in Cass'

head, and she firmly thrust it aside. *Of course she'll be back. She has to come back because ... well ... I can't imagine life without her anymore.*

Cass shook herself out of her gloomy thoughts and forced herself to concentrate on the conversation swirling around her. Rianne and Randy had moved from teasing each other to talking about the children's Christmas party on Ebeye scheduled for the second week in December.

"Wait until you see the Marshallese kids," Rianne said enthusiastically. "They're adorable with their straight, jet-black hair and huge brown eyes."

"Nobody's ever done a party for them before, right?" Cass picked up a potato chip and nibbled at it.

Rianne shook her head. "Not that I know of. At least not one teenagers were ever invited to participate in. Your parents are so cool for setting this up."

"They're looking forward to it even more than we are," Cass said. "I think Mom said twenty-two kids have signed up to go. She'll be handing out the assignments at this Sunday's meeting."

"I hope she has me down for buying and wrapping gifts." Rianne gave a shiver of anticipation. "I can't imagine anything more fun than getting toys and stuffed animals for those kids. It's really going to make Christmas meaningful this year."

"I want to help out with the games at the party," Randy put in. "I've been thinking about what might be good to play."

Cass' gaze shifted between the brother and sister, and her heart swelled with fondness for them. "If you want me to, I'll tell Mom your preferences when I get home."

The Thayers nodded in unison, their pleased expressions warming Cass all the way through.

"There's nothing like having an in with the youth group leaders." Randy laughed. "I hope you don't feel used."

"Me? Nah." Cass dismissed the thought with an airy wave. "If you can't pull a few strings for your friends, who can you pull them for?"

The clock struck three before Cass decided it was time to head home. Standing up and stretching, she shot an irritated look at the window.

"I'd hoped the rain would let up if I stayed long enough. Obviously, it's here to stay. Unless I plan to camp out in the middle of your living room, I might as well accept the fact I'm about to get very wet."

"Didn't you bring your poncho with you?" Rianne followed Cass through the living room toward the front door.

Cass shook her head. "It wasn't raining when I left my house."

Randy, who'd accompanied them, laughed. "Don't you know you never leave home without a poncho during the rainy season?"

"I do now." Cass grimaced at the rain lashing the door and prepared to make a mad dash for it. "Well, here goes nothing. Thanks for lunch. I'll talk to you later, Rianne."

"Wait," Rianne said quickly. "I have an extra poncho you can borrow."

Suddenly, Cass laughed. "That's okay. When I was little, I used to beg my mother to let me play out in the rain. I especially wanted to ride my bike so I could splash through the biggest puddles I could find. Here's my chance to ride in the rain to my heart's content, and there's nothing Mom can do about it."

Rianne playfully shoved her toward the door. "Whatever floats your boat. You're one weird chick, but I must be even weirder because I'm crazy about you."

With a final laugh, Cass let herself out. The force of the rain in her face briefly took her breath away, and she had to squint to find her way across the lawn to her bike. The moment she got on the bike and started pedaling, however, the discomfort lifted and exhilaration set in.

With the wind whipping her soaked hair and her clothes plastered to her skin, Cass realized she was having a ball. *If my friends back home could see me now, they'd think I'd lost it.* She giggled and thought, *So what? They're there, and I'm here. This is my life, and I'm going to make the most of it.*

Cass decided not to go straight home. Instead, she cruised past the elementary, middle, and high schools, then paused for several minutes to watch the gusts whipping the waves into a frenzy off the northeast tip of the island before finally wending her way to the house. By the time she arrived, there wasn't a centimeter of dry skin left anywhere on her body.

Mom was in the kitchen when Cass squished into the house. Her eyes widened in alarm.

"What happened to you?"

Cass stopped to smirk at her, and puddles immediately formed around her feet. "Isn't it obvious?"

"You know what I mean," Mom said, slightly irritated.

Cass wagged a chiding finger at her. "Aren't you the one who always says it's important to ask the right question?"

Mom sighed. "All right then, why aren't you wearing a poncho?"

Even though it was futile, Cass swiped at the water dripping down her face. "Because I didn't bring one with me."

"Couldn't you have borrowed one from Rianne?"

"I could have." Cass' face lit up with an impish smile. "But I didn't want to. I decided it would be more fun to ride home without any protection. Although," she confessed, "I didn't come right home. I was enjoying myself so much I took a couple of side trips."

"Why in the world—" Rolling her eyes, Mom interrupted herself, "Never mind. I don't want to know. The important thing is you're here now. Hurry up and change into some dry clothes. Dad and I want to talk to you."

Cass instantly grew wary. "Why? What's going on now?"

"My, my, aren't you a suspicious little thing?" Mom patted Cass' cheek then made a show of wiping her hand on her shorts. "Go on and change. We'll talk as soon as you're done. And don't worry," she advised as Cass reluctantly began to move. "I think you'll like what we have to propose."

Not unless you're going to tell me you've decided to lock Tabitha in her room to keep her from getting on the plane to Oregon I won't, Cass grumbled silently.

Curiosity got the better of her, however, so she took a quick shower and got dressed in record time. When she returned to the living room, Dad was in the recliner and Mom in the rocking chair so Cass flopped down on the couch.

"So, what's up?" she demanded.

Mom and Dad exchanged looks before Mom answered. "Dad and I have been talking, and—"

"Uh-oh," Cass broke in. "That's usually a bad sign."

Mom frowned at her. "And it's usually bad when children interrupt their parents. Anyway, we've been talking and have decided to ask you if you'd like to fly back to Tennessee for winter break."

Cass' jaw dropped open. She didn't blink as she looked back and forth between Mom and Dad, and a full minute elapsed before she found her voice.

"You're kidding, right?" she croaked.

"Of course we're not kidding." Mom looked put out at the suggestion.

"We're dead serious," Dad said. "The trip is yours, if you're interested."

"But why?" Cass forced herself to blink. Her face tightened with suspicion. "Are you trying to get rid of me?"

"Not at all," Mom said quickly. "In fact, I don't like to think about you going. Do you realize it'll be the longest the two of us have ever been apart if you decide to take us up on our offer?"

"Then why are you even suggesting it?" Cass asked, bewildered.

"Your Mom and I feel it's only fair if Tabitha's going to take a trip that you have the option of taking one too." Dad smiled at Cass. "Feel free to turn us down. Our feelings won't be hurt."

"Wait a minute. Who said anything about turning you down?" Now that the initial shock had passed, Cass was rapidly warming to the idea. "I was just telling Rianne today I didn't know what I was going to do with Tabitha gone for two whole weeks. I said it would be nice if I could clear out and give y'all some privacy, but—good heavens!—I never imagined something like this being a possibility."

"So you're saying you like the idea?" Mom asked.

"Like it?" Laughter bubbled up from Cass, and she wrapped her arms around herself in glee. "I love it!"

"You realize this will be your Christmas present, don't you?" Dad said. "You won't find much under the tree come Christmas morning."

"Who cares?" Cass still couldn't quite believe they were serious. "You can consider this Christmas and my birthday gifts all wrapped up into one."

"Fair enough." Nodding, Dad turned to Mom. "Is there anything else you want to say?"

"Just that since you want to go, we'll make the arrangements with Mamaw and Papaw about getting you to and from the airport and where you'll stay. Oh, and you might want to call Janette, and make sure she doesn't have any plans for the time you'll be in Jonesborough. Ask her if she'll get the word out to your other friends so they can start making plans for getting together."

"I will." The enormity of Mom and Dad's offer suddenly

hit Cass, and she leaped up from the couch to hurry over to Mom. Throwing her arms around Mom's neck, she cried, "Thank you! I don't believe you're doing this." Going to Dad, she repeated the gesture. "Y'all are the greatest!"

Dad patted her back. "You're pretty special yourself."

To Cass' surprise, tears welled in her eyes and overflowed to stream down her cheeks. "At least you don't have to worry about whether or not I'll come back." The attempted joke ended on a loud sniffle. "I wouldn't trade you two for all my friends back home, plus Papaw. And you know how much I love Papaw."

Mom got up from her chair and joined them in a group hug. "Thank-you. That's good to know. Believe me, I wouldn't let you go if I thought there was even the slightest chance you wouldn't come back."

Cass raised her head to look Mom directly in the eyes. "Then why are you letting Tabitha go?"

Startled, Mom could only gape at her. Cass turned to Dad.

Dad shrugged, but Cass could see the pain in his eyes. "Hmm. Good question. We'll have to think about that and get back to you."

Cass didn't want to push that particular issue any more. "It's too late for me to call Janette since it's—" closing her eyes, she did some rapid calculations, "—almost midnight there. I'll call her tomorrow." She smiled, her expression bemused. "I still can't get used to being a day ahead of them. It's yesterday, which means they just finished celebrating Thanksgiving while we're already halfway through our leftovers." She shook her head. "Weird."

"It is one of the stranger things about life here on Kwaj," agreed Mom. Laughing, she patted Cass' wet hair. "But then again, so are you. Riding around in the middle of a storm. Honestly. What am I going to do with you?"

"Enjoy me while you can?" suggested Cass with a sassy

grin. "I'll be off to college in a couple of years, and then life will be so boring you won't be able to stand it." She grinned impishly and ran off to her room before either of them could contradict her.

Five minutes later, they yelled down the hall that they were going next door for a Scrabble tournament and would be home later. The moment the door shut behind them, Cass let out a whoop.

"I'm going home!" she proclaimed to the ceiling. Stretched out on her bed, she kicked her legs and flung out her arms. "I thought it would be years before I saw Tennessee again, but I'll be there in six weeks! Hallelujah!"

"What's all the shouting about?" a voice yelled from the back of the house.

Mortified at having been caught in loud celebration, Cass fervently hoped Tabitha hadn't brought Kira home with her. "Uh ... I ... you see ..." she stammered.

Tabitha appeared in the doorway, and to Cass' relief, she was alone. "Uh ...what?" she teased.

Rolling up to a sitting position, Cass scooted back to lean against the wall. "I was rejoicing in some fantastic news Mom and Dad just gave me."

"Oh, yeah? What is it?"

Still unable to quite believe it, Cass took a deep breath and blurted, "They're flying me home for winter break."

Stunned, Tabitha didn't say anything for a few seconds. "Wow," she finally breathed. "And you had no idea this was coming?"

"Not a clue." Cass couldn't hold back the grin that began spreading from ear to ear. "To say I was shocked is an understatement, but it was the best shock I've ever received."

Tabitha's forehead puckered in a small frown. "So you're happy about going?"

"Happy?" Cass echoed. "I'm way more than happy. I'm on cloud nine."

"But that means Mom and Dad will be here alone," Tabitha pointed out.

"Gee, you're quick," drawled Cass. Her eyebrows met above her nose in a scowl. "You have a problem with that?"

Tabitha absently brushed at the damp tendrils of hair clinging to her cheeks. "I guess not. It's just—" she hesitated. "I guess I was counting on you being here while I was gone so they wouldn't be—I don't know—lonely."

Cass gave her an amused look. "They'll have each other. I doubt they'll be too lonely."

"That's not quite how I meant it." Staring down at the hands tightly clenched in her lap, Tabitha tried again. "I figured you being here would keep them from missing me too much."

"Ah." Understanding dawned on Cass, and she nodded wisely. "Now I get it. You're allowed to go off and have a good time, but I'm supposed to stay here and keep the folks company so you don't feel so guilty about choosing your mother over them."

Tabitha's head snapped up and her eyes narrowed to angry slits. "That's not fair."

"No?" Cass remained unruffled. "Then how would you put it?"

"I ... it's not ... you know ..." she stopped. "Never mind. You wouldn't understand."

"Try me." Cass fixed Tabitha with a steady gaze that soon had her squirming. "I'm actually pretty bright. When people speak slowly enough and use little words, I usually comprehend what they're saying."

"Very funny," muttered Tabitha. "Does Janette know you'll be home·in January?"

"You're hoping to distract me, aren't you?" Cass smirked at the flash of annoyance that passed across Tabitha's face.

"Okay, I'll play along and pretend it worked. No—by the time Dad and Mom told me the plans, it was too late to get in touch with Jan. I'll call her tomorrow."

"Do you think she'll be as excited as you are?"

"Of course." Despite the assurance in her voice, a flicker of doubt flared in the pit of Cass' stomach. Unnerved, she went on the offensive. "Why wouldn't she be? After all, she's my best friend."

"I thought Rianne was your best friend," Tabitha said quietly.

"She's my best friend here." Even though Cass knew Tabitha was baiting her, she couldn't resist responding. "Janette's my best friend back home."

"Huh. You could have fooled me." Tabitha made a show of examining her fingernails. "With the way you've been complaining about her lately, I figured your friendship was pretty much over."

Cass wanted to argue with Tabitha, but in all honesty, she couldn't. "I'll admit we're not as close as we were, but I'm sure this trip will patch things up. We just need to spend some time together, talking and hanging out like we used to. A few days of that, and I'll guarantee you everything will be back to normal."

"If you say so." Tabitha didn't sound convinced.

Stung by her lack of faith, Cass flung at her, "You haven't seen your mother in years, and you think that's all it will take to fix things with her. Why should it be any different with Janette and me?"

Tabitha drew in a sharp breath and glowered at Cass. "I wish you wouldn't keep throwing my mother in my face. You don't know what I hope happens so quit acting like you do."

"Don't you want this trip to jump-start your relationship?"

Shrugging, Tabitha chewed on her thumbnail. "I don't

know. All I know for sure is that it's something I have to do. I'm trying not to plan anything so I'm not disappointed whatever way it goes."

"Oh." Cass paused. "That's smart of you. Maybe I should do the same thing with my visit to Tennessee."

A wry smile curved Tabitha's lips. "Wow, you mean I actually taught you something?"

Cass returned her smile. "Yeah. Hard to believe, huh?" She acted as if she were about to get up. "Maybe I should circle the date on the calendar."

Tabitha was the one who stood. "Don't bother," she advised. "I'm sure I'll teach you a lot more stuff before I'm finished."

Cass snorted. "Don't count on it, Sis," she called after Tabitha as she left the room.

CHAPTER 17

The following morning, Cass was up at dawn. Mom had said she could call Janette as soon as she got up, and Cass was too keyed up to sleep any longer. Padding into the kitchen and dialing the familiar number, Cass realized her palms were sweaty. Grimacing, she wiped them on her nightshirt.

There's nothing to be nervous about, she sternly told herself. *It's just Jan. Good old Jan. I don't care what Tabitha tried to tell me. Janette and I are friends forever. She'll jump for joy when I tell her I'm coming home.*

The phone started to ring on the other end, and Cass' grip on the receiver tightened. When she realized her fingers were cramping, she forced herself to relax.

"Hello?"

Even across the thousands of miles separating them, Cass recognized Janette's voice, and she grinned. "Jan, it's me. Cass."

There was a pause because of the satellite transmission before Janette replied, "Hey, Cass. What are you doing calling? Is something up?"

Cass couldn't be sure, but Janette didn't sound all that excited to hear from her. Taking a deep breath, she forced a cheerful note into her voice. "Something's definitely up, beginning with my spirits. Guess what."

"I have no idea." There was a muffled conversation in the background then Janette came back on the phone. "Look, I hate to rush you, but I don't have time to play guessing games. Lauren's here, and we were just about to head over to the mall. It's the biggest shopping day of the year, you know."

Cass' good mood instantly evaporated. It was obvious Janette didn't want to be bothered with her. For just a second, she thought about hanging up without saying anything about the trip, then telling her parents she'd changed her mind about going.

"In that case, I won't keep you," Cass forced herself to respond cheerfully. "I just wanted to let you know I'll be home in January."

"For good?" Janette sounded shocked. "What happened?"

"No, not for good, silly." Cass' laugh was hollow. She wondered what Jan's reaction would be if she were heading home for good. "For a visit. My parents are flying me to Tennessee for winter break. I'll be there the last two weeks in January."

"Well ... good."

Gee, could you possibly sound any less enthusiastic? Cass thought darkly.

Aloud, she chirped, "You bet it's good. In fact, it's great. I can't wait to see everybody. I hope you'll let everyone know I'm coming in so we can set up some get-togethers."

Janette didn't respond to her broad hint, asking instead, "Will you be staying with your grandparents?"

Cass was finding it more and more difficult to keep a rein on her temper. The conversation wasn't going at all like she'd hoped it would. She decided to give it one more try.

"I'll stay part of the time with them, of course. Then I

was thinking I'll spend the rest of the time at your house. If it's all right with your mother, that is," she added.

There, she thought, *it doesn't get any plainer than that. Let's see what she does with it.*

The silence on Janette's end lengthened until it became downright awkward. When she finally spoke, her voice was strained. "I'll ... uh ... check with her. It might not ... I mean ... maybe you'd better not count on staying here. I'm not sure how my mother will feel about it. She's been kind of tense lately."

"Okay." Cass suddenly wanted nothing more than to end the call. "Ask her and get back to me. I'd also appreciate it if you'd check around and see if anyone is interested in spending time with me while I'm in."

"You bet!" Janette replied with exaggerated enthusiasm, and Cass wondered if she had caught on to Cass' sarcastic tone. "And keep your fingers crossed. I might be able to talk my mom into letting you bunk here a couple of nights."

"Whatever." Cass found herself swallowing a lump the size of a golf ball that seemed to have lodged in her throat. "I'll call you in a couple of weeks to see what the plans are. You and Lauren have a good time at the mall."

"We will." Janette hesitated a few seconds then added quietly, "I'm sorry I didn't come across as more gung-ho about your trip. You just took me by surprise, that's all. I'm really glad you're coming."

"Yeah, same here. Bye, Jan."

Cass didn't wait for Janette's farewell. Hanging up, she folded an arm against the wall and leaned her forehead on it.

O Lord, she started to pray, then stopped. The pain and anger were almost choking her. She took a few deep breaths, then straightened and headed to the cupboard where the cereal was kept. Since she was up, she might as well eat breakfast.

She was on her way back to her room when she met

Mom coming out of the bathroom. Not wanting to talk about her conversation with Janette, Cass mumbled a greeting and was about to duck into her room when Mom placed a hand on her arm.

"Good morning." Mom smiled as she pushed back the sleep-tousled hair from her forehead. "You were up with the birds, weren't you?"

"There aren't any birds on the island to be up with," griped Cass. She tried to walk away, but Mom held fast.

"What about the sandpipers?" she asked.

Cass' snort told her exactly what she thought of sandpipers. "They're the sorriest excuses for birds I've ever seen. They hardly ever fly, and they don't sing. They peep."

Mom sighed softly. "Did you call Janette?"

Cass nodded.

"And?" Mom prompted when it became apparent Cass wasn't going to elaborate.

"And nothing." Taking advantage of Mom's relaxed grip, Cass pulled her arm away. "I told her I'm coming. She said good. I asked about staying with her, and she said she'd check with her mother. Then she and Lauren had to get to the mall so I said goodbye." She shrugged. "End of story."

"Hmm." As Cass turned to go into her bedroom, Mom caught her by the sleeve. "Come have breakfast with me."

"I already ate."

"Then you can watch me eat. I want to talk to you."

"Mom, I don't feel like talking."

"Tough." Mom tugged on her sleeve to turn her then, with a gentle push, sent her toward the kitchen. "I know you're upset, and I'm not going to let you disappear into your room to brood. You know you'll feel 100 percent better after we talk so don't argue."

Cass gave in with a heavy sigh. "Okay, fine. We'll talk. But I'm not happy about it."

"Really?" Mom said in mock surprise. "And here I

thought you were thrilled at being given the opportunity to bare your soul."

They moved into the kitchen and Cass sat down at the table. Mom bustled around for a while, preparing herself some breakfast. Cass grew edgier by the minute until Mom finally sat down across from her. "All right, give," Mom said. "What really happened when you talked to Janette?"

Drawing designs on the tabletop, Cass avoided her eyes. "It went exactly like I said. We couldn't talk very long because Jan and Lauren had to leave."

"Is that what upset you?" Mom bit into her toast.

For the first time, Cass met her gaze. "No. I've gotten used to Janette having her own life, especially since I have a pretty good one going here. I don't get jealous anymore about her spending time with other people."

"Then what is the problem?" Mom asked.

"Who says there is one?"

Mom raised an eyebrow. "I say there is. Now quit playing games and tell me what's wrong."

Too tired to keep putting up a fight, Cass gave in. "Janette was about as enthusiastic as a dead fish about my trip. She didn't whoop and holler the way I thought she would. She didn't say a word about us spending time together. When I hinted around about getting the group together, she totally ignored me. I've been thinking if that's the way it's going to be, maybe you and Dad should save your money and not bother sending me home."

There, she'd said it. Cass looked at Mom out of the corner of her eye to gauge her reaction.

Mom calmly sipped her juice. "I'm sorry Janette wasn't happier about the visit. But sometimes it's hard to tell how somebody feels over the phone. Maybe she was more excited than you realized."

"I doubt it." Cass slumped in her chair and crossed her arms over her chest. "I always know what she's thinking, and she wasn't at all thrilled about me coming. It's almost enough to make me want to stay here."

"That's the second time you've said that," commented Mom. "Are you serious about not going if Janette doesn't show more enthusiasm?"

Shrugging, Cass rubbed an imaginary stain on the table. "There doesn't seem much point in going if she's not interested in spending time with me, do you think?"

"What about the chance to see Papaw and Mamaw and Uncle Larry and Aunt Linda?"

"It would be nice to see them, especially Papaw," Cass said wistfully. "But would it really be worth the money to send me in January when we're all supposed to go sometime this summer?"

"It would if it makes you happy." Mom wiped her mouth with a napkin. "Look, you don't have to decide right this minute. Take some time to think about what you want to do. A word of advice though. Don't base your decision only on your conversation with Janette. There's a lot more to this trip than just seeing her."

"Like what?"

Mom grinned. "Like not having to be stuck here with Dad and me while Tabitha's gone."

Cass reddened. "What makes you think I'd consider it being stuck with y'all?"

"Sweetie—" Mom fixed her with a shrewd gaze. "Don't forget I was a teen-ager once upon a time. Hanging around with my parents wasn't exactly my favorite thing to do when I was sixteen."

"That's because you had Mamaw for a mother," Cass pointed out. "I love her to death, but she's the original dragon lady. Talk about stubborn and opinionated."

"Sounds a lot like somebody else I know." Mom laughed when Cass glared at her. "Face it, you and my mother are cut from the same cloth. That's why the two of you don't get along very well. You're too much alike."

Cass groaned, only partially in jest. "Like I wasn't depressed already. I think I'll go back to bed and start the day over. Maybe it'll improve with a second go 'round. It sure can't get any worse."

"You're so cranky when you first get up." Standing, Mom came around the table to lean her cheek on top of Cass' head and loosely slide her arms around her neck. "But I love you, Cassandra Aileen."

Cass laid her hand over Mom's and squeezed. "I love you, too, Donna Maureen." The exchange was a leftover from her childhood, and it never failed to comfort her. "But—" She pushed back her chair, causing Mom to release her and step out of the way. "I'm still heading off to bed. See you again around ten o'clock."

Try as she might, Cass couldn't go back to sleep. She tried lying on her back. She tried lying on her stomach. She put the pillow over her head then scrunched it up under her cheek. After thirty minutes of tossing and turning, she gave up and flopped over onto her back with a sigh.

This isn't working, she thought darkly. *And it's all Jan's fault. She could've at least pretended she was pleased about my visit. But no, I guess she and Lauren have gotten so close that she doesn't consider me her best friend anymore. Although,* she was forced to admit, *she's not exactly my best friend either. Still, it'll be fun to see her. I mean, if she called to tell me she was coming to Kwaj, I'd be jumping for joy.*

Frustrated, Cass decided to take a shower to try and stop thinking about Jan. She felt somewhat better half an hour later when she headed out to the kitchen to see what was happening. Dad sat at the table, finishing breakfast, while Mom talked on the phone. Cass sat down next to Dad. She nodded in Mom's direction.

"Who's she talking to?"

"Your grandparents. They're talking about your trip."

"Oh, good." Cass could barely refrain from jumping up and down in joy. "I'll bet Papaw's walking on air at the news."

Mom beckoned to Cass over Dad's shoulder and whispered, "Do you want to talk?"

Cass nodded emphatically. She got up while Mom bid her parents farewell and waited impatiently for her to finish. Her mother could take longer to say goodbye than anybody she'd ever known. In this case, nearly three minutes passed before Mom handed her the receiver.

"Hey! Who am I talking to? Papaw or Mamaw?"

"What's happened to your grammar since you moved?" came Mamaw's reply. "You should have asked to whom you were speaking."

Cass rolled her eyes and grinned to herself, half in irritation and half in pleasure. Other things in life might change, but her grandmother never would.

"Hello, Mamaw. I'm sorry I offended you by asking such an ungrammatical question. I hope you can find it in your heart to forgive me."

"Don't get smart with me, young lady," Mamaw scolded, although with obvious affection in her voice. "I'm glad you're coming to visit us so I can straighten you out."

"Well, you think you'll be able to?" Cass asked impishly.

Mamaw laughed. "Laws, I've missed you. I can't wait to see you, child. For some strange reason, everyone else seems a tad bit afraid of me. But not you. You've always stood up to your old Mamaw."

"That's because I know that underneath that ornery act you put on, you're ... well ... actually it's not an act. You really are ornery." Cass enjoyed hearing Mamaw laugh. "But since I'm known to be ornery every now and then myself, it doesn't intimidate me like it does other people."

"We are two peas in a pod," agreed Mamaw. "Heaven help the man you marry. Speaking of which, your Papaw's breathing down my neck, signaling me to hurry it up so he can talk to you. I'll be counting the days until you're here, Sweetheart."

"Same here, Mamaw. I love you." Following her grandmother's response, Cass eagerly awaited the sound of Papaw's voice. When it came, a lump formed in her throat the way it always did at the beginning of a conversation with her grandfather.

"Well, as I live and breathe, if it isn't my favorite granddaughter. How are you doing, Sassafras?" boomed Papaw.

Cass grinned at hearing the nickname only he was allowed to use. "I'm fine, Papaw. How are you?"

"Happier than a tick on a hound dog, now that your Mom tells me we're going to be seeing you before long. As soon as we hang up, I'm going to set right down and make a list of things for us to do while you're here, starting with you and me spending some quality time at the Main Street Cafe. You haven't forgotten the Main Street Cafe, have you?"

"Papaw," Cass scolded, "how could you even think such a thing? It's where we've had lunch one Saturday a month for as far back as I can remember."

Papaw laughed. "I didn't really think you'd forget. I was just testing you. Are you excited about coming back home?"

Cass realized talking with her grandparents had done a great deal to restore the original enthusiasm she'd felt for the trip, and she nodded. "So much that I can hardly stand it."

"You can't be any more excited than your Mamaw and I are. I'm looking forward to telling your aunt and uncle. In fact," decided Papaw, "I do believe I'll be a regular Paul Revere, going through town telling everyone, my granddaughter's coming, my granddaughter's coming."

"It's not like anyone outside the family will care," drawled Cass. "Or even know who you're talking about."

"No matter," Papaw said breezily. "I won't be doing it for anyone but myself. I'm so happy I could bust."

"Papaw, you make me feel so loved." Cass told herself to remember to thank her mother for this phone call. It went a long way toward cheering her up after the conversation with Janette. "I'm counting the days until I see you."

"That's nothing, sugar. I'm counting the seconds. I'll let you go now. Tell Steve and Tabitha that we love them."

"I will. You tell Aunt Linda and Uncle Larry and the kids the same from me." Cass' heart leaped as she added, "See you in a little over six weeks."

"See you too, Sassafras."

Cass hung up the phone and wandered back out to the dining room. Mom, Dad, and Tabitha sat at the table; their conversation stopped when Cass appeared.

"Papaw says to tell you—" she looked at Dad then at Tabitha, "—and you that he and Mamaw love you."

"I like your grandparents." Tabitha frowned. "Although your grandmother is sort of scary."

Recalling that part of the discussion with Mamaw, Cass grinned. "True, but you get used to it after a while. Besides, they're not just my grandparents. They're yours too."

Mom smiled at Cass. "That's right. Just as you're related to Steve's parents now. We're going to arrange for you to see them while you're in Jonesborough."

Cass didn't mind sharing her relatives with Tabitha, but she wasn't sure she liked acquiring new ones of her own, especially ones she was expected to visit. "But I hardly know them," she objected.

"Then this will be a wonderful opportunity for you to get to know them."

Cass just made a face at Mom. "Whatever," she mumbled. She had six weeks to come up with a way to get out of visiting the Spencers. Surely that was long enough to devise a plan.

CHAPTER 18

"I'm so glad it's almost Christmas!" Tabitha exclaimed, then frowned when she saw Cass' face. "What are you being such a Scrooge about? If your face froze like that, you'd wind up scaring little kids for the rest of your life."

"How could it freeze?" Cass said darkly. "It's almost ninety degrees. It's more likely my face will melt."

Tabitha nodded sagely. "Ah, now I get it. You're in one of your 'it can't be Christmas without snow' moods. They seem to be occurring more frequently. What are you up to? About one a day now?"

Cass frowned. "That shows how much you know. It doesn't have to snow for it to feel like Christmas. I hardly ever remember having a white Christmas back home. But at least the temperature should be in the forties." She fanned herself. "Sweating up a storm doesn't exactly put me in a holiday mood."

Tabitha tilted her head to one side and regarded Cass with a playful gaze. "You want something to get you in the spirit? I have just what the doctor ordered. Hey, guys!" she called to the others scattered about the lagoon. "Cass needs some cheering up. Get over here."

"Geez Louise, what now?" muttered Cass as Micah,

Logan, Kira, and Rianne obediently came up the beach to the pavilion.

"What's up?" Micah immediately went to stand by Tabitha. Droplets of water glistened in his dark hair and spiked his eyelashes.

"Cass is seriously lacking in holiday spirit," Tabitha informed him. "I thought serenading her with a few Christmas carols might do the trick."

Logan sat down beside Cass at the aluminum table where the remains of their picnic lunch were still in evidence. He helped himself to a handful of pretzels. "Will having us sing perk you up?"

Cass made a face at him. "Hardly. I've heard you sing, and it makes me want to cry, not laugh."

Logan pressed a hand to his chest in a gesture of injured pride. "I'm hurt. I'll have you know I sang in the chorus back in my old high school."

"Which explains the heartfelt thank-you note the chorus director gave you when you left," retorted Cass.

Logan scowled at her while their friends laughed. "Keep it up, and you can kiss your Christmas presents goodbye," he warned.

"Gee, and I was so looking forward to the pack of gum and the paper clips you were planning to give me." Cass stuck her tongue out at him.

Before Logan could respond, Kira stepped in. "Okay, I'm putting a stop to this. Honestly, the way you two carry on, you'd think you were brother and sister, not boyfriend and girlfriend." She turned to Tabitha. "You got me out of the water to come up here and sing. If we're going to sing, then let's get it over with. Otherwise, I'm going back to swimming."

"I want to sing," declared Rianne. She anchored her blonde hair behind her ears, folded her hands in front of her, and hummed a note.

Wincing, Micah clamped his hands over his ears. "What are you doing?"

Rianne smiled serenely. "Warming up, silly." She hummed a few more notes then announced, "Okay, I'm ready."

"If there were dogs on the island, they'd be howling their fool heads off by now." Kira elbowed Rianne in the ribs. "You may look like an angel, but you sure don't sing like one."

"What I lack in talent, I more than make up for in enthusiasm."

With that, Rianne took a deep breath and broke into a rousing rendition of "It's Beginning to Look a Lot Like Christmas." After hesitating a couple of seconds, the others joined her. Cass sat with her head in her hands while they entertained her. At the end of "The First Noel," she applauded loudly, hoping they'd get the hint she wanted them to stop. But it wasn't until they went through "Rudolph The Red-Nosed Reindeer" twice that they finally bowed and pronounced the show over.

"There." Rianne plopped down onto the bench next to Cass. "Don't you feel a lot more Christmasy now?"

"Oh, you bet," drawled Cass. "See these tears in my eyes? That's how moved I am by your performance."

"Well," sniffed Kira, "I, for one, can tell when I'm not appreciated. I'm going back in the water." She started down the beach.

"Don't go away mad," Cass called after her. When Kira acted as if she were returning to the pavilion, Cass added impishly, "Just go away."

"You are not nice," Kira said, flouncing back and pretending to sulk in a corner.

"I know," Cass said, hanging her head in mock shame. "My new year's resolution is to be a better person."

"Oh, no!" Logan said, and they all turned to stare at

him. "How will we recognize her if she's nice?" he asked everyone but Cass.

Micah laughed. "Ooh—score one for the redhead."

Cass scowled at him. "I'm a red-head too, you know."

Micah shrugged. "In that case, score one for the redhead everyone here likes."

"Hey!" Cass protested above the chorus of appreciative laughter Micah's remark had produced. "What is this? Gang-up-on-Cass day?"

"No, but it wouldn't be a bad idea to have one every now and then," observed Logan.

"Whose side are you on?" Cass good-naturedly growled at him.

Grinning, Logan blew her a kiss. "Yours, of course. Sorry. I let peer pressure get the better of me for a couple of moments there."

After taking another handful of pretzels, he passed the bag around to the others. Chips and icy cans of soda dug out of the cooler soon followed, and all thoughts of swimming were abandoned. Everyone gathered around the picnic table to discuss the Christmas party they'd be hosting tomorrow after church.

"I'm looking forward to seeing Ebeye." Cass plucked a potato chip out of the bag Rianne held. "Have y'all been there? What's it like?"

Everyone but Logan nodded to indicate they'd visited the neighboring island. Cass noticed varying degrees of distaste on each face.

"I've gone twice." Kira gave an involuntary shudder. "It reminded me of pictures I've seen of Third World countries."

"That's a good way of putting it," her brother agreed. "It's very backward, not at all like here. There are no paved roads and the houses are mostly tin huts."

"When I went, none of the kids I saw wore shoes,"

Rianne said. "And their clothes were ragged, like they'd been passed down from kid to kid to kid."

"And it smells." Tabitha wrinkled her nose. "They let the garbage pile up before they do anything about it and not all the houses have indoor plumbing."

Cass' fantasy of being able to tell everyone back home that she'd visited a genuine tropical island complete with natives vanished in a puff of smoke. "It sounds awful. I'm not sure I even want to go now."

Tabitha fixed her with a steely stare. "You're going, and that's that."

"Besides, it's not as bad as most people make it out to be." When the others murmured their disagreement, Rianne added, "Okay, Ebeye itself isn't a nice place. But the people are wonderful, especially the children." Her expression softened. "They're shy at first. Once they warm up to you though, they're all over you. They have the biggest brown eyes and the sweetest smiles. And they're not spoiled like the kids back on the mainland. The littlest thing means so much to them. I remember giving one little girl a pack of gum. You'd have thought I'd handed her the moon, the way she hugged me. It made me want to come back here and buy out Surfway then cart everything over there. I'm always hearing people complain about the poor selection at Surfway and Macy's, and it really bothers me. I bet the Marshallese who live on Ebeye wouldn't complain about it. They'd appreciate the items our stores provide because they know what it's like to do without."

The group was silent after her outburst, and Rianne ducked her head in embarrassment. "I'm sorry. I didn't mean to lecture."

"No, you're right," Micah said quickly. "We—or at least I—do tend to take things for granted. I need to be reminded on a regular basis how good I've got it."

"Have you ever thought about being a missionary?" Logan asked quietly.

Rianne stared at him, her eyes wide with amazement. "What in the world made you ask that? Have you been reading my mind?"

Laughing, Logan shook his head. "Call it a lucky guess. Or maybe an educated one. It's not just the things you're saying now. It's other conversations. You care a lot about people, especially the ones the rest of the world considers to be less fortunate. You come across as someone who wants to do something to help. You don't just want to discuss it for a little while then forget about it."

"I'm no saint," Rianne said, shaking her head. "But you're right. I do care. Lately, I've been thinking more and more about going into some kind of mission work. Maybe becoming a doctor or something, so I can go to underdeveloped countries and help provide medical care. And share the Gospel, of course."

Touched by Rianne's words, Cass affectionately bumped shoulders with her. "I'm proud to be your friend. I'm not kidding. You are a genuinely good human being."

Rianne frowned slightly. "I said I'm not a saint. Different people have different talents according to the way God made them. Some people paint. Others are math whizzes. I care." She laughed. "Unfortunately, that's about all I do. Obviously, the rest of you think I'm tone-deaf."

"We don't think that at all." Cass hesitated, then grinned. "We know it."

They stayed at the beach until late in the afternoon, heading home only when several other families arrived for a cookout.

"That was fun." Tired from the day in the sun, Tabitha rode with one hand casually steering the bike.

"Uh-huh." Cass gave her a teasing smile. "You and Micah are the cutest couple. I'll have to be sure to take a picture of you two back to Tennessee with me."

Tabitha frowned. "Are you sure that's a good idea?"

Cass' head jerked around in her direction and her eyes narrowed. "What do you mean?"

Looking uneasy, Tabitha stammered, "You know ... seeing as how Micah is part black. Won't that bother some people?"

"What is it with you?" snapped Cass. "Not everyone from the south is prejudiced, and my friends definitely aren't or they wouldn't be my friends. Got it?"

Tabitha nodded meekly. "Got it." She cleared her throat and added, "How about bringing the picture Micah and I had taken at the fall formal to show your friends? I think we look pretty good in that one."

Recognizing the offer as Tabitha's way of apologizing, Cass replied, "Good idea. But don't be so modest. Y'all don't look pretty good. You look spectacular."

"You're bringing lots of pictures of Logan, aren't you?"

Cass grinned. "You know I am. Except I don't know how many I'll show around. I'm mainly taking them for me to look at when I get to missing him so much that I can't stand it."

"Same here," Tabitha said, sighing. "I'm starting to wonder why I agreed to this trip. Kira told me a couple of days ago that they're all heading to Hono for a week. If I weren't going to see Beth, they'd have asked me to go with them."

"That would have been fun."

"Tell me about it." The corners of Tabitha's mouth drooped even more. "This would have been Micah's and my first and last winter break together as an official couple, and I'm ruining it by going to Oregon." Letting go of the handlebar, she made a scale out of hands and pretended to weigh the matter. "Let's see. Oregon with Beth or Honolulu with Micah." One hand dropped into her lap. "Looks like Micah and Hono win."

"Only they don't," Cass reminded her. "There's no way you can back out of the trip to see your mother." She hesitated, unsure that was a correct statement. "Is there?"

"No," Tabitha said darkly. "I hinted around to Mom and Dad the other night that I might not want to go to Oregon after all. They informed me in no uncertain terms that since I have my ticket and new clothes, I'm going."

"I'm glad you approached them first because I've been thinking about seeing if I could cancel my trip to Tennessee." At Tabitha's questioning glance, Cass explained, "For the same reason you want out. I hate the thought of passing up two whole weeks with Logan, just to spend them with a bunch of people I'm not sure I have that much in common with anymore."

"Your last phone call with Janette didn't go any better than the one at Thanksgiving?"

Cass shook her head. "It's like she wants to tell me not to come, but she can't bring herself to do it. So she does the next best thing. She says nothing at all when I bring up plans to do stuff together. Most of the time, I feel like I'm talking to a brick wall."

"I might actually prefer that to the conversations I have with my mother." Tabitha's tone held a note of impatience. "She goes on and on about all the places we're going to go and the things we're going to do. I'm starting to wonder if I'm going to get any sleep while I'm up there."

"Sounds like she's planning to cram all the years she's missed with you into two weeks," Cass said.

"That's what I'm thinking too." Tabitha sighed. "If there's going to be any cramming, I'd rather cram the months I'm going to be away from Micah while he's in college into those two weeks."

"Did I tell you Logan's paperwork has finally been submitted to West Point?" Cass asked, half sad, half excited. "The guidance counselor and the army officer he's been working with both say he has a good chance of getting an appointment."

"Wow. That's a tough school to get into. He said one time that they generally get between twelve and fifteen thousand applications, and they only give out twelve hundred appointments."

"Which will give us the perfect reason to throw him a party if he gets in. Talk about an accomplishment. Of course, my heart will be breaking but I'll be a good sport and act like I'm happy for him."

"You *will* be happy for him," Tabitha sternly ordered. "I don't really know what the deal is with his family, but I know they don't have any money. That's why his dad getting this job was such a blessing. Logan told me one time that the only way he'd be able to go to college would be to attend one of the service academies or get a full academic scholarship."

"Okay, I'll be happy for him," agreed Cass. They had reached their house, so as they wheeled their bikes into the backyard, she added with a saucy smile, "But I'll be sad for myself."

CHAPTER 19

The next morning, Cass could hardly wait for the worship service to conclude. The boat was leaving for Ebeye at one, which meant they'd have just enough time to get home, change, eat lunch, and head to the marina.

In the middle of the first hymn, Cass shivered with excitement. Except for a rowboat, she'd never been on a boat before. In a couple of hours, she'd be on one skimming across several miles of ocean. Anticipation, mixed with nervousness, made her shiver again.

Tabitha shot her a curious look. "Are you cold?" she whispered.

Cass shook her head. "Excited, and also a little scared."

"Of what? The party?"

"No, the trip." Cass' reply drew a frown from Mom.

Tabitha raised her eyebrows. "If you think twenty minutes in a boat is something to be scared about, what are you going to do when you're flying across the country by yourself?"

At Mom's warning "shh," Cass decided not to respond. In her head, however, she darkly replied, *Thanks, like I needed to be reminded of that this morning. I just want to think about one trip at a time. Once this one's over, I'll start dreading the next one.*

The moment the service ended, Cass and Tabitha slipped out the side door and met Logan, the Alexanders, and the Thayers.

"We certainly have a beautiful day for the party." Kira glanced heavenward, where not a single cloud marred the azure sky.

"And for the boat trip." Randy rubbed his hands in glee. "I'm really looking forward to that."

"What's the final count on how many of us are going?" Logan asked.

Squinting, Cass thought a moment. "I think Mom said there'll be twenty-three kids and six adults."

"That's wonderful." Rianne clapped her approval of the number. "I was wondering on the way to church though, what about a Christmas tree?"

"Pastor Thompson talked with the pastor on Ebeye and he's got it covered," Tabitha said. "Someone donated an artificial tree that they set up in the community center and decorated yesterday afternoon."

Cass frowned. "I wish the kids could experience a real Christmas tree. There's nothing like the smell and the look of a real tree. A fake one just doesn't cut it."

"You heard how much the real trees they shipped in from Hono cost," Rianne reminded her. "Only a handful of people can afford to pay ninety dollars for a tree. The rest of us have to make do with an artificial one."

"Yeah, but I've never had a fake tree before. It's depressing. We haven't even put it up yet, and I already hate it," Cass whined.

"Uh-oh," Logan said. "Are we going to have to sing to you again?" He eyed the others. "What do you say, guys? Should we do 'Frosty The Snowman' or 'Joy to the World' first?"

Groaning, Cass held up her hands in surrender. "Please, anything but that. Look—" she produced the biggest smile she could, "—I'm happy again. There's no need for you to sing."

"I can't wait to get to Ebeye," grumbled Rianne. "I'll bet the kids will appreciate our singing."

"Only if they're hard of hearing." Cass' retort earned her a pout from Rianne, and she stuck out her tongue in response.

It was an excited group of teens and adults that gathered at the marina just before one o'clock. A couple of the guys wore Santa caps and most of the girls were dressed in reds, greens, and whites. Randy had attached bells to his wheels so he jingled every time he moved. The atmosphere was quite festive as the crowd milled about the dock, waiting to board the water taxi to Ebeye.

Even in the midst of the throng, Cass and Logan managed to find a quiet spot all to themselves.

"Are you nervous about the boat trip?" Logan asked, standing close to Cass.

Although she hated to admit she was afraid of anything, Cass nodded. "A little. This is the first time I've ever been in a boat. And it's not like we're going out on a lake." She gestured with her chin at the expanse of water stretching all the way to the horizon. "It's the Pacific Ocean."

"We won't be going out into open water," Logan reminded her. "We're cutting across the lagoon."

The look Cass gave him brimmed with scorn. "Is the lagoon deep? Are there sharks and other scary sea creatures in it? Have boats been known to capsize in lagoons?" Logan was forced to nod affirmatively to each of her questions, and she jeered, "See? You even agree I have something to worry about."

Logan summoned up his most charming smile. "Will it make you feel any better if I promise to stay by your side throughout the entire trip? I also give you my solemn vow to save you, even at the risk of losing my own life if the boat sinks."

Cass grinned. "Who said chivalry is dead?" she teased. "It's an honor to take you up on your offer, kind sir."

"Man, you'll fall for anything." Logan shook his head. "Don't you know I was just making sure I got to sit next to you on the trip?"

"Don't you know a setup when you see one?" Cass shot back. "I acted scared so you'd offer to sit by me."

Logan expelled a sigh of disgust. "I can't win with you. No matter what I say, you always find a way to top me."

"True, but I have to admire the way you keep trying. Besides," Cass leaned close to add, "I really am a little anxious about the trip. If you don't mind playing hero, I don't mind being the damsel in distress."

Logan ducked his head and scraped his foot along the dock. "I'll be your hero any day." Although his manner was joking, he sounded serious. "It's nice to be needed."

Before Cass could respond, Dad blew a whistle to get everyone's attention. Mortified, Cass and Tabitha, who stood nearby with Micah and Kira, exchanged chagrinned glances.

"Where in the world did he get the whistle?" hissed Tabitha.

"Who knows? The important question is, does he plan to use it all afternoon to keep us in line?"

"Not if I have anything to say about it." Tabitha's mouth was set in a determined line. "Once we're on the boat, I'm going to get the thing away from him and toss it overboard."

"I'll help you," vowed Cass.

Once everyone was settled on the boat, Cass was relieved to see there was room left over. She'd been worried it would be a tight fit, and the boat would sink under the sheer weight of its occupants. Realizing it could easily accommodate at least twenty more passengers, she relaxed.

She and Logan chose spots on the bench that ran the length of the left side of the boat. Rianne sat next to her while Kira, Micah, and Tabitha sat on the other side of Logan.

Cass' stomach did a slow roll when the engine rumbled to life, and she gripped Logan's hand. He turned to her with a reassuring smile.

"Remember," he murmured, "I won't let anything happen to you."

Cass attempted a laugh that came out more nervous than amused. "Let me get this straight again. If we go down, you'll fight sharks, jellyfish, sea snakes ..."

"Eels, killer whales, stingrays, and anything else that lurks beneath the surface," Logan completed the list for her. "And all for you."

Sliding her sunglasses down her nose so she could look him in the eyes, Cass repeated skeptically, "Killer whales? Don't they live in arctic waters?"

"Everybody knows they vacation in the South Pacific." Logan puffed out his chest. "Besides, I used to be a Boy Scout and our motto was 'Be prepared.' I'm not saying there are any killer whales roaming around the lagoon. But in case there are, I want to be ready."

Cass raised a skeptical eyebrow. "What are you planning to do if you run into one? Temporarily blind it with your shirt?"

Logan glanced down at his wildly colored Hawaiian shirt, then looked back at Cass with an injured expression. "I wanted to look like I was in a holiday mood, and this was the cheeriest thing I could find." He fingered the hem of the shirt where pink, fuschia, and orange splotches swirled in a dizzying pattern. "Do you think it's too much?"

Realizing he was genuinely concerned, Cass relented. "No, I was just giving you a hard time. The shirt's great. If I squint, it sort of looks like Christmas tree lights."

Logan's face instantly brightened. "That's what I thought."

Once the boat was underway, Cass found herself wondering why she'd been so uneasy about the trip. The water beneath the hull ranged from pale green to emerald, and it was as smooth as glass. Not a single wave rocked the craft.

As they left Kwaj behind, Cass craned her neck to see the island from a different perspective. From this distance, it looked like a white-fringed jewel set against a turquoise background, and she felt a new appreciation for both its beauty and vulnerability. There was so much water and so little land.

Too soon for Cass, the trip was over as the boat slowed to approach Ebeye's pier. Eager for her first look at the island, Cass stood up and leaned over the rail. Beside her, Rianne did the same.

"The thing I like about Ebeye is that it looks like a real tropical island," Rianne said. "Kwaj has been transformed into Smalltown, U.S.A." At Cass' sidelong glance, she hastily added, "I'm not saying that's a bad thing. I wouldn't want to live on Ebeye. Every now and then though, it's nice to visit."

"Even with the smells?" Cass wrinkled her nose at the odors the breeze carried to them.

Rianne shrugged. "They're part of what life is like here."

Cass smiled. "You have a good attitude." Her nose twitched at the aroma of decaying vegetation that grew stronger the closer they got to land. "But I'm afraid I won't be following your example. Yuck! I wish I had a cold and couldn't smell whatever that stuff is." She waved her hand in front of her face. "Whew! It's going to be a long afternoon."

"You get used to it after a while. Then you hardly even notice it."

Cass fixed her with a dubious stare. "I'll believe that

when it happens."

To Cass and Tabitha's dismay, Dad blew the whistle again. Leaning back, Cass sent Tabitha a scolding look.

"I thought you were going to get that thing away from him."

Tabitha's gaze darted to Micah, and she grinned. "I sort of got distracted. Sorry."

"I'm not," declared Micah. "Sitting next to you was the highlight of the trip."

"Oh, puh-leeze!" Kira pretended to gag. "I think I liked it better when you two were just friends. Sometimes you're so cutesy, you make me want to throw up."

Draping his arm around her shoulder, Micah pulled her close to loudly kiss her cheek. "Gee, Sis, I love you too."

Kira tried to look annoyed, but her twitching mouth gave her away. "Oh, you." She gave Micah a playful shove. "Just because that works on Tabitha doesn't mean it'll work on me."

Before either Tabitha or Micah could respond, Dad launched into a series of instructions about what to do once they disembarked. He enlisted the help of several of the guys to carry the boxes of gifts and baked goods to the community center. Logan and Micah were among those chosen, and they hurried to join the group surrounding Dad.

As the boat docked, Tabitha, who'd slid next to Cass, nudged her. "Look at the kids. There must be a hundred of them."

Cass' heart leapt at the sight of the children crowding the shore. A sea of dark hair and gleaming smiles stretched as far as the eye could see. Most of the children were jumping up and down and waving in their excitement, and Cass found herself waving back.

This is going to be fun! she realized. *Lord, thank You for giving Mom and Dad the idea to do this or else I wouldn't be here, seeing all these beautiful faces.*

In her eagerness to wade into the horde of children, Cass positioned herself to be one of the first off the boat. Rianne was right behind her.

"Can't wait, huh?" Rianne sounded smug. "I thought you'd change your tune once you saw the kids. They're hard to resist, aren't they? The smells don't seem so important compared to them."

"Don't gloat." Cass stepped aside so Rianne could move next to her. "Let's just enjoy this instead."

The moment the line of passengers began snaking its way down the gangplank, a cheer rose from the Marshallese children. Cass couldn't hold back her grin. She couldn't recall the last time she'd felt this good. The expressions on the faces of those around her told her they were enjoying the welcome as much as she was.

Wading into the crowd, Cass immediately attached herself to two little girls who couldn't be more than five. They clasped her hands with a grip that said they didn't plan on letting go any time soon. A few feet away, she saw that Tabitha had a pair of boys in tow. Likewise, all the members of the youth group soon found themselves being led to the community center by miniature personal escorts.

The community center, a Quonset hut, was nestled among a stand of palm trees. The area around the building was swept clean and divided into sections by shells embedded in the sand.

Ceiling fans whirred inside the building, but they didn't do much to dispel the heat. It wasn't long before everyone was sweating. Even Rianne, who usually looked as cool as a cucumber, was wilting. Catching Cass' eye, she smiled, shrugged, and pulled her shirt away from her sweaty skin.

Tabitha, still accompanied by the boys, joined Cass and her companions by the window. "It's a sauna in here."

Because the girls refused to let go of her hands, Cass lowered her head to wipe her cheek on her shoulder. "I'm afraid your clothes are never going to be the same after this," she said, referring to the shirt Tabitha had loaned her in honor of the event.

One of Tabitha's boys tugged on her hand until she looked down at him. When he saw he had her attention, he grinned and winked. Tabitha burst out laughing.

"Whatever happens to my clothes," she assured Cass, "it'll be worth it to have spent time with these angels."

The party was up and running within ten minutes of the group's arrival. Christmas carols played in the background while those who'd volunteered to lead the games organized the children into groups. While some went outside to play, others stayed behind for their turn at the refreshments. Cass and Tabitha waited in line with their kids until it was their turn at the table.

Picking up two paper plates, Cass asked the girls, "What do you want to eat?"

Even though they didn't understand English, they quickly caught on that she was offering food. She could hardly keep up with them as they raced down the length of the table, choosing brownies, cookies, and candies. When their plates were piled high, she directed them to an empty corner and sat with them, enjoying their expressions as they sampled the treats. Tabitha joined her a few minutes later with the two boys.

"I wish we could talk to them," Tabitha said to Cass as the foursome talked among themselves in Marshallese.

"At least enough so we could find out their names." Cass tapped one of the girls on the shoulder. When she turned, Cass pointed to herself and said, "Cass." She repeated her name until understanding dawned on the little girl's face.

Setting down her plate, the girl spread her hand on her chest and said slowly and distinctly, "Poma."

151

Thrilled, Cass echoed, "Poma?"

The girl nodded. Laying a hand on her companion's arm, she declared, "Lani."

Cass placed her hand on Lani's jet-black hair. "Lani."

Her smile could have lit up the darkest cave, but it was nothing compared to the glow spreading throughout Cass' body. Seeing the success Cass had achieved, Tabitha went through the same routine with the boys and found out their names were Naka and, to their great amusement, Bob.

"Bob?" Cass murmured to Tabitha. "What kind of name is Bob for a Marshallese kid?"

"Maybe his parents wanted something different." Tabitha laughed. "You know, like Cassandra or Tabitha."

Cass returned her smile. "I see your point."

When it was time for the groups to switch, Cass and Tabitha led their little ones outside. Intrigued by his wheelchair, Lani and Poma made a beeline for Randy. When they reached him, they stuck their fingers in their mouths and stared, wide-eyed, at him. Randy set them to giggling by rolling forward a few inches to make the bells jingle.

"Showoff," teased Cass, coming up behind the girls. "What are you trying to do? Steal them away from me? How am I supposed to compete with a musical wheelchair?"

"What can I say? When you've got it—" Randy wiggled his eyebrows at her, "—you've got it."

Tabitha and Cass spent the next thirty minutes helping their charges participate in the events. Naka and Bob wound up taking first place in the three-legged race while Poma and Lani kept getting in line to compete in the balloon toss. They were drenched, but happy, by the time Cass herded them back inside the hut.

After another round of refreshments, everyone in the youth group lined up to entertain the children by enthusiastically singing Christmas carols. "Jingle Bells" was the most requested number, especially when Randy got into the act with his wheelchair. Pastor Thompson finally quieted the proceedings down by having the group sing "Silent Night."

When they had finished singing, the group sat down and Pastor Thompson began to tell them the Christmas story. The pastor from Ebeye translated everything he said, and Cass loved watching the faces of the kids as they heard about this Christ Child who was born in conditions much like they lived in. Cass was so glad that they could be here not just to distribute toys and other gifts—but to give them the best gift of all: the news of a Savoir that was born into this world.

After he was done speaking, Pastor Thompson led them all in singing "Joy to the World," and then they passed out the gifts they had brought. Cass was touched by the joy Poma and Lani displayed when she handed them their presents. Lani tore into hers while Poma took her time examining the wrapping before carefully removing it. She gasped when she opened the box and saw the stuffed pink bunny inside.

She looked at Cass, her eyes enormous in her solemn face. Patting her chest, she breathed, "Poma?"

Taking the bunny out of the box and placing it in the child's hands, Cass assured her, "Yes, for Poma."

As Poma clasped the bunny to her, crooning a Marshallese melody, Cass exchanged a satisfied smile with Tabitha. Bob and Naka were busy with their new toys, and Lani had taken off running with her baby doll. It was a rare moment of peace in the midst of the hectic afternoon.

"This is what Christmas should be about," Tabitha observed, glancing around at the gleeful children. "Giving, instead of getting."

"You can say that again," Cass fervently agreed.

Before she could say anything else, she felt a featherlike tap on her shoulder. Since she was sitting on the floor, all she needed to do was turn her head, and she was eye to eye with Poma. "Yes, sweetie?"

Clutching her bunny in one arm, Poma slipped the other one around Cass' neck and laid her head on her shoulder. Cass' breath caught in her throat, and she drew the child close for a long hug. When Poma drew back, she gave Cass a final, brilliant smile before hurrying away to show off her gift to her friends.

"Now that," Cass declared when she was able to speak, "is why I'm having girls when I get married. They're just cuddlier than boys."

"Oh, I don't know." Tabitha's lips curved in a saucy smile. "Micah can be pretty cuddly."

Cass laughed. "If you're going to talk about grown-up boys, that's another matter entirely. I don't have any complaints about Logan in that department."

At 4:30, it was time to head back to the boat. Pastor Thompson gathered everyone together for a final prayer, then the crowd filed out of the community center and headed for the marina. Most of the children skipped alongside them.

Cass found Lani to give her one last hug. The girl rewarded her with a lip-smacking kiss and a long speech in Marshallese that Cass translated as "thank you." When she located Poma, the child insisted on walking to the marina with her. Once there, she flung her arms around Cass' legs and held on for dear life until a Marshallese woman pried her off. The last Cass saw of Poma, she was weeping and stretching out her arms to her. It was almost enough to make Cass decide to move across the lagoon to Ebeye. As she steered Cass up the gangplank onto the boat, Tabitha reminded her that Mom and Dad were talking about holding an Easter party and she'd see Poma again then.

As the boat pulled into port at Kwaj, Micah stood up and waved his arms to get everyone's attention.

"Before we dock and go our separate ways," he declared, "I think we should let Mr. and Mrs. S. know how much we appreciate them setting up this party. If it weren't for them, we'd have spent the afternoon doing our usual stuff, and we would've missed out on something really special. So let's hear it for the Spencers."

Her heart swelling with pride, Cass joined in the applause and cheers for her parents.

As the family biked home from the marina, Cass deliberately fell behind so she could observe the other three without them realizing it. Studying their backs, she thought about how dear Dad and Tabitha had become to her and how much her admiration for Mom had increased since the move to Kwaj.

Jesus, she prayed, *I can honestly say I'm glad You brought me down here. Six months ago, I couldn't imagine a better life than the one I had in Tennessee, but, as usual, You knew best. I love my family. I love my life. But, most of all, I love You. In two weeks, we'll officially celebrate Your birth, but, right now, I feel so full of the joy and wonder of the season, I'm about to pop. Thank You for one of the absolutely best days of my life.*

CHAPTER 20

The following Friday evening, Micah and Logan were invited to the house for dinner and to help decorate the Christmas tree. Dad grilled hamburgers, and they ate on the lanai with the surf providing background music.

As the sun began its descent, Logan pushed away his plate and sighed with contentment. "That was a great meal."

"No kidding," Cass said. "You had three hamburgers. Hasn't anyone ever told you it's rude to eat that much?"

"Hasn't anyone ever told you it's rude to point out how much somebody's eaten?" Logan responded immediately with a smile.

"Good one," approved Dad.

Cass whirled on him with a mock scowl. "Hey! Whose side are you on?"

"Look," Dad pointed out, "I'm usually outnumbered three to one around here. It's nice to have another male around to throw my support behind."

Mom patted his arm. "Poor Steve. Nobody knows the torment you live with day in and day out. You're a real trouper, putting up with us the way you do."

Cass and Tabitha laughed, so Dad turned to Micah and

Logan. "You see what I mean? There's too many of them. I can't catch a break."

Micah nodded his understanding. "They gang up on you, and you can't do a thing about it."

"Finally!" Dad lifted his arms heavenward in a gesture of praise. "Somebody understands." Lowering his arms, he asked Micah, "Would you consider letting me adopt you?"

"I'm sorry, sir," Micah said quite seriously. "I appreciate the offer, but then I'd be dating my sister and that would be way too weird."

As the others burst into laughter, a blazing pink blush appeared on Tabitha's cheeks. Cass grinned at her in sympathy.

Once supper was over, and Cass, Logan, Tabitha, and Micah had finished with the dishes, everyone gathered in the living room to begin trimming the tree. Mom selected several Christmas CD's for Tabitha to load in the stereo while the boys helped Dad string the lights. After a few moments, Cass disappeared back into the kitchen.

"What are you doing?" Mom called as the opening strains of "The First Noel" lilted from the stereo.

Cass poked her head around the corner. "Making hot chocolate. We always have hot chocolate when we decorate the tree. It's a tradition."

Smiling, Tabitha looked over at Logan. "Remember the beginning of the school year when you had your mother make me hot cocoa because I told you I'd never had any? That was so sweet of you."

"I didn't think it was sweet," Cass called from the kitchen. "I thought he was hitting on you."

"Let's not talk about that time period," Micah suggested with a pained expression. "Half the time, I didn't know what was going on. I couldn't figure out who liked who. I prefer things the way they are now."

"Amen to that," agreed Logan.

Leaving the hot chocolate to simmer, Cass rejoined the others in time to help Mom unwrap the ornaments they'd shipped from home. Dad had also brought out the box of decorations he and Tabitha had collected over the years, and Cass eyed the two cartons with skepticism.

"This is going to be one cluttered tree," she remarked.

Tabitha frowned at her. "Maybe we should have bought another one," she said darkly. "Then you and Mom could've decorated yours your way, and Dad and I could've decorated ours our way."

An awkward silence abruptly settled on the room, broken only by the cheerful melody of "Deck The Halls." Cass looked at Mom as if to ask, *what did I say?*

Dad cleared his throat and started to speak, but Tabitha raised her hand to forestall him. "You don't have to say anything. I know that was uncalled for. When Cass said that about the tree, the first thing I thought was that we'd have to leave off some of the ornaments. I was afraid they'd turn out to be ours, and I overreacted. Sorry, everybody. I didn't mean to ruin the mood."

"Nothing's ruined," Mom reassured her. "Plus, I hope you realize we'll either fit all the decorations on the tree or display the ones we can't around the house."

"Fair enough." The tension in Tabitha's face vanished. She turned to Cass. "Do you have a favorite ornament, one you always make sure you get to hang?"

Although Cass was still a little miffed, she hid it well. "Yup. Mine's a kitten in a stocking. Papaw gave it to me when I was … five, I think."

"My favorite is a snowman." Tabitha smiled over at Dad. "It had a carrot nose, but I broke it off one year. I'd taken it off the tree and was playing with it, which was something Dad had told me not to do. When I realized I'd broken its nose, I quickly put it back, facing the wall so Dad wouldn't see. He discovered what I'd done when he took down the tree." She rubbed the seat of her shorts. "I couldn't sit down for a week."

"Don't exaggerate," Dad said with a laugh. "I don't want people thinking I beat you. It was more like two or three days."

Once the lights were in place, Cass, Tabitha, and Mom began hanging the ornaments. Dad and the guys helped hang the decorations near the top of the tree, but mostly they just sat and watched. After a while, Dad disappeared into the kitchen and returned with a tray of cookies and jug of hot chocolate. Everyone paused to get something to eat and admire their handiwork.

"Looking good, ladies," Dad said. "Have you hung your favorite ornaments yet?"

"No." Tabitha pointed to two sitting off to one side on the end table. "Cass and I decided to wait until you were here."

"I'm honored. Thank you." Dad walked to the bookcase where earlier he'd set out the camera. "Tabitha, you go first, and I'll get your picture while you're hanging your snowman."

She obediently picked up the ornament and carried it to a spot on the left side of the tree. She posed with a broad smile while Dad snapped two pictures in quick succession.

"Okay, Cass, your turn," he announced.

Wishing she didn't have an audience, Cass got her ornament and took it to the opposite side. "How's this?" she asked, feeling stiff and uncomfortable.

"Uh … fine." Dad said hesitantly.

"Hey, Cass," Logan called.

"What?" With her eyes trained on the camera, her smile remained frozen in place.

"You're so pretty, you could be the angel on top of the tree."

"You need your eyes checked, pal," Cass couldn't help retorting.

Her stiff smile shattered and was replaced with a genuine grin. Dad fired off two rapid shots.

"Way to go." He slapped Logan's back. "How did you know the right thing to say?"

"Lucky guess, Mr. S." Logan grinned over at Cass. "Plus, telling the truth. She does look like an angel."

"Aww, how sweet," Mom and Tabitha cooed while an embarrassed Cass hid her face in her hands.

When the tree was finished, Dad unplugged the lights while Mom turned off the lamp next to the recliner, plunging the room into darkness. On the count of three, he plugged the lights back in.

"It's lovely." Mom slipped her arm around Dad's waist. "Our first Christmas tree together."

"It's the prettiest it's ever looked," declared Tabitha. "I like the extra decorations."

"Not bad for a fake." Cass' nod was satisfied.

Tabitha leaned around Micah to glower at her. "Is that the best you can do?"

Cass thought for a moment then amended her statement to, "It's really not bad for a fake."

"I give up." Tabitha flung her hands up in defeat.

Scooting around Logan so she was next to Tabitha, Cass draped her arm across her shoulders. "No, you don't. You'll never give up as long as you have any hope at all of changing me."

"You know me too well," Tabitha complained, although her eyes danced with mischief. "You drive me crazy, you know."

Cass shrugged. "It's a rotten job, but somebody has to do it."

Tabitha rested her hand on Cass' shoulder. "What did I ever do without you?"

"Not much, is the best I can figure."

Fixing her with a stern gaze, Tabitha ordered, "Cut out the one-liners. I'm being serious here. As corny as it sounds, you and Mom are the best Christmas gifts I could have ever asked for."

"And you and Dad—" Cass hesitated as she fought the urge to crack a joke, "—mean the world to me," she finished softly.

In the stillness that followed, Dad began reciting softly from Luke 2, " 'In those days Caesar Augustus issued a decree ...' "

" 'And there were shepherds living out in the fields nearby,' " Mom picked up the story after Dad paused.

They all joined in when she got to the song of the host of angels, " 'Glory to God in the highest, and on earth peace to men on whom His favor rests.' "

Cass remembered the joyful look on the faces of the children of Ebeye, and knew the same look was on her face. In her heart she knew it didn't matter what the weather was like outside, or what type of tree they had, or what ornaments they hung on the tree. All that mattered really was that night long ago when Jesus had been born.

"I know I'm a week early," Dad murmured, "but Merry Christmas, everybody."

"Merry Christmas," the others chorused.

Their hands linked, the family, plus Micah and Logan, stood in a semicircle around the tree and soaked up the joy of the season.

CHAPTER 21

I don't want to go. I don't want to go.

The chant seemed to have taken up permanent residence in Cass' head as the day she and Tabitha would be leaving drew steadily closer. They were now down to less than twelve hours before they boarded the plane that would whisk them away from Kwaj, and the chant had become a deafening chorus.

"Are you okay?" Logan's concerned voice penetrated Cass' thoughts.

She blinked and turned distracted eyes to him. "Huh? I mean, yes, I'm fine." She produced an artificial laugh. "You know how it is. I keep going over all the mental lists I've made, checking to see if I've forgotten anything."

"Well, have you?" They were sitting on a bench across from the library, and Logan slid his arm along the back of the seat.

She shivered at his closeness. "No."

"Then stop worrying about it," Logan said. "This is the last chance we'll have to be together for two weeks, and I want you here with me, not a million miles away."

"You are coming to the airport in the morning to see me off, aren't you?" Cass asked.

Logan emitted a mock groan. "I guess. Even though your plane does leave at six." He dropped the pose. "Wild horses couldn't keep me away. I want mine to be the last face you see before you get on the plane."

"Oh, Logan." Sighing, Cass rested her head on his shoulder. "I wish I were staying here."

"Shh." Logan's arm slipped from the bench back to encircle Cass. "It's okay. It's just for two weeks. You'll be back before you know it."

His bleak tone didn't match the upbeat words and Cass smiled in the dark. "You don't believe that any more than I do." She raised her head to look him in the eyes. "But I appreciate you trying to make me feel better."

"Anytime." He looked up. "Just think, it won't be long before you'll be looking at the stars over Tennessee."

"It won't be the same," whispered Cass.

"Why not?"

"Because you won't be there to share them with me." Cass settled her head back on Logan's shoulder. "I wish you were going with me, so I could show you off to all my friends."

"What's there to show off?" scoffed Logan. "If I looked like Micah, that would be one thing, but I'm pretty ordinary."

"You are not!" Cass said immediately. "I like your looks." She giggled. "After all, there's a lot to be said for red hair and freckles. Plus, you're the sweetest, most thoughtful guy I've ever met."

"Aw, go on." When Cass didn't say anything else, Logan urged, "I mean it. Go on, tell me more. A guy can't hear enough good things about himself."

Cass elbowed him in the ribs. "Men and their egos," she pretended to huff. "It's like you're bottomless pits. All the compliments in the world aren't enough to fill you up."

"And that's a bad thing?" teased Logan.

Ignoring him, Cass lifted her legs to gaze at her sandal-shod feet. "It's so weird to think I won't be wearing flip-flops for two weeks. I'm going to have to worry about socks and shoes, not to mention gloves and jackets. Life here is a lot simpler than life on the mainland. For one thing, you don't need nearly as many clothes."

"And some people get by with even less than others." Shaking his head, Logan let out a long, low whistle. "Did you see what Alison Ross was wearing today? If her skirt were any shorter, it would have been a belt."

"You looked!" Cass rounded accusingly on him, although her lips twitched with amusement.

"There wasn't any way I could avoid it." Logan lifted his hands in a helpless gesture. "I came out of economics class and there she was, walking down the hall in front of me. I tried looking at the ceiling, but her skirt was like a magnet. It kept drawing my eyes back to it."

"Great." Folding her arms, Cass assumed a very convincing pout. "How do you expect me to feel okay about leaving you for two weeks when I know Alison's running around in micro miniskirts?"

"What if I promise not to look for longer than—oh, say—two, three minutes tops?"

Cass sniffed and considered his offer. "Well, okay," she grudgingly agreed. "As long as you also promise not to drool."

Logan lifted his hand as if taking a solemn oath. "Absolutely no drooling," he vowed. Dropping the pose, he asked earnestly, "You do know I'm just kidding around, don't you? You're the only girl for me."

"I think I know it, but—" Cass sighed with pure contentment, "it's always nice to hear."

Taking Cass' hand, Logan began playing with her fingers. "We've never talked about this, but did you leave a special guy behind in Jonesborough?"

Even though Cass knew she shouldn't tease him, she couldn't resist the impish spirit that took control of her. "Well, now that you mention it, yes, I did."

Logan grew very still. "Oh. Wha—" He swallowed hard and tried again. "What's he like?"

"Actually, a lot like you." Cass grinned in the darkness. "He's kind and caring and just as cute as he can be."

"I see." It took a moment for Logan to speak again. "How long have you known him?"

"All my life." Stifling her smile, Cass asked in her most innocent voice, "What's wrong? You've gotten awfully quiet all of a sudden."

Logan cleared his throat. "What would you say if I asked you not to see the guy while you're home?"

"Oh, I'm afraid I couldn't agree to that." The laughter Cass had been suppressing began to bubble over. "I mean, how do you think my Papaw would feel if I told him I wasn't going to see him? It would break his heart."

It took a second for Logan to catch on. "You mean you've been talking about your grandfather? Whew! For a minute there, I thought I was going to have to figure out some way to beg, borrow, or steal the airfare to Tennessee so I could keep an eye on you."

Cass pressed a hand to her chest and purred in her most syrupy drawl, "You'd go to all that trouble for little ol' me?"

Laughing, Logan tapped her nose. "Don't give me that southern belle routine. You have me right where you want me, and you know it."

Cass' lips curved in a flirtatious smile. "Oh, really? And where is that?"

"Head over heels in—" Logan paused, and Cass' heart cartwheeled, "—like with you."

Cass was torn between disappointment and relief. The rational side of her knew they hadn't know each other long enough to be talking about love, but her romantic side couldn't help thinking a declaration of love from Logan would have been the perfect send off.

Before Cass could decide how she felt, Logan stood and pulled her to her feet. "We'd better head back. Your parents were very clear about wanting you home by nine-thirty. The librarian just left, which means it's some time after nine."

"The evening really flew by." Holding Logan's hand, Cass crossed the street with him to retrieve their bikes from the rack outside the library. "I hope the time in Tennessee goes just as fast."

Logan shrugged. "But you should try to enjoy each day you're home, so you don't have any regrets when you get back here."

"I guess you might have a point." Cass climbed on her bike, and she and Logan started down the road. "And I suppose making the best of my time in Jonesborough would be a better way to spend Mom and Dad's money."

"Well, I'd feel better if you missed me at least a little bit."

"I'll do better than that," promised Cass. "I'll miss you a lot. In fact, I'm sure I'll even be able to work up a few tears over you."

"Cool." Cass could tell he was smiling by the tone of his voice. "I'm not into crying myself, but I probably won't be fit to live with while you're gone."

"I can live with that." They rode in silence for several seconds then Cass asked, "Is it okay if I call you?"

"I'd like that. In fact, if my parents said it was okay, I was planning to surprise you with a call. I thought I'd get your grandparents' number from your mom after you left tomorrow."

"You can still surprise me," Cass assured him. "Since I won't know when you're calling, it'll count as a surprise."

They arrived at the Spencer house in time to run into

Micah as he was leaving. He paused at the edge of the lawn to wish Cass a safe trip.

"I thought you were coming to the terminal to see Tabitha off in the morning," remarked Cass.

Micah avoided her eyes. "That hasn't been decided."

Cass frowned. "When are you planning to make up your mind? Our plane leaves at six."

"Cass," Logan jumped in, "don't you think whether or not Micah is at the airport is between him and Tabitha?"

Cass rounded on him, ready to argue, then recognized the truth of his question. "You're right," she conceded. Turning back to Micah, she added, "If I don't see you tomorrow, have a great time in Hono with Kira and your Mom."

"I hope your trip home is everything you want it to be," replied Micah.

Lifting his hand in farewell, he climbed on his bike and pedaled away. Cass and Logan exchanged puzzled glances.

"I'd better get inside to Tabitha and see what's up." Cass lifted her leg over her bike and started wheeling it across the grass to the backyard.

Logan followed her. "Do you think I should run by Micah's house on the way home?"

Cass shrugged. "I have no idea."

"I'll probably stop by and see if he wants to talk," Logan said as he leaned his bike against the side of the house.

After Cass set hers on its usual place on the lanai, she turned, and Logan held out his hands to her. She took them, and they gazed at each other in the meager light of the crescent moon.

"I'm going to miss you," whispered Logan.

"I'll miss you more." Cass squeezed his hands and tried to smile.

Logan laughed softly and shook his head. "Everything's a competition with you."

"Yeah, I'm twisted that way."

Cass took a step closer and raised her head, silently inviting a kiss. Logan didn't hesitate. Leaning forward, he placed his lips over hers. When the kiss ended, they sighed simultaneously, which made them both laugh.

"See how perfect we are together?" murmured Logan. "We even sigh at the same time."

"We're a match made in heaven all right." Cass reluctantly let go of his hands and began backing toward the house. "I'll see you in the morning."

"I'll be the one in the cowboy pajamas."

Cass giggled. "I'll be the one pretending not to know you." Reaching the door, she paused. "Thank you for a fun evening. Good night."

"Sweet dreams."

Once inside, Cass spent a few minutes talking with Mom and Dad then went in search of Tabitha. She found her stepsister sitting on her bed and staring into space.

"Knock, knock." Cass pretended to rap on Tabitha's bedroom door that stood open.

Tabitha shifted dull eyes from the wall to Cass. "What do you want?"

Slipping into the room, Cass closed the door behind her and leaned against it. "What's going on with you and Micah?"

"Why?" Although Tabitha's expression didn't change, her eyes narrowed. "Did he say something to you?"

"Logan and I met him as he was leaving, and he said he didn't know if he'd be at the airport in the morning." Cass frowned. "I thought that had been decided weeks ago."

"I thought so too." Looking down at her lap, Tabitha picked at imaginary pieces of lint on her shorts. "Then he started acting weird tonight."

When she didn't go on, Cass prompted, "Weird how?"

"He said stuff like, maybe my trip is for the best—that

we should use the break to figure out how we really feel about each other." Tabitha's voice faltered and she took a deep breath. "He said the time apart will be good training for when he leaves for college, that it'll show us how well we'll handle the separation."

"Gosh." Cass slumped against the door. This didn't sound like the Micah she knew. "What's gotten into him?"

Her expression bleak, Tabitha lifted her shoulders then let them fall. "I wish I knew. When I asked him if he even wanted to come to the terminal to say goodbye to me, he said he didn't know. That's when I about lost it."

"I can understand why." The look Cass gave Tabitha overflowed with sympathy. "What did you do then?"

"I told him maybe it would be best if we called it a night." Tabitha lifted stricken eyes to Cass. "The worst part is, he agreed. He kissed me when he dropped me off, but I didn't feel like his heart was in it."

"Oh, Tabitha." Cass walked to the bed and, sinking down beside her stepsister, slipped a comforting arm around her waist. "I don't know what to say. Maybe he's more upset about you leaving than he wants to let on, and this is his way of coping."

"I asked him about that, but he didn't say anything. So," Tabitha loudly exhaled, "who knows what's going on in his head?" As if rallying, she shook herself and sat up straighter. "I'll tell you one thing. If it's over between Micah and me, I won't have much reason to come back after the two weeks with my mother are up."

Cass drew back to fix her with a stern look. "Don't talk like that," she ordered. "Nothing's over between you and Micah. But even if it were, you'd still have a million reasons to return to Kwaj."

"Other than the family, name one," Tabitha challenged.

"This is your home. Your friends are here. It's where you go to school." Frustrated because Tabitha didn't look convinced, Cass waved her arms. "Like I said, there are millions of reasons for you to come back."

With her chin tilted at a defiant angle, Tabitha rebutted each of Cass' points. "Home is where the heart is. If my heart isn't here anymore, anyplace can be home. I can always make new friends. People change schools all the time, and it doesn't kill them. Look at you."

Too tired to think of more arguments, Cass jumped up and stalked to the door. "This is a stupid conversation. Micah will be there in the morning. You'll see. Now, I'm going to bed."

"Cass, wait!"

Cass turned around. Tabitha gave her a grief-stricken look. "I'm sorry," she said softly. "It's just—" She started crying.

Cass hesitated for a moment, then pushed her anger aside to go back to Tabitha's side. Slipping her arms around her, she held Tabitha's shaking form close to her.

"What's the matter with me?" Tabitha said, her voice so thick with tears that Cass could barely understand her. "Is there something about me that pushes people away? Is that why my mother left all those years ago? Or is it that she and I are alike? Are we afraid of getting too close to people so we pull back?"

"Oh, Tabitha, no," Cass said firmly, holding her tighter. "Not at all." She had no idea how to convince Tabitha how wrong she was, so she just whispered, "Shhh. It'll be okay. I promise." Then silently she prayed with all her heart that it would be.

CHAPTER 22

Little conversation took place in the taxi that transported them to the airport early the next morning. Tabitha stared down at the floor, not saying a word. Cass snuggled next to Mom, depressed at the thought of leaving her. Dad hummed an unrecognizable tune that grated on Cass' nerves, but she didn't have the heart to tell him to stop.

As Cass got out of the taxi, she quickly scanned the area in front of the terminal for the guys. She grinned when both Micah and Logan detached themselves from the wall near the door and started toward them.

Cass elbowed Tabitha. "See?" she said. "I told you he'd be here."

Tabitha gave her a wry grin. "For once I don't mind hearing 'I told you so.' I don't think I'd have gotten on the plane if he didn't show up."

"That would've gone over real well with the parents. Speaking of which—" Cass glanced around and saw them unloading the luggage from the taxi. "Shouldn't we give them a hand with the suitcases?"

"No way." Tabitha slipped her hand into Micah's outstretched one. "My hands are full at the moment."

They walked off to stand by themselves, so Cass and

Logan turned back to Mom and Dad.

"I'll get that," Logan offered to Mom as she leaned down to heft one of Tabitha's suitcases.

Mom stepped aside to allow him to do so, smiling gratefully. "I told the girls to limit their packing to two suitcases each. I should have also limited them to less than five hundred pounds per piece."

"You're not kidding." Logan pretended to stagger under the weight of Tabitha's luggage. "Arnold Schwarzenegger would have a hard time carrying these."

Mom and Cass took care of the carry-on baggage while Dad and Logan muscled the suitcases into the terminal. Mom eyed Micah and Tabitha as the group passed them on the way inside.

"I see they made up from last night," she murmured to Cass.

"Did Tabitha tell you there was a problem?" Cass asked cautiously.

Mom gave her a wry smile. "Tabitha came in from their date looking like she was on the verge of tears and went straight to her room without speaking to her father or me. That's usually a sign that things aren't going well."

"They had a minor disagreement," Cass responded, waving vaguely. "But obviously they worked it out." She nodded at Logan's back. "I think he might have had something to do with that. He said he was going to stop by and talk with Micah on his way home last night."

"I did," Logan said over his shoulder.

"Hey!" Cass protested. "This is a private conversation between my mother and me."

"Then don't hold it loud enough for half the island to hear," Logan retorted good-naturedly.

While Dad checked her and Tabitha in, Cass wandered off to a corner with Logan. She leaned against the wall and gazed up at him.

"What are you smiling about?" she asked suspiciously.

"I can't remember ever seeing you in jeans." Logan stepped back and eyed her. "You look cute." Grinning, he pointed at her feet. "Wow—and sneakers too. It's like you're turning into a mainlander right before my eyes."

Cass tugged self-consciously at the shirt she'd paired with her jeans. "I know. I feel sort of funny, like my clothes are strangling me or something. They're so heavy."

"By this time tomorrow, they'll feel normal."

"I hope so." Cass glanced around the terminal. "Oh, good. Here come the Nishiharas. I'm glad they're flying with us to Honolulu and putting me on the plane to California. I just hope I find the right plane from there to Knoxville."

"You'll do fine." Logan squeezed her hand. "You're a lot more capable than you give yourself credit for sometimes."

"Thanks." Cass' attention was caught by Micah and Tabitha coming in the door. "What did you and Micah talk about last night?"

"Uh … well … he sort of swore me to secrecy."

Cass' eyes widened in alarm. "Was it something bad? Something Tabitha should know about?"

"No, nothing like that," Logan said quickly. "It's just sometimes guys need to talk to each other without having to worry about it going any further. You know, like girls do. You wouldn't want me to know everything you and Tabitha talk about, would you?"

"Well … no," Cass admitted reluctantly. She peeked again at the other couple. "And they seem to be doing okay, so I guess you're not hiding some deep, dark secret."

"Not me." Logan shrugged. "We just sat around and talked guy stuff for a couple of hours. I gave him some advice. And voila!" He gestured across the building. "There you see the results."

Cass grinned up at him. "So now you're in the business of handing out advice, are you?"

Logan puffed out his chest. "What can I say? When you've got, you've got it."

"And you, mister, are full of it." Laughing, Cass led him by the hand over to where her parents stood with Ed and Lois Nishihara. "Good morning," she greeted them. "You know Logan, don't you?"

The Nishiharas nodded. Ed checked his watch.

"We should be boarding in about five minutes," he announced. "Unless there's a last-minute rush, it doesn't look like there'll be that many of us on the flight."

Cass estimated there were approximately seventy people milling about the terminal and decided that not all of them were passengers. "Good. I like to be able to stretch out when I'm flying. I hate feeling cramped, especially on the military planes that don't have any passenger windows."

"That's what we'll be flying this morning," Lois said. "Then your flight to San Francisco will be on a regular jet."

As Tabitha and Micah joined the group, Cass noticed that Tabitha clung to Micah's hand as if she were drowning and it was a life preserver. *We're going to have to use a crowbar to pry them apart and get Tabitha on the plane,* she thought wryly to herself.

A flight attendant came over the loudspeaker, announcing that the plane was ready to be boarded. A swarm of butterflies immediately began soaring and dipping in the pit of Cass' stomach. By the look on Tabitha's face, she was experiencing a similar reaction.

Dad caught Cass close in a bear hug. "I'll be praying for you, sweetie. Call us the minute you get there."

"I will." Cass swallowed the lump that had formed in her throat. "You and Mom have fun pretending you're childless."

"I have a feeling I'm not going to enjoy it nearly as much as I thought I would." Dad released Cass then curved a hand around her cheek. "I love you. Tell your grandparents hello for me."

Not trusting herself to speak, Cass merely nodded. She dreaded turning to Mom, knowing her mother well enough to know she'd be crying.

"Don't even think about getting on that plane without telling me goodbye," Mom teased, despite the tears welling in her eyes.

"A girl can dream, can't she?" Cass shot back.

Mom pulled her in for a tight hug, and Cass found herself hanging on for dear life.

"I hate that I'm going," she whispered fiercely against Mom's hair. "Whose stupid idea was this anyway?"

"Uh ... that would be Dad and me." Mom laughed.

"Please let me stay," Cass begged, wondering what she'd do if Mom agreed.

Mom snorted. "Yeah, right. And the minute the plane took off, you'd be whining and carrying on about being stuck here with us." She pulled back and set Cass away from her. "So, shoo. Get on the plane and have yourself a wonderful time. Give everybody back home my love."

Sniffling pitifully, Cass assured her, "I will. Take care while I'm gone."

"You bet," Mom said, and Cass turned away to head for the door leading to the tarmac. "I love you, Cassandra Aileen," Mom called after her.

Cass' head snapped around and fresh tears spilled from her eyes. "I love you too, Donna Maureen." Then, gripping Logan's hand, she started again for the door.

They joined Micah where he stood just beyond Tabitha who stood with her arms entwined around Dad's neck, her face buried in his chest. Dad was rubbing her back.

"Everything will be fine," Cass heard him say to her. "No matter what happens, don't forget we love you, and we're behind you 100 percent."

"What if ... if ..." Tabitha stopped.

Dad gently disentangled her arms from around his neck and framed her face between his hands, brushing away her tears with his thumbs. "God is in charge of all the what if's. You don't need to worry about them."

"B-but do you think I'm do-doing the right thing?" stammered Tabitha.

Dad nodded. "Yes, I do. Just keep praying while you're in Oregon, and you'll be amazed at how well things turn out." Dad kissed her cheek and motioned to Micah. "Why don't you walk her to the door?" he suggested.

Cass hugged Logan one last time and gave him a quick kiss on the cheek before she and Tabitha turned and headed toward the plane. Once on board, they located their seats midway down the cabin and sat down to watch the rest of the passengers file on board.

Tabitha nudged Cass. "Look, there's Hannah O'Malley," she said, wiping the last of her tears from her cheeks. "I wonder where she's going."

"Maybe to look at colleges," Cass said. "Graduation's not that far away."

"How can you talk so calmly about graduation?" Tabitha said darkly. "I can't even think about it without wanting to cry."

Cass felt beneath her for the two ends of the seat belt. "Not talking about it isn't going to keep it from happening."

"Yeah, but isn't it going to kill you when Logan leaves for college?"

"I'm not looking forward to it," Cass conceded. "But who knows what things will be like by then? A lot can change in a few months."

Tabitha halted her quest for her own seat belt to peer intently at her. "Are you planning some kind of change?"

Cass shook her head. "No, but I wasn't planning on moving down here either, and look what happened."

"True." Tabitha hesitated. "Actually, I'll let you in on a little secret. I'm keeping my options open."

Cass wasn't sure she liked the sound of that and scowled. "What's that supposed to mean?"

Tabitha fastened the two ends of her seat belt and settled back in her seat. "Just that I've decided to hear my mother out instead of automatically turning her down if she asks me to spend more time with her."

Even though she'd been anticipating this possibility, it still took Cass' breath away to hear Tabitha state it out loud. "Does Dad know?"

Tabitha made a face. "I said it was a secret, remember?"

Cass stared down the aisle, frowning.

"Did I upset you?" Tabitha asked after a moment. "You're not saying anything, and that's unusual for you."

Cass just wished she could avoid the subject. "I can't believe you even have to ask if I'm upset. Of course I'm upset. This two-week separation is bad enough. The thought of it turning into something longer makes me sick to my stomach."

"Oh," Tabitha said lamely.

Cass took advantage of her silence to buckle her seat belt and tighten it with a vicious tug. If only the pilot would hurry up and take off, she could curl into a ball and pretend to sleep. That way, she wouldn't have to talk to Tabitha for the rest of the trip.

The intercom crackled and the pilot came on to inform the passengers that they'd be taxiing to the runway momentarily. The flight attendant, a young female soldier, closed and secured the plane's door, shutting out the sunlight. Cass breathed deeply to ease the claustrophobic feeling the windowless compartment gave her.

"Are you scared?" Tabitha asked quietly.

It took Cass a few seconds to respond. The idea that Tabitha might choose her mother over the family struck

Cass as the ultimate betrayal. Still, it wasn't reasonable to think they could spend five hours cooped up in a plane together and not exchange a single word. For the sake of harmony, Cass choked back her anger.

"I'm not scared exactly," she replied. "It's the window thing. I don't like not being able to see outside."

"What's there to see?"

Stung by Tabitha's nonchalant attitude, Cass bristled. "For one thing, Mom, Dad, and the guys. I know they're standing outside the terminal, waiting for the plane to take off. Wouldn't you like one last look at Micah?"

Tabitha's expression turned wistful. "That would be nice." She shook herself. "Once we're airborne, though, we're over water from here to Hawaii. It's not exactly exciting scenery."

"Anything's got to be better than looking at this for the next five hours." Cass gestured at the cargo netting on the walls.

Tabitha dismissed her complaint with a breezy wave. "If I know you, you'll be asleep most of the time anyway."

The plane lurched into motion and their conversation ceased, which was just fine with Cass. She hated fighting with Tabitha, especially if ... Cass swallowed hard against the lump that suddenly formed in her throat. If Tabitha opted to stay with her mother, this would be the last time they were together. Cass didn't want the memory to be bitter.

Cass turned to Tabitha at the same moment her stepsister looked at her. She was taken aback to see tears streaming down Tabitha's cheeks.

"What's the matter?"

"I'm so scared," whispered Tabitha. She kept her face averted so the other passengers couldn't see she was crying. "It took every ounce of courage I had to leave Dad and get on the plane."

"Because you're not sure you're coming back?"

A fresh crop of tears accompanied Tabitha's nod.

"Look—" Cass had to raise her voice to be heard over the whine of the engines. "Nobody's forcing you to stay with your mother. In the first place, you don't even know for sure she's going to ask you to. And secondly, you don't have to say yes if she does."

"But I have to be fair," Tabitha insisted. She waited to continue until the plane had roared down the runway and lifted off. "Let's say she asks me to stay a few months so the two of us can get better acquainted. How can I tell her no?"

"Like this." Exaggerating the words, Cass said slowly and distinctly, "No, Beth, I'm not staying with you. I'm going home, where I belong."

"And that's another thing. What am I supposed to call her?"

"Well," Cass drawled, "her name is Beth, so I'm thinking that's what I'd go with."

"But she's my mother," argued Tabitha. With the plane airborne, she twisted in her seat to face Cass. "I can't call her by her first name."

"What choice do you have?" Cass' piercing gaze was unwavering. "You're not going to call her Mom, are you? You already have a Mom. Do you think it'd be fair to her to call another woman by her name?"

Tabitha's tears had stopped, but her smile was still slightly watery. "I can remember when you hated me calling your mother Mom."

"That was then, and this is now," Cass replied briskly. "Stick to the subject. If you're not comfortable using your mother's first name, you'd better figure out what you are comfortable with. After all, you'll be face-to-face with the woman in—what?—about twelve hours."

Tabitha frowned. "Approximately. So what do you suggest?"

"I already gave you my suggestion."

"I suppose I could start out calling her Beth and see where it goes from there," Tabitha said hesitantly.

"Sounds good." Cass shifted position, trying to get more comfortable. "When do you think they'll be bringing us something to eat? I'm starved."

Tabitha wiped away the last of her tears with the back of her hand and laughed. "Doesn't anything affect your appetite?"

"Sure. When I'm upset, I tend to eat even more." Cass craned her neck to see if she could locate a flight attendant to ask about breakfast.

"You don't seem upset," Tabitha said.

Cass slumped back in the seat. "That's because I'm not. Leaving was hard, but now that we're on our way, I'm kind of excited. After all, I'm getting to see Papaw and the rest of my family and friends. What could possibly be the down side of that?"

"Being away from Logan?" Tabitha arched an eyebrow at her.

"Okay, it'd be more fun if he were coming with me," acknowledged Cass. Then she shrugged. "But he's not, and I refuse to spend the next fourteen days pining away for him. Besides," she went on with a curious glance at Tabitha, "I'm not the one talking about being gone for a couple of months. If you're so crazy about Micah, how can you even think of staying away one second longer than you have to?"

A faint blush worked its way up Tabitha's neck to her cheeks. "It's not as simple as you're making it sound."

"So explain it to me. I'm not going anywhere for the next five hours." Cass turned in her seat to face her.

Tabitha closed her eyes and leaned her head back against the seat. "Last night with Micah threw me for a loop," she began after a moment of hesitation. "Everything was fine when he picked me up. But as soon as we left the house, he got really quiet. I kept trying to get him to talk, but he total-ly clammed up. We were going to get something to eat then take in a movie. Supper was so awful though, that I suggest-ed we skip the movie and go to Eamon Beach to talk."

"And?" Cass prompted when Tabitha fell silent.

Opening her eyes, Tabitha rolled her head to gaze at Cass. "That's when he told me he thought this trip would be good for us. He said, with college coming up for him, we need to find out how we're going to deal with being apart. I asked him if that meant he was glad I wasn't going to Hono with him. He never really answered me, but I'm scared it does. I don't know." She passed a hand across her eyes. "Maybe he's hoping to meet somebody else while he's in Hawaii. We have been dating for almost five months now. He could be getting tired of me."

Cass vehemently shook her head. "No way! He was mis-erable about you leaving. Anybody could see that."

"Then why didn't he act like it last night?" persisted Tabitha. "He was cool as a cucumber about me going away, telling me to have fun and not to worry about writing or calling."

Cass frowned. "Maybe he thought he had to act tough so you wouldn't see how much he was hurting. Some guys are like that. Besides, the important thing is that he showed up this morning and practically glued himself to your side until you had to get on the plane."

"That was nice," Tabitha admitted. "But it made every-thing more confusing. I can't tell how he really feels. Did it kill him to see me leave? Or was he happy to get rid of me?"

Cass pressed her fingers to her temples. "Ouch. My head feels like it's about to explode. I'm tired of analyzing every-thing. Can't we just sit here for a little while and pretend that our lives are uncomplicated?"

Tabitha grinned. "It may be asking too much. But, sure, let's give it a shot."

CHAPTER 23

When the Nishiharas stopped by to check on Cass and Tabitha twenty minutes later, they were happily sorting through pictures from the Christmas party on Ebeye that Cass had put in her carry-on bag.

"You ladies seem to be getting along fine," Lois Nishihara remarked. "I'm glad to see no one's crying."

Cass avoided looking at Tabitha, for fear they might start giggling. "We got over being sad as soon as the plane lifted off," she assured Lois. "The only problem we're having now is that we're about to collapse from hunger. Do you have any idea when they're going to start serving breakfast?"

"I asked about that before we got up," replied Ed. "They're heating the meals now, so it should be any minute."

"Good." Cass stretched and rubbed her midsection. "I'm afraid if my stomach keeps growling, people are going to think we're having engine problems."

The Nishiharas laughed. Lois patted Cass' head.

"Hang in there. In the meantime, if either of you needs anything, you know where to find us." She made a vague gesture behind her. "We're back there somewhere."

"That certainly narrows it down," Cass whispered to Tabitha as the couple moved on.

"Shh," Tabitha ordered, giggling. "They might hear you."

After a breakfast of eggs and sausage, they settled in for the duration of the flight. Cass reached into her carry-on bag for a book Mom had bought her for the trip. It was by one of her favorite authors, but Cass found it impossible to keep her eyes open.

When she awoke a short while later, she discovered Tabitha had taken her book. After watching her for a few minutes, it became obvious her stepsister was only pretending to read because she never turned a page.

"What are you staring at?" Cass asked. "There aren't any pictures."

Tabitha jumped. The book fell to the floor, and she bent to retrieve it. When she straightened up, her face was flushed.

"I didn't know you were awake. What were you doing? Spying on me?"

Here we go again, thought Cass. *Grouchy Tabitha is back.*

"Look, Tab, I don't want to—" Cass began.

Tabitha held up a hand to interrupt her. "One of the first things I told you when we met was not to call me Tab."

"Oops. I forgot." Cass gave a careless shrug. "What's the big deal about the nickname anyway?"

"It's what my mother called me when I was little," Tabitha reluctantly confessed. "Since I didn't like to be reminded of her, I decided shortly after she left to use my full name."

"Then why is it still a problem?" wondered Cass. "After all, you and Beth seem to be getting along great now."

Tabitha sighed. "The memories of what it was like after she walked out are still painful. I don't like anything associated with that time period." She hesitated before saying in a low voice, "Whenever we talk on the phone, she calls me Tab and it gives me a queasy feeling."

"Have you told her that?" Cass asked.

Tabitha shook her head.

"Why not?" As well as she thought she knew Tabitha, there were still times when Cass couldn't figure her out at all. "For pity's sake, you're not shy about telling everyone else how you feel about being called by the right name."

Tabitha was silent for a few minutes. When she finally spoke, Cass had to strain to hear her. "I guess I'm worried I might make her mad if I say something. I'd have to go into why I don't like being called Tab, and she might not like hearing it still bothers me that she walked out on us."

"Are you serious?" Cass exploded, making Tabitha jump. "How do you expect to build any kind of relationship with Beth if you can't be honest with her? What are you planning to do? Show up and act like everything's great, that her leaving didn't have the slightest impact on your life? There's a real solid foundation for a meaningful relationship."

"I don't—"

"You have no intention of confronting your mother about what she did," Cass continued, ignoring Tabitha's interruption. "Now that she's back in your life, you're so afraid of losing her again you'll do anything to make sure she sticks around this time. That's why you're considering staying on with her if she asks you to, isn't it? You still think you did something to make her leave, and you're hoping if you're a good little girl, it won't happen again."

Tabitha turned a pleading face to Cass, her breath coming out raggedly. "Please stop. I don't want to listen to this."

"Tough." Cass had no intention of stopping. "Somebody should have made you listen years ago, or at least when this all started again with your mother. You're not to blame for her leaving. I know people have told you that before, but maybe this time you'll get it through your thick skull. You didn't make your mother leave. Your Dad didn't make her leave. Beth left of her own free will because she couldn't hack it as a wife and mother. She's the one with the problems, not you and Dad."

"I know that up here." Tabitha touched her forehead. "But I can't seem to convince myself in here." She placed her hand over her heart.

"Like Mom says when it comes to faith, sometimes you have to go with what you know to be true in your head, even if you don't feel it yet." Cass jostled Tabitha's arm. "It's time you started acting like you know your mother was in the wrong. Stop being scared of saying or doing the wrong thing. Be yourself. If she doesn't like you as you, too bad. It's her loss. Again," she added pointedly.

Tabitha quirked a wan smile at her. "Has anybody ever told you that you should go into coaching? You're pretty good at giving pep talks."

"I'm better at giving them to other people than I am to myself," confessed Cass. "Before I fell asleep, I kept telling myself to quit worrying about what's going to happen with Janette and take whatever comes as being for the best."

"What do you mean, being for the best? When things don't turn out the way you want them to, how can that be for the best?"

"Awhile back, Mom and Dad gave me this verse from Romans about God bringing good out of every situation for those who love Him," explained Cass. "I still don't completely understand it, but Mom said it means that God's in charge, no matter what happens."

Tabitha nodded slowly. "Good advice, but of course," she added with a wry smile, "it's easier said than done. Most of the time when I try to trust God and leave things in His hands, it doesn't last very long. I start to get anxious because He doesn't seem to be moving fast enough so I take back whatever problem I've given Him."

"Welcome to the club." Cass uncrossed and re-crossed her legs, then announced, "I've got to get up and walk around. I'm not used to sitting still this long."

"I'll go with you," Tabitha volunteered. "We can check in with the Nishiharas. Let them know we're still on the plane."

Cass stood up and stretched. "Very good. See? You can be funny when you put your mind to it."

"Gee, thanks," drawled Tabitha. "That means so much coming from a professional comedian like you."

"Wow, sarcasm too." Cass stepped into the aisle. "Is there no end to your talents?"

They made several passes up and down the aisle, stopping to talk with people they knew. They made arrangements with Ed and Lois to accompany them to the baggage claim area so the couple could retrieve their luggage before they, in turn, escorted the girls to the gates their flights would be leaving from.

"I feel like we should pin notes to our shirts with our names and flight numbers written on them in case we get lost," Tabitha said as they walked away from the Nishiharas.

"They do treat us like a couple of little kids," agreed Cass. "I mean, we could wait in the main terminal while they get their luggage, instead of tagging along behind them all over the airport."

Tabitha stifled a giggle. "Yeah, but we might wander off and get lost. How would they explain that to Mom and Dad?" Mimicking an adult voice, she carried on a pretend conversation. "We're sorry, Steve and Donna. We have no idea what happened to the girls. We left them alone for two minutes. When we got back, they were gone. We have half the airport looking for them though, so they should turn up any second now."

Although Cass laughed, she felt guilty. "We're not being very nice. They are doing us a favor, after all."

"That's true." Having reached their seats, Tabitha slipped into hers first. "We ought to be more gracious."

"It's hard to graciously make fun of people." Cass sank down into the seat on the aisle.

"Maybe we can figure out how when I get back," Tabitha suggested.

Cass turned to her with a hopeful expression. "So you are coming back then?"

Tabitha instantly tensed. "I don't know. Don't push me, okay?"

"Just promise me you'll pray about it before you make any decisions." Realizing the flight was almost over, Cass felt a sense of urgency about getting Tabitha to at least promise that much.

"Of course I'll pray," she said darkly. "Give me a little credit, will you?"

"All right, but only a little." Surprising herself, Cass slipped her arm through Tabitha's. "I want you to also promise me that you won't forget what we mean to each other. I know I'm not related to you the same way your little brother and sister are, but we do have a bond."

"I know." Suddenly the plane began its descent to the runway, so Tabitha reached over to clasp Cass' hand. Without speaking a word, Cass knew what she was thinking. *This was the last time they'd be together for two weeks, and possibly longer.* It was enough to bring a lump the size of a golf ball to her throat.

"You take care of yourself, you hear?" Cass whispered sternly. "Don't be afraid of letting your mother get to know the real you. I happen to think you're a terrific person. A little too snotty and uptight sometimes for my taste," she couldn't resist adding, earning herself a strangled laugh. "But, all in all, a really special human being."

Tabitha responded by squeezing Cass' hand. "I want you to take your own advice when it comes to Janette. If she starts laying a guilt trip on you that it's your fault the friendship is falling apart, get in her face and tell her off. You don't have to take that from her, not after the way she's treated you the past several months."

"Yes, ma'am." Cass grinned.

The plane set down with a shuddering bump, and the girls were pressed against their seats as the pilot applied the brakes. Once the pressure eased, they turned to each other with solemn faces.

"This is it." Tabitha took a deep breath. "I'll be praying for you while you're in Tennessee. Please pray for me."

Cass nodded stiffly, afraid that any more movement would start her crying. "Every day and twice on Sundays," she tried joking. She lost it when Tabitha produced a wobbly smile. Grabbing her stepsister close, she implored, "Don't stay in Oregon. Please come back to us."

She later decided it was the worst moment of her life when Tabitha merely shrugged, unable to give her that assurance.

CHAPTER 24

"Grandma!"

"Hello, dear. I'm glad you finally made it."

Twelve hours after boarding the plane on Kwajalein, Tabitha walked off another plane in Oregon, straight into her grandmother's arms. Despite her fatigue, she summoned up a cheery smile and an enthusiastic greeting. "You look great! You've lost weight since the last time I saw you."

Stepping back, Tabitha surveyed her grandmother from head to toe. "Your hair's different. I like it."

Grandma self-consciously patted her salt-and-pepper curls. "I decided to stop dying it. What you see is my natural color."

"It looks good." Slipping her arm through her grandmother's, Tabitha leaned over and kissed her cheek. "It's wonderful to see you again." She glanced furtively around. "You're here by yourself, right?"

Grandma nodded, although her lips tightened. "Of course. That's how I told your father it would be." She hesitated before revealing, "Your mother wasn't at all happy about the arrangement. She called shortly before I left for the airport to ask one last time if she could accompany me.

I told her in no uncertain terms that she could not. Your father trusts me to keep my word, and that's exactly what I plan to do while you're here. I assured Beth I'd bring you to her house bright and early tomorrow morning."

"Good." Relieved that she had another few hours to prepare herself for meeting her mother, Tabitha bent down to pick up the carry-on bag she'd dropped while greeting Grandma. "What do you say we get my luggage and hit the road? I'm exhausted."

"Your room is all ready for you." Grandma smiled at Tabitha. "Do you remember it from the last time you visited?"

Tabitha briefly closed her eyes in order to envision the room Grandma had told her years ago she decorated specifically for her. "Yes, I do. The furniture was white and the bed had a pink-and-green striped canopy. The wallpaper was patterned with pink rosebuds and green vines and the curtains were lace. I loved it. I remember thinking it was a fairy-tale room, something fit for a princess."

Grandma's grin creased her lined face. "You do remember," she said excitedly. "I'm so pleased." She glanced shyly at Tabitha. "Perhaps it was rather silly of me, but I didn't change a thing. The room is exactly the way you left it. I'm sure you'll find it rather childish now, but I recalled how delighted you were with it before and couldn't bear the thought of redecorating."

Tabitha patted Grandma's arm. "I'm glad you didn't change anything. I would've been disappointed if you had. Besides," she went on, "you have another granddaughter. Sunshine's a little young right now to appreciate the room. But I bet when she gets older, she enjoys it just as much as I did."

Grandma's heavy sigh told Tabitha that she wasn't so confident. "She will if Beth and I are still on speaking terms."

"Oh." Tabitha wasn't sure if she should ask Grandma what she meant, then decided she had a right to know what was going on in the family. "Are you and my mother having problems?"

Grandma rolled her eyes and sniffed. "When do we not have problems? Not that there's anything going on at the moment," she added hastily. "It's just that we continue to experience ups and downs in our relationship. I had hoped by now we'd be getting along better, but it doesn't seem to be happening. I don't know, perhaps I'm to blame."

Although Tabitha didn't see her grandmother often, she did feel a great deal of loyalty to her. After all, Grandma had done her best to maintain a relationship with Tabitha, despite Beth's behavior.

"I find it hard to believe any of what goes on is your fault. Beth doesn't have a very good track record when it comes to relationships. It seems to me if anybody is to blame, it's probably my mother."

Grandma gave her a grateful smile. "I appreciate your support. Truly I do. But I think it's best we don't talk any more about the situation. I wouldn't want you to think I'm trying to influence you concerning your mother."

In a flash of understanding, it occurred to Tabitha that her grandmother didn't like her mother very much. The realization made her uneasy. Grandma's opinion mattered to her, but Tabitha didn't know how to come right out and ask her if what she suspected was true. In the end, she opted to say nothing and chatted about unimportant subjects as she and Grandma made their way to the baggage claim area.

Tabitha's two suitcases were the first ones spit out onto the conveyer belt. After claiming them, she followed Grandma out to the parking lot. The moment the airport doors hissed open, a blast of arctic air took Tabitha's breath away.

"Wow!" exclaimed Tabitha. "Even the air in our freezer back home isn't this cold."

Her brow furrowed with concern, Grandma paused on the sidewalk. "If you prefer, you can wait inside while I get the car. Then I'll swing by and pick you up."

Tabitha squared her shoulders and lifted her face to the icy wind that brought tears to her eyes. "No, I'll be fine. But it'll take some getting used to. When I left Hono, the temperature was eighty-six degrees. What do you suppose it is here?"

"I listened to the news on the drive here and it was nineteen. I'm sure it's gone down a couple of degrees since then." Grandma turned up the collar on Tabitha's denim jacket for her.

Tabitha shivered. "No wonder I'm freezing." She jutted her chin in the direction of the parking lot. "Let's go find your car before I turn into an icicle."

Fortunately, Grandma had parked in a spot close to the building. Within a couple of minutes, Tabitha was huddled in the front seat of the car, impatiently waiting for Grandma to turn on the heater. She watched in amazement as her breath turned into miniature cloud puffs.

"I forgot it does this when it's cold." She laughed. "I remember when I was little, I'd pretend I was smoking. I thought I was so cool until Dad told me to cut it out."

"Your Dad is a good man." Grandma started the engine and checked the rearview mirror before backing out. "He's raised you right."

"Yes, he has." Using her sleeve, Tabitha wiped away the condensation on the window. "I'm really blessed to have a father like him."

Grandma slid her a glance out of the corner of her eye. "I like hearing you use the word 'blessed' instead of lucky or fortunate. Your father is a blessing from God."

"So is my Mom." Tabitha felt her cheeks flame. "I mean

my stepmother."

"You call her Mom?" When Tabitha acknowledged that she did, Grandma nodded with satisfaction. "That's good. It means she's made you feel you're one of hers. She must be a very special woman to have accomplished that in such a short time."

An unexpected wave of homesickness washed over Tabitha. "She is. Right from the start, I've felt like she loves me just as much as she loves her daughter." She laughed. "Of course, that didn't sit well with Cass. For a while there, she was wildly jealous. Actually, we both were," she added honestly. "Dad was just as good about accepting Cass as Mom was about accepting me. Neither of us was used to sharing our parents so it got pretty tense sometimes. I don't know how we kept from getting into knock-down, drag-out battles over it."

Grandma quirked an eyebrow at her. "I imagine your parents had a lot to do with keeping the situation under control. Obviously, Steve and Donna are well suited to each other and are doing an excellent job of helping you girls adjust to the changes in your lives." Grandma sounded as pleased as she looked. "I've prayed long and hard for God to provide your father with a helpmate. It seems my prayers have been answered."

The motion of the car was making Tabitha drowsy. With her head lolling against the seat back, she peered over at Grandma. "You really like Dad, don't you?"

"I think the world of Steve," Grandma said.

"You don't hold him responsible at all for what happened between him and my mother?" To her surprise, Tabitha heard herself asking a question she never, in a million years, would have asked under normal circumstances.

She was relieved when Grandma didn't seem to mind answering her. "Absolutely not. Steve's conduct when he was married to Beth was beyond reproach. I was proud to have him as a son-in-law. I'm not saying he was perfect, but I believe he did his level best to be a good husband and father. Neither he nor you deserved the way Beth treated you."

"Wow." Tabitha turned to face Grandma, impressed. "You don't pull any punches when you talk about what happened. You call 'em like you see 'em."

Grandma glanced away from the highway to smile at her. "That's because I'm sixty-three years old, dear. I'm too old to play games with the truth. Perhaps if I'd been less indulgent when your mother was younger and more straightforward with her about her shortcomings, she might have turned out differently. I don't blame myself for the things she's done, but I do believe I have to share some of the responsibility. I wasn't as tough with Beth as I should have been."

"Just so you know, I don't blame you one iota for what she did," Tabitha said quickly. "And neither does Dad. He always speaks very highly of you."

Grandma didn't say anything for a moment. When she finally spoke, her voice was soft and trembled slightly. "I'm glad to hear that. It means more to me than you'll ever know."

The singing of the tires on the pavement began to lull Tabitha to sleep. Fighting to stay awake, she yawned and forced herself to look out the window at the scenery flashing by. All she could see, however, was snow and an occasional house set far back from the road.

"I forgot how deserted it is around here. And I thought we lived out in the middle of nowhere," she joked.

"I prefer living like this. I had my fill of big cities when your grandfather was alive." Grandma's voice took on a nostalgic tone. "We always talked about retiring in the country. Since he was from Oregon, we bought a piece of land out here, intending to build on it when he retired.

Unfortunately he died before that could happen, but I still had the house built and moved here by myself."

"Are you lonely?" Tabitha asked softly.

"Sometimes," Grandma admitted. "Most of the time, however, I'm quite content. I like my privacy. Plus, I come and go as I please without answering to anybody."

"Gee, I hope I'm not too much of a disruption while I'm here," teased Tabitha. "I'll do my best to stay out of your way."

"You, my dear, are never a bother." Grandma smiled at her. "You've always had a very special place in my heart."

"Thank you." Not knowing what else to say, Tabitha shifted her attention to looking out the window. After several seconds, she asked, "How much longer?"

"About thirty minutes. Why don't you try to sleep?" suggested Grandma. "You don't have to stay awake to keep me company." Leaning forward, she turned on the radio and classical music filled the car. "Go ahead and sleep. We'll be home before you know it."

Although Tabitha tried to fight her drowsiness, within five minutes she was curled up in a ball against the door, sound asleep.

CHAPTER 25

She woke to Grandma shaking her, her soft voice announcing, "Wake up, sleepyhead. We're almost there."

Tabitha uncurled herself and stretched before sitting up straight in the seat. Her eyes grew wide as she peered out the windshield. "Hey, I know where we are. Your house should be coming up on the right any second now."

"Very good," Grandma said. A moment later, her smile disappeared and a deep frown puckered her forehead. "I don't believe it," she muttered. "What is she doing here?"

"What? Who?" Tabitha glanced from Grandma's face to the driveway she'd slowed to turn in to. A van took up most of the space. "Do you know who that belongs to?"

"Yes." Grandma stopped the car, shut off the engine, and jerked up the emergency brake. "Your mother."

Tabitha's heart slammed against her chest. "But I thought I wasn't supposed to see her until tomorrow." She glanced wildly around, as if looking to escape.

"You weren't. Not surprisingly, Beth decided to take matters into her own hands." With a gusty sigh, Grandma opened her door, admitting a rush of cold air. "I should have expected this. She was determined to see you tonight so here she is. Your mother doesn't take no for an answer."

"Is she in the house or waiting in the van?" Although her grandmother had started to climb out of the car, Tabitha remained frozen in her seat.

"The lights are on in the house, so I imagine she's there." Grandma glanced over her shoulder at Tabitha. "I know this is a shock, but you can't sit in the car the rest of the night. Come on," she coaxed. "Let's get you inside. If you're not ready to see your mother, why don't you head right upstairs while I send her home? I'll explain to her that we're sticking to the original schedule."

With a tremendous effort, Tabitha managed to shake off her temporary paralysis. She slowly grasped the door handle. "She doesn't have to leave. I'll talk to her. What difference would a few more hours make?"

Taking a deep breath, Tabitha opened the door and swung a leg out of the car. The moment she did, the front door to the house flew open, and a woman appeared in the halo of the porch light.

"Tab! Oh, my baby, my baby! You're really here! My darling, precious baby!" Her wild mane of hair streaming behind her, Beth flew down the steps and raced across the lawn. Reaching Tabitha, she didn't hesitate a second, but grabbed her in a bone-crushing embrace. She alternated between jumping up and down and rocking from side to side as she crooned, "My baby. My sweet, wonderful baby."

Too stunned to react, Tabitha merely stood there with her arms stiff as boards at her sides. Over her mother's shoulder, she sent Grandma a mute appeal for help.

Coming around the front of the car, Grandma gently but firmly disentangled Tabitha from Beth's arms. "Now, dear," she chided her daughter, "don't strangle the poor child. Give her room to breathe and a chance to get her bearings."

"I can't." Beth reached again for Tabitha, but Grandma quickly stepped between them. "It's been so long. Nobody knows how much I've ached to hold this precious baby of mine."

Overwhelmed by the emotional display, Tabitha didn't know what to do. Part of her wanted to scramble back into the car and head straight to the airport. Another part longed to throw herself back into her mother's arms.

With a visible effort, Beth got herself under control. Her eyes continued to glitter feverishly every time she looked at Tabitha, but she didn't make any attempt to seize her again.

"All right then." Grandma kept a wary eye on Beth as she moved toward the trunk to unlock it. "We need to carry Tabitha's things inside and get her out of this frigid night air. She's not used to it, and the last thing we want is for her to take sick."

"You're right." Beth turned to Tabitha to shoo her into the house. "You go on in, and we'll see to your belongings. Go on," she urged when Tabitha hesitated.

Grandma nodded. "It's okay. We'll take care of your things."

Dazed, Tabitha stumbled toward the house. She couldn't believe her mother had shown up after being told not to. It bothered her to realize how willful Beth was, and she didn't look forward to telling Dad what she'd done. She knew her father wouldn't like it one bit that Beth had taken matters into her own hands.

As Tabitha came through the front door, she halted in her tracks. Standing in the hallway, clutching a blanket and rubbing his eyes, was Peace. He gave Tabitha a tentative smile.

"Hi."

"Hello." Tabitha looked over her shoulder, hoping to see Grandma and Beth right behind her. They weren't, which meant she was on her own with her half-brother.

"I'm Peace," the little boy announced.

"I know. I'm Tabitha."

Peace nodded. "Tab," he corrected her. "Mom said you was coming."

Tabitha studied the little boy. His blue eyes reminded her of her own, and his blonde hair fell to his shoulders in soft waves.

"Why're you lookin' at me like that?" Peace demanded, his brows drawn together in a scowl.

Tabitha shook herself. "I'm sorry. I didn't mean to stare." When Peace looked confused, she opted to change the subject. "Where's your little sister?"

"Sunshine sleepin'." Peace pointed a pudgy finger at the dimly lit room off to the left. Tabitha remembered it was the living room. "In there."

Before Tabitha could think of a response, she heard her grandmother and mother coming up the front steps. She expelled the breath she'd been holding in a whoosh of relief. She and Peace might be related, but she had no idea what to say to him.

"Mom!" Peace shouted when he spied his mother. "Tab's here."

"I know." Dropping the suitcase she carried, Beth reached out to tousle the boy's hair while, at the same time, taking Tabitha's hand. "I see you've met your bother. What do you think? Isn't he wonderful?"

Once again, Tabitha found herself tongue-tied, this time because she'd gotten her first glimpse of her mother in the bright light of the hall. It was like looking into a mirror. True, there were similarities between her and Mom, but this was remarkable. Except for the wrinkles, Beth's face was identical to the one that stared back at Tabitha every morning in the bathroom mirror.

I wonder how Dad feels when he looks at me, Tabitha wondered, a surge of sympathy for her father welling up inside her. *It has to be hard for him, but he's never said a word.*

She suddenly realized Beth had asked her something.

Blinking, she confessed, "Sorry, I wandered off for a couple of seconds there. What did you say?"

"I asked you what you think of Peace." Beth drew the boy to her side, and he curled an arm around her leg as he leaned against her. "I know I'm biased, but I'm wondering if you consider him as glorious a child as I do."

"He's very cute." Tabitha recognized what a lame response that was and tried again. "He speaks quite well for his age."

"That's because he's a genius." Cupping Peace's chin, Beth tilted his head up so she could smile down at him. "Aren't you, son? Aren't you the smartest boy that ever lived? Don't you make Mommy proud because of how brilliant you are?"

Uncomfortable with Beth's praise, Tabitha searched for something to distract her. "Uh … he said Sunshine's asleep in the other room."

Her ploy worked. Pushing Peace away, Beth tugged urgently on Tabitha's hand. "He's right. She is. Come see my other miracle. Honestly, I should have had a dozen kids. I make such incredible children." She beamed over her shoulder at Tabitha. "Especially you. I mean, look at you. You're gorgeous and, from what you tell me about your schoolwork, intelligent. That can't all come from just your father."

Beth's reference to Dad bothered Tabitha. He was married to Mom, and Tabitha didn't like hearing another woman talk about him, even if she had been married to him once. She was spared the need to comment by Beth dragging her across the living room to the spot on the floor where a baby lay curled up on a blanket.

Tabitha's heart melted at the sight of the child. "Oh, she's adorable." Sinking to her knees, she gently rubbed Sunshine's back.

"Of course she is," chirped Beth, kneeling down beside Tabitha. "She looks exactly like me."

"Beth." Grandma's exasperated voice came from behind them, and Tabitha turned to look up at her. "How many times have I told you not to put her on the floor? It's too cold and hard."

"She's lying on a blanket," Beth said, sounding slightly irritated.

"A very thin blanket," Grandma pointed out.

"Sunshine's tough." To Tabitha's surprise, Beth scooped the baby up in her arms and jiggled her awake. "Aren't you tough?" she asked the baby who whimpered in protest. "Just like your Mommy."

"Beth, don't," Grandma ordered sharply. "Leave her be. Here," she held out her arms. "Let me take her. I'll fix up a place for her on my bed."

Beth stopped shaking Sunshine and handed her to Grandma. "Where will you sleep then?"

Grandma gave her a sharp look. "What do you mean? Aren't you going home tonight?"

Beth's laugh was a trill of disbelief. "Are you kidding?" She slipped her arm around Tabitha's waist and squeezed. "You expect me to just up and leave my baby now that we've been reunited after all these years?"

Tabitha suddenly felt dizzy. The combination of the trip and her mother had finally gotten to her. Her head reeled, and the only thing she wanted was to find someplace to lie down before she fell down.

"Grandma?"

The older woman stopped fussing with Sunshine's blanket and instantly focused her attention on her other granddaughter. "Yes, dear?"

"I think I need to go to bed, if that's okay."

"Of course it's okay." Shifting Sunshine to her other arm, Grandma held out her hand to Tabitha. "Come with me, and I'll help you get settled in your room."

Beth leaped to her feet. "No, let me." She threaded her

fingers through Tabitha's. "After all, this is the first time in years that I'll be able to tuck my daughter into bed."

The last thing Tabitha wanted was to have her mother come with her, but she didn't say anything. With a wan smile, she allowed Beth to lead her from the room. After a brief stop in the hallway to gather her luggage, she trailed her mother up the stairs to the bedroom Grandma had decorated for her all those years ago.

To Tabitha's discomfort, Beth plopped herself down in the middle of the bed. She seemed to watch every move Tabitha made as she opened one of the suitcases in search of her pajamas and toothbrush. Desperate for privacy, Tabitha wracked her brain for some way to get her mother to leave.

"What do you suppose Peace is doing while you and Grandma are up here?" she finally asked.

Beth shrugged. "I don't know." She fluttered an airy wave. "Whatever he's up to, he's fine. He's a very resourceful little guy. He knows how to take care of himself."

Probably because he knows you're not going to do it for him, Tabitha thought bitterly.

Aloud, she said, "Don't you think you ought to check on him?"

Beth refused to take the hint. "Nope. He has a healthy set of lungs. I'll hear him bawl if there's a problem."

Since Beth wasn't going to budge, Tabitha decided she'd leave. Gathering her things, she edged toward the door. "I'll just take these into the bathroom with me and change there."

"Fine." Beth patted the bed. "I'll be right here when you get back. Maybe I can brush your hair while we chat a bit," she suggested.

"I'm really pooped," Tabitha hedged. At Beth's disappointed expression, she added, "But I'll see how I feel after I get ready for bed."

Hurrying into the bathroom, Tabitha shut the door then leaned against it with a sigh of relief. She'd managed to escape her mother for a few minutes anyway. She hoped it was long enough to gather her wits about her in preparation for facing Beth again. Almost immediately, there was a knock at the door.

"Yes?" Tabitha asked warily.

"It's me, dear."

Grateful to hear Grandma's voice instead of Beth's, Tabitha opened the door a crack. "What's up?"

Grandma lowered her voice to a whisper. "How are you holding up? Do you need me to shoo Beth out of your room?"

"I'm—" Tabitha passed a shaky hand across her eyes, "—feeling kind of steam rolled, and I could really use some time to sort things out. If you could get rid of Beth, I'd definitely owe you one."

Laughing softly, Grandma reached through the crack to pat her cheek. "You don't owe me a thing. It's on the house. You just get ready for bed, and leave your mother to me."

True to her word, Grandma somehow convinced Beth to go away by the time Tabitha emerged from the bathroom. Hearing her mother chatting with Peace downstairs, Tabitha scampered across the hall and ducked into her bedroom. Turning off the light, she slid into bed and pulled the covers up to her chin.

Please don't let Beth come upstairs, she implored God. *I've had all I can take for one night. I'm on overload right now. A* violent shiver rocked her. *Brr! I'm also freezing. Why in the world did I think coming here was a good idea?*

Little by little, Tabitha forced her tightly closed eyes to open. A branch scratched at the window to her left, and she rolled over onto her side to gaze at it. A hill rose behind the tree, and the glow from the moonlight hitting the snow reminded Tabitha of a moonlit beach. She bolted upright, her hand flying to her mouth.

"I forgot to call Dad," she gasped. "He must be frantic by now."

Flinging off the covers, Tabitha sprang out of bed. Heedless of the cold, she rushed barefoot to the door. When she yanked it open, she was startled to find her mother standing on the other side.

"Goodness!" Beth laughed and stepped back. "Where are you going in such a hurry?"

"I need to call Dad," explained Tabitha. "I was supposed to call him the minute I got here. He's probably worried sick."

Beth's eyes narrowed ever so slightly. "Now, now." She took Tabitha's hand and tucked it into the crook of her arm. "Don't make such a big deal out of one little slip-up. I'm sure Steve will understand you got caught up in the excitement of seeing your grandmother and me again." She tightened her hold when Tabitha started to inch away. "However, if you're concerned he might be angry, I'll be happy to call him for you and let him know you arrived safe and sound."

Tabitha's jaw dropped. She could just imagine Dad's reaction if he picked up the phone to find her mother calling on her behalf. Besides, she wanted to talk to him and Mom. It seemed like forever since she'd left them at the airport that morning.

"I'll call." Tabitha removed her hand from Beth's arm.

"Be sure to tell him I said hi," she called as Tabitha started down the stairs. "Also thank him for sending you to me. Although it would've been nice if he'd done this years ago, instead of waiting until you were nearly grown," she added with a brittle laugh.

Tabitha halted on the steps and slowly turned to face her mother. "You never asked to see me before."

Beth's eyebrows arched. "Is that what he told you?"

Shaking her head, she moved to the top of the stairs. "I hate to be the one to break it to you, Tab, but he lied. In the beginning, I asked him every month if I could see you. No," she corrected herself, "I begged him to let me see you. He wouldn't allow it. After a while, I quit asking. I couldn't take the constant rejection. When you turned sixteen though, I decided it was now or never. If we were ever going to re-establish a relationship, I'd have to give it one last shot. Fortunately, this time I was able to deal directly with you without having to go through your father." She spread her hands in gesture of unbridled joy. "Obviously, it made all the difference in the world because here you are."

Staggered by her mother's revelations, Tabitha clung to the railing, afraid she might fall if she let go. "That's not true. You never asked to see me—not once—after you left."

Beth shook her head and gazed sadly down at Tabitha. "I know it's hard to accept, but your father's been lying to you all these years."

"No!" There was such a crushing weight pressing down on her chest that Tabitha found it difficult to breathe. "Dad doesn't lie."

Beth came down one step, then stopped when Tabitha shrank from her. "Steve hates me for walking out on him," she said softly. "He used you to hurt me. He lied about me in court so the judge wouldn't award me custody, then he took you halfway around the world where I couldn't get to you, no matter how hard I tried." Her eyes filled with tears, and she choked back a sob. "And believe me, I tried. When you opened your door a few minutes ago and found me standing there, that's what I'd come up to tell you. I couldn't let one more second go by without you knowing the truth about what happened. I didn't abandon you."

"But you wrote me a letter saying you did and that you were sorry," Tabitha reminded her.

"Because I knew the only way Steve would let you visit

would be if he thought I'd keep silent about what really occurred. I counted on you showing the letter to him." Beth walked down another step. "The only thing that mattered to me was getting you here so I could finally tell you the facts about my so-called abandonment."

Fear and confusion swirled through Tabitha. *Either she's lying or Dad is. If Dad's been lying to me all these years, then my entire life is based on a falsehood. If Beth's lying then something really spooky is going on, and I should probably get out of here pronto.*

Aloud, she announced in a trembling voice, "I'm calling Dad and asking him."

Beth shot her a skeptical look. "Do you honestly think he'll tell you the truth? Of course he'll say I'm lying. I have no proof I tried getting in touch with you. I'm sure he burned the letters and gifts I sent."

"What about Grandma?" challenged Tabitha. "She must know if you really did all the stuff you say you did."

Crossing her arms, Beth propped her hip against the railing. "My mother and I had very little to do with each other after Steve and I divorced. It wasn't until I had Peace that we resumed a relationship. She has no idea what I did or didn't do all the years in between."

How convenient, a voice sneered in Tabitha's head. She thought it sounded a lot like Cass, and, for a moment, she desperately wished her stepsister were there. She'd know what to do. *But she's not here,* Tabitha reminded herself. *It's up to you to figure out how to handle things.*

Squaring her shoulders, she repeated, "I'm calling Dad."

Beth shrugged and gestured toward the hallway below. "Be my guest. But I'm warning you, he's going to deny everything."

Tabitha started down the stairs with Beth on her heels. Spinning around, she announced, "You're not allowed to listen in. I want to talk to Dad alone."

Beth raised her hands and assumed a hurt expression. "Fine. You don't have to jump all over me." Reaching the bottom of the steps, she flounced off to the living room. "I know when I'm not wanted."

Grandma, who was entertaining Peace in the living room, watched Beth throw herself onto the sofa. She turned to Tabitha with a questioning look. "What's going on?"

Despite the strain she was under, Tabitha summoned up a reassuring smile. "Nothing. I was in bed when I remembered I need to call Dad. The phone's in the kitchen, right?"

Grandma nodded. "Close the door if you'd like some privacy. And take as long as you want."

"Thanks."

Dad answered the phone on the first ring. "Hello?"

Relieved to hear his voice, Tabitha slumped against the counter and blinked away the tears that sprang to her eyes. "What were you doing? Sitting on top of the phone, waiting for it to ring?" she teased.

"Just about," Dad admitted. "How are you, sweetie? How was the trip?"

"I'm fine, and so was the trip. Grandma met me at the airport."

"Just Grandma?"

Tabitha nodded, then remembered Dad couldn't see her. "Yes, although Beth called at the last minute and asked to come."

Dad inhaled sharply. "I'm glad your grandmother had the sense to turn her down. Have you talked to Beth yet?"

"Uh ... actually yes." Tabitha hesitated, knowing Dad would be angry at hearing she was here. "She was at the house when we got here. Grandma was pretty mad, but there was nothing she could do about it."

"Be sure to tell her I don't blame her for Beth's actions.

So—" Dad said, then paused. "What do you think of your mother?"

Not sure how to respond, Tabitha settled for, "It's a little too early to say. I'll let you know after we've spent more time together. Peace and Sunshine are pretty cute, though."

"Having seen their pictures, I imagine they are."

Tabitha smiled, knowing instantly from his simple remark that he'd told her the truth through the years about her mother. A mean, sneaky person would have made a nasty comment about his ex-wife's kids. Dad was anything but mean and sneaky. He was the one who'd stuck by her and raised her, never once complaining. Tabitha was ashamed of herself for having doubted him for one second.

"Sweetie, are you there?"

Dad's anxious question reminded Tabitha they were in the middle of a conversation. "I'm here." She straightened. "You should know Beth told me a pack of lies about you being the one who kept us apart."

There was a moment of hesitation on his end, but his voice was calm when he responded. "Do we need to discuss anything she said? Would you like me to talk to her?"

"Nope." Warmed by his support, Tabitha smiled. "I know what's true and what isn't."

"Will you be okay spending time with her after this?" Dad asked quickly. "You don't have to stay with her if she makes you uncomfortable."

Tabitha twisted the telephone cord around her finger as she considered her options. "As of right now, I want to go ahead with the plans," she finally replied. "I'll see how I feel, though, if she keeps on lying."

"Mom and I will be praying for you," Dad assured her. "Hang onto that thought, and you'll be fine."

"I know. Is Mom there? I'd really like to talk to her, " Tabitha asked just as Beth came into the kitchen. She fervently hoped Beth hadn't heard her request, but it was too late to do anything about it if she had.

"Of course she's here. Where else would she be?" quipped Dad. "However, before I hand you over to her, let me remind you how much I love you. I started missing you the moment you walked on the plane, and I won't stop until you return."

Tabitha swallowed the lump in her throat. "Same here. I love you, Dad. Bye." While she waited for Mom to come on, she was acutely aware of Beth puttering nearby, filling a cup with juice and rummaging in the refrigerator for something to eat.

I know what she's doing, and I won't let her bully me into acting differently with Mom, Tabitha vowed to herself. *I'll be myself, no matter how uncomfortable she makes me.*

"Hi there," came Mom's cheerful greeting. "Is this one of my two favorite world-travelers?"

Hearing her lifted Tabitha's spirits. "Hi, yourself. It sure is." She pretended to sulk, "Although I'd like it better if I were your favorite, not just one of them."

"Boy, you girls take sibling rivalry to new heights."

"What can I say? Cass and I are overachievers. We try to excel at everything we do." Tabitha abruptly dropped the bantering. "How are you and Dad? Do you miss us?"

"Desperately." There wasn't an ounce of joking in Mom's tone. "We had our first spat this afternoon, which we chalked up to the stress of you two being gone."

"Oh, Mom." Forgetting about Beth, Tabitha squeezed her eyes shut and wished herself home. "I miss you both so much. I'm counting the hours until I return."

"Don't do that," Mom gently commanded. "Try to enjoy yourself while you're there, okay?"

"I guess." Tabitha opened her eyes and discovered Beth was gone. "I'll call you the day after tomorrow. If you see Micah, tell him I said hi. I love you."

"I love you too, sweetie. Get a good night's sleep so you're raring to go tomorrow. Bye now."

"Bye," Tabitha whispered, holding onto the phone for several seconds after Mom hung up.

Grandma was alone in the living room when Tabitha returned. At the girl's quick glance around, she explained, "Beth took Peace upstairs to put him to bed."

"That's where I'm headed." Tabitha began to sidle out of the room. "Good night."

"Before you go," Grandma said, patting the arm of her chair, "come sit with me and chat a few minutes. I promise I won't keep you long. I realize you're tired."

Tabitha walked over to the chair and perched on the arm. "What do you want to talk about?"

Instead of answering, Grandma asked, "How are your parents?"

"They're okay." Tabitha grinned. "Mom said they really miss us. She said they had their first quarrel today."

Grandma laughed. "Worrying about your children can do that." Reaching up, she encircled Tabitha's waist with her arm. "You don't have to answer this if you don't want to, but I have to ask. Did your mother say something earlier to disturb you?"

Tabitha briefly considered not responding, then decided she owed Grandma the truth. "Yes." As best she could, she related her conversation with Beth.

Grandma's face tightened until she looked as if she'd just bitten into a lemon. "I see." She nodded curtly when Tabitha finished. "I was afraid she'd pull something like this. I'll speak to her about it first thing in the morning."

Tabitha placed a calming hand on Grandma's shoulder. "Don't. I'll handle it. She has to know she's not dealing with a child anymore. I'm old enough to fight my own battles."

Grandma gazed up at her in admiration. "You're a

remarkable young woman, Tabitha Joi Spencer. I'm proud to call you my granddaughter."

"God, Dad, and Mom get all the credit. In that order."

After kissing Grandma, Tabitha stood and ran up the stairs two at a time. Despite the late hour and the talk with her mother, her heart was light. Dad and Mom missed her. Grandma was proud of her. Life was good. Before falling asleep, Tabitha thanked God for giving her the strength to see her through the last couple of hours, as well as whatever the next two weeks might hold.

CHAPTER 26

Tabitha awoke the next morning to the sound of a baby crying. Disoriented and unable to recall where she was and why a baby would be crying, she rubbed the sleep from her eyes and peered about the unfamiliar room. Recognizing the canopy over her head, everything came back to her, and she scrambled from beneath the covers. From the sound of it, Sunshine was up and running, which meant it was time to meet her little sister.

Pausing long enough to slip on her robe, Tabitha followed Sunshine's ruckus down the stairs and into the kitchen. She found Beth and Peace at the table and Sunshine in a highchair while Grandma toiled at the stove. Peace's face lit up at the sight of Tabitha, and Sunshine instantly stopped crying to stare, round-eyed, at this stranger. Beth pointedly ignored her.

"Good morning, everyone," Tabitha chirped, waving to Peace and Sunshine.

Peace returned her wave. Sunshine continued to regard her with a solemn gaze. Beth said nothing, but Grandma turned from the stove.

"Good morning, dear." Using a spatula, she gestured at the frying pan. "I'm fixing bacon and eggs. Are you interested?"

"Am I ever!" Tabitha's stomach growled at the mere mention of food. "Usually I can't hold a candle to my sister, Cass, when it comes to eating. But I believe I'd give her a run for her money if she were here this morning."

"Stepsister," Beth coolly corrected her.

"Excuse me?" Hoping she hadn't heard what she thought she'd heard, Tabitha gave her mother a chance to take back her comment.

Lifting icy blue eyes to Tabitha's, she replied, "Cass is your stepsister, not your sister. I thought you were one of those ultra-religious people. Isn't it lying to call someone your sister when she's not?"

Tabitha's mouth opened and closed several times as she tried to think of a response. All the while, Beth sat there, coldly staring her down.

Grandma came to Tabitha's rescue. "Don't quibble, Beth. Tabitha told me last night how close she and Cass are. I, for one, think it's wonderful she feels so strongly about Cass that she considers her a sister."

"A lie is a lie," declared Beth. "Technically, Tab and that girl aren't related. Therefore, it's an untruth for her to refer to the girl as her sister."

"Look who's talking about lying," Tabitha amazed herself by purring.

A venomous smile curled Beth's lips. "I was wondering when you'd get around to that. I guess your Dad and *Mom* filled your pretty little head with all sorts of vicious stories about me when you talked to them last night." She didn't seem to notice Peace's whimper from across the table. "Naturally," she continued, "you hung on their every word, accepting whatever they said as the gospel truth. Did it ever occur to you to give me the benefit of the doubt? No, of course not." She cackled bitterly. "You decided long ago I was the bad guy, and nothing's going to change your mind."

As their mother's voice grew louder, Peace and Sunshine became more agitated. Peace started banging his spoon on the table, and Sunshine let loose with a wail. Abandoning her cooking, Grandma hurried to comfort them.

"That's enough, Beth. Look what you're doing to the children. If you have something to say to Tabitha, take it in the other room."

Beth slammed her hands down on the table, shoved back her chair, and rose. Glaring down her nose at Tabitha, she demanded, "Well? Are you willing to deal with this like an adult? Or would you rather stay here and hide behind my mother?"

Despite the nervous fluttering in her stomach, Tabitha realized she was amazingly calm. Listening to her mother, she found it hard to believe Beth was thirty-eight years old. She sounded more like a petulant child than a grown woman.

"I'll be happy to discuss the situation with you," she informed Beth in an unruffled voice. Stepping aside, she motioned toward the door. "After you."

Once in the living room, Beth sat down on the couch and patted the cushion next to her. "Why don't you sit here?" she suggested with her most winsome smile. Apparently, she had decided to change her game.

"No, thanks." Tabitha deliberately chose the chair farthest from the couch. "I'd rather sit over here."

Although Beth's mouth pursed with irritation, she responded mildly, "Suit yourself. Now—" she rubbed her hands together, "—let's see if we can get this little problem cleared up so we can enjoy the rest of your vacation."

"I don't consider you lying about my father to be a little problem." Tabitha stared at her mother until the woman looked away.

Beth giggled nervously. "Perhaps I could have chosen a

better way to describe the situation," she conceded. At Tabitha's curt nod, she continued, "Hard as this is for me to admit, I do have a confession to make."

"Go on," Tabitha prompted when Beth fell silent.

"I will. Give me a moment. This is very hard." Clasping her hands together in her lap, Beth leaned forward to peer earnestly at Tabitha. "I ... I ... lied last night about Steve keeping you from me. He never did that. In fact, he used to try to get me to contact you. I was the one who kept us apart, not your father."

"You never wrote me letters or sent me gifts?"

Her mother shook her head. "Other than those few occasions when I remembered your birthday, never."

"Then why did you say you did?" Tabitha couldn't mask the disgust she felt for Beth. "Why in the world would you try to turn me against Dad?"

Hanging her head, Beth replied in a small voice, "You're going to find this difficult to accept, but I did it because I love you so much." At Tabitha's derisive snort, her head jerked up. "It's true. I love you with all my heart. I always have. I realize it was wrong to lie to you, but I was desperate to figure out some way to get you on my side. I thought if I could convince you Steve's been lying, you'd feel sorry for me. Your pity might grow into love. I planned to own up to what I'd done after I was sure of your feelings for me."

Tabitha shook her head in bewilderment. "That's crazy."

Beth shrugged. "People do crazy things when they're desperate. And I was desperate—I still am—for you to love me."

Sighing, Tabitha stared out the window at the falling snow. "Why now?"

"Excuse me?"

Tabitha swung her gaze back to her mother. "For years, you had nothing to do with me. Now all of a sudden you show up, claiming to love me and wanting me to love you back. I want to know what happened to make you want me in your life again."

"That's a good question." Beth leaned back against the cushions and crossed her legs. "I guess it all started after Peace was born. Being with him, taking care of him, I proved to myself I could be a good mother."

Thinking about some of Beth's parenting techniques, Tabitha snorted softly.

"Having Sunshine confirmed for me just how terrific a mom I am when I put my mind to it," Beth continued. "It made me realize all I had missed out on with you. I can't tell you how much I regret not seeing you grow up. I wasn't there when you started school or went to your first party. I don't know when you lost your first tooth or who your first boyfriend was. I decided a few months back it was time to correct my past mistakes. That's what prompted me to write to you." Her expression softened. "And you so kindly wrote back. Your letter meant everything to me. I carried it in my wallet for weeks, so I could take it out and read it whenever I felt the urge."

Although her suspicions remained, Tabitha found herself wanting to believe her mother. "What do you expect out of this visit?"

Drawing her legs up beneath her, Indian-style, Beth leaned her elbows on her knees and propped her chin on her hands. "First and foremost, I want you to realize I'm your mother and not that woman your father married. Plus, Peace, Sunshine, and I are your real family, no matter how hard you try to pretend the one you live with is."

Her words made Tabitha's blood run cold. *So that's what this is about,* she thought. *She's jealous. She doesn't care about being my mother. All she wants to do is make sure nobody else is.*

"Wow, it really bugged you last night when you heard me call Donna *Mom,* didn't it?" Tabitha's eyes never left Beth's face.

"Of course it did," her mother huffed. "I have feelings too, you know. Ever since my mother told me Steve had remarried, I've been expecting something like this to happen. Even though he made some halfhearted attempts to keep me in your life, I'm sure he jumped at the chance to have Donna replace me in your affections. I'll even bet he was the one who suggested you call her Mom."

Tabitha held up a hand to interrupt. "That's enough. I won't listen to you talk about Dad that way. You're forgetting he's the parent who stayed when you got tired of mothering and took off. Do you think that was easy? Believe me, it wasn't. But he hung in there with me because, unlike you, he loves me more than he loves himself. Plus," she went on, raising her voice when Beth tried to break in, "he did his best to maintain some kind of relationship between you and me, even when you couldn't be bothered. When I was little, he used to buy presents and cards for Christmas and my birthday and pretend they were from you. The only reason he stopped was because I finally caught on when I was eight. And, last but not least, it was my idea—not Dad's, not Donna's, not the man in the moon's—for me to call her Mom. I couldn't wait to have a mother. Thanks to you, it had been a long time since I had one. Not that I ever really did. Mom's been more of a mother to me in the past eight months than you ever were."

Beth's face hardened into a furious mask. "You're just as cold and heartless as your father," she sneered. "I don't know why I bothered to contact you in the first place. I should have known it would turn out like this. I let Steve have you too long. He brainwashed you."

Tabitha responded with an incredulous laugh. "You're the one who's brainwashed. You've convinced yourself you're a good mother and that you've earned the right to be in my life. I hope, for Peace and Sunshine's sakes, that you have changed your ways. But I worry that when the going gets tough with them, you'll get going. Again," she added pointedly.

Beth's face flushed a deep crimson. "I'll never walk out on my babies. And do you want to know why? Because I love them in a way I never loved you."

As hard as it was for Tabitha to hear that, it settled the issue once and for all of whether or not she could have a relationship with her mother. Instead of being angry, she felt at peace. Beth was who she was and Tabitha couldn't change that. To her surprise, she found herself smiling.

"I pray it's true, that you do love them in a way you weren't capable of loving me when you were younger. They're terrific kids. I'm sorry I won't get to know them." Getting up, Tabitha crossed the floor to stand in front of her mother. "I'm going to call Dad and tell him what's happened. He and I will decide what to do about letting me stay here with Grandma or flying back to Kwaj. Either way, I won't be seeing you again. Have a nice life. Take care of Peace and Sunshine. I'd appreciate it if you'd send me pictures of them every now and then." She leaned down and kissed Beth's cheek. "Just so you know, I forgive you for what you did. I love my life, and your leaving is what made it possible."

For a brief moment, Beth looked like she was about to cry. "This is it then? We're not going to give it a try?"

Tabitha shook her head. "No. We're too different. We don't believe in the same things. I wish you only the best, and I honestly don't hold any grudges against you. But—" she shrugged, "—I have my life, and you have yours."

"But I love you, and I want a relationship with you," protested Beth.

Tabitha just looked down at her, full of pity. "I truly don't believe you know what love is," she murmured before turning and walking out of the room.

A short while later, she heard a door close and went to

the bedroom window that faced the front yard. She watched as Beth buckled Sunshine and Peace into their car seats. Without a backward glance at the house, Beth climbed behind the wheel, backed down the driveway, and was gone.

Tabitha was still standing at the window when Grandma knocked on the door.

"Come in," Tabitha called without turning around.

Grandma came up behind her and laid her hand on her shoulder. "How are you doing?" she asked softly.

Tabitha placed her hand over Grandma's and squeezed. "I'm fine. It was hard, but I think I did the right thing."

"Yes, you did," agreed Grandma. "I knew from the start that Beth's reasons for contacting you and getting you up here were selfish. I prayed you'd realize it and that you wouldn't be hurt too badly when you did. I trust my prayers have been answered."

Letting the curtain fall, Tabitha turned around. She smiled tenderly at her grandmother. "Yes, they have. Thank you for praying for me. From now on, though, concentrate your prayers on Sunshine and Peace. They're going to need them a lot more than I will."

"I'm afraid you're right." Grandma looked as sad as she sounded.

Tabitha gently squeezed her arm. "Hey, look on the bright side," she teased. "It seems you're going to have me to yourself for the next couple of days while Dad and I figure out what to do with me."

Grandma's grin lit up her face. "Now that's a happy thought. Why don't you call your Dad while I finish cooking you some breakfast?"

Tabitha put her arms around her grandmother and hugged her. "I love you." Her lips curved in an impish grin. "Your daughter, on the other hand …"

Grandma shook her finger at her, but grinned. "Don't be

fresh." Placing her hands on Tabitha's back, she pushed her toward the door. "Go call. I'm anxious to know how much longer I get to have you here."

Laughing, Tabitha sashayed toward the door. "You know, I like this. I feel so wanted." She smiled to herself when Grandma laughed.

On her way downstairs to the phone in the kitchen, Tabitha paused a moment to whisper, "Lord, I had no idea things would turn out the way they have. Thank You for keeping me strong when I talked to Beth. Bless her and the children. And please make sure I get home safely. I can't wait to see Mom and Dad again. Oh, and Cass too. I realize I don't just love her like a sister. I love her because she is my sister, and I want to tell her that face to face."

CHAPTER 27

"I'll bet anything Tabitha's having herself a wonderful time in Oregon while nothing—absolutely nothing—is going right for me here," Cass grumbled to herself as she lay in bed early on the third morning of her stay.

Still not over her jet lag, her days and nights remained mixed up. The sun hadn't risen yet, and the room was pitch-black. *And cold,* Cass added with a shiver. *I forgot what it was like to be this cold. I wonder if I always disliked it this much.*

Sitting up, she propped the pillows behind her and leaned back against the headboard. With much tugging, she finally arranged the covers so she was completely enveloped except for her head. Once that was accomplished, she settled down with a gusty sigh, ready to review the events of the past forty-eight hours.

Grimacing, Cass recalled stumbling off the plane in Knoxville at six o'clock Saturday morning. Fortunately, Papaw was waiting with open arms and his welcoming bear hug lifted her spirits and eased her weariness. They chatted nonstop on the two-hour drive back to Jonesborough, catching up on all the news. Mamaw greeted them with a hearty breakfast, and after a nap and a shower, Cass was ready to face the day. Her first call was to Janette. Thinking about their conversation left Cass with a hollow feeling in the pit of her stomach, and she kicked the covers.

I wonder if Jan could have been any less excited to hear from me, she mused. *Instead of rushing right over here so we could spend the day together, she had to run by Lauren's first because she'd promised to help her pick out something to wear for her date that night. Then she stopped by Carly's to drop off a couple of CDs she'd borrowed. By the time she got here, I couldn't help wondering why she even bothered coming at all. It wasn't like she cared one iota about how my life's going. All she wanted to talk about was herself and the parties she goes to every weekend.*

Cass stretched, then immediately pulled her hands back under the quilt. At night, her grandparents cut the heat back to what she considered a subfreezing level. Since Papaw probably wouldn't be up for another hour, it would be that long before the furnace kicked on. She shivered and burrowed deeper into her cocoon as she resumed mulling over the past couple of days.

Saturday night, she had accompanied Janette to a party thrown by a guy named B.J. Although Cass knew him, she was surprised when Jan said they were going to his house because he was somebody they used to avoid. He and his friends were among the wilder groups at school, and Cass had been uneasy as she followed Jan into his house.

Her uneasiness mounted by the second. B.J.'s parents obviously weren't home, and many of her former classmates roamed freely throughout the house with cans of beer or glasses of something Cass could only wonder about. Her jaw dropped when Janette accepted a beer from a passing partier, nonchalantly popped the tab, and drank deeply. When Cass raised an eyebrow, Janette just grinned and offered her a sip. Cass took a hasty step back and raised her hands.

"No, I … uh … well … no." She mentally kicked herself for feeling like she needed to explain. The person who should be explaining herself was Janette, and Cass decided to tell her so. "Since when did you start drinking?" she demanded in a frosty tone.

Instead of looking ashamed, Jan had the nerve to laugh in her face. "Since I quit acting like a prude and grew up."

Stung, Cass bristled. "Are you calling me a prude?"

Janette shrugged and took another drink. "If the title fits …"

"Well, I never." Propping her hands on her hips, Cass glared at Janette.

"Maybe that's your problem," Jan said, her tone very chilled. "You never."

To her dismay, Cass felt her cheeks flame and tears well in her eyes. "What's going on with you? Can't we find a quiet corner someplace so we can sit and talk?"

Finishing the beer, Janette carelessly tossed the can aside. It hit the floor and rolled until it ran up against a chair. "This is a party. People have fun at a party. They don't have serious discussions. We can talk tomorrow."

"You mean after church?" asked Cass.

Jan arched an eyebrow at her then burst into giggles. "Yeah, right. After church." She continued to laugh as if Cass had said something tremendously funny.

"I'd like to go back to my grandparents' house."

"So go." Jan flapped her hand in an airy wave.

It wasn't easy, but Cass held onto her temper. "I can't unless you drive me. You brought me here, remember?"

"I'm not going anywhere. At least not until my curfew." Leaning close to Cass, Janette bumped shoulders with her. "Come on, lighten up. I was a little uncomfortable at these parties in the beginning too. Then I learned to relax and go with the flow. You'll be amazed at how much fun you can have when you're not standing around, being all critical."

Although Cass berated herself for not standing up to Jan, she passed a hand across her eyes and heaved a deep sigh. "Maybe, but I'm not going to give it a try tonight. The trip took more out of me than I realized. I'm exhausted. If you don't want to take me home, I'll call Papaw. He'll be happy to come get me."

Irritated, Janette threw her hands up in the air. "Don't call your grandfather. You want him to know about the party?"

"He already does." Cass was confused. "I told him where we'd be."

"That's just great." Jan shook her head and snorted. "What if it gets back to B.J.'s parents that he threw a party while they were out of town? Even worse, what if your grandfather tells my mother? She thinks we were going to the mall then to a nine o'clock movie. Way to go, Einstein."

"Hey, it's not my fault you lied to your mother," protested Cass. "And it won't be my fault if you get caught and she grounds you. If you didn't lie, you wouldn't have to worry about her finding out. You never used to lie."

"I never used to do a lot of things," retorted Jan. "So please spare me the lecture. Look, if you're serious about wanting to leave, get your coat. I'll drive you. The sooner I get rid of you, the sooner I can get back here and enjoy myself."

The memory of the silent drive back to her grandparents' house and her frosty parting with Jan made Cass' heart ache. She still couldn't believe things had turned so ugly so fast between them.

Although she was disappointed, Cass wasn't surprised that Janette hadn't attended church yesterday. When Cass called, Jan apologized for not being able to get together and used having to write a history paper as her excuse. She told Cass she'd call after school on Monday, but Cass didn't hold out much hope of hearing from her.

As the sky began to lighten with streaks of gold and rose, an idea popped into Cass' head. *I could ask Papaw to drive me over to the high school so I could follow Jan around from class to class.* But a second later, she dismissed it. *No, I can't do that, not without clearing it with Jan first. Besides, I'm on vacation. Why would I want to ruin it by spending part of it in school?*

Cass frowned. The day stretched ahead of her, and she had no idea how she would pass the time. She could go to the mall, but it wouldn't be much fun by herself. Mamaw and Papaw would be more than happy to do something with her, but she wanted to be with people her own age. She thought longingly of Tabitha.

"I hope your trip is turning out better than mine," she whispered to her distant stepsister. "If I'd known it was going to be like this, I never would've gotten on the plane."

Another thirty minutes passed before Cass heard Papaw get up and head downstairs. A short while later, the whoosh of the furnace signaled heat was on the way. When her nose stopped tingling from the cold, Cass pushed back the covers and climbed out of bed. Retrieving the flannel robe draped over the footboard, she shrugged into it and padded down the steps in search of Papaw. He welcomed her with a grin when she tracked him down in the kitchen.

"Good morning, Sassafras." Having switched on the coffee maker, he started for the refrigerator. "How did you sleep?"

"I slept fine." Cass slid into a chair at the table. "I just didn't sleep much. I hope I get over this jet lag soon. It's about to kill me."

Papaw's eyes twinkled behind his glasses. "Not that you're exaggerating."

"Have you ever had jet lag?" Cass good-naturedly shot back. When Papaw shook his head, she chided, "Then you have no idea how bad it can be. My body clock is all messed up. I could barely stay awake in church yesterday morning. Then by last night, I was raring to go."

Papaw lowered his voice to confide, "I found myself nodding off a couple of times during the sermon too. Do you think your Mamaw would believe me if I claimed jet lag as my excuse?"

Cass laughed. "Sometimes I wonder if anyone's ever managed to fool her."

"I wouldn't know because I was always too scared to try. She's rather intimidating, that wife of mine." Papaw's tone was affectionate. "But the good Lord never created a finer woman. She'd go to the ends of the earth for the people she cares about."

"I know. It makes me glad I'm one of them." Cass perked up as Papaw took a carton of eggs from the refrigerator and set it on the counter. "What are you making?"

"Scrambled eggs." Papaw got out the milk and butter. "Are you interested in joining me in a bite of breakfast?"

"Interested?" echoed Cass. "I'm way beyond interested. That's another thing about jet lag. I'm hungry all the time."

"That's not jet lag." Papaw set a cast-iron skillet on the stove to heat before taking out a bowl to break the eggs into. "That's boredom."

"What do you mean?" Cass' tone was wary. Papaw had always been able to read her like a book, but she wasn't sure she wanted him to know what was going on.

He gave her a sage look over his shoulder. "Don't play games with your ol' Papaw. You're not pleased with the way things have been going so far."

"Are you talking about Jan?" Cass decided to proceed cautiously. Maybe Papaw didn't know as much as she thought he did.

"Jan, your other friends, just being here in general." Papaw splashed several generous dollops of milk into the bowl with the eggs. "I reckon this visit is turning out to be more of an eye-opener than you anticipated."

"I'm having a good time." Even Cass could tell her declaration lacked any real conviction.

"Uh-huh." Papaw whisked the egg and milk mixture to a froth. "That explains why you're spending all your time with Mamaw and me."

"I love being with you and Mamaw." This time Cass managed to sound a bit more convincing. "You're the main reason I decided to make the trip."

Papaw turned from the counter to stare searchingly at her. "Is that a fact? You flew halfway around the world to spend the better part of your time with a couple of senior citizens?"

"Well, when you put it that way," Cass hedged.

"Huh," Papaw grunted with satisfaction. "Now we're getting to the heart of the matter. Let's stop beating around the bush. What's happened between you and Janette? Mamaw and I reckoned you'd be with her twenty-three-and-a-half hours a day, but you've hardly seen her since you arrived."

"She's been kind of busy," Cass mumbled. She avoided Papaw's piercing gaze by tracing patterns on the scarred tabletop.

Papaw's snort let her know he didn't buy her excuse. "Try again," he said tartly. "And how about telling the truth this time?"

Cass knew she was cornered, and she slumped in her chair. "Okay, but it's no big deal. It's just that we've both changed a lot in the past several months. We don't have that much in common."

"Is that so?" Papaw's raised eyebrows arched above his spectacles. "Isn't it peculiar that Mamaw and I were just remarking to each other last night on how little you've changed? Except for being more mature, that is."

Cass momentarily brightened. "You think I'm more mature?"

Papaw nodded. "No doubt about it. You've grown up a good bit since we last saw you." He swung back around to the stove, dropping a slice of butter into the pan. "So I can't help but wonder if it's you or Janette who's changed so much that your friendship doesn't work anymore."

While Papaw poured the eggs into the skillet, Cass got up to set the table for the two of them. She knew Mamaw well enough to know she wouldn't wake up for at least another hour.

"If I tell you something about Jan, do you promise not to tell anybody?" Cass asked in a small voice as she took two plates out of the cupboard. "Especially her mother."

"I can't make a promise like that." Papaw scraped the spoon around the pan to loosen the eggs. "If she's involved in something dangerous, I'm honor-bound to let her mother know."

Wondering what to do, Cass set the plates on the table and moved to the silverware drawer for utensils. "Okay, here's the situation," she began when she finally made up her mind, "Jan's been doing a lot of partying. You know the one she took me to Saturday night? The guy's parents were out of town and everybody was drinking."

"Including Janette?" Papaw asked softly.

"Yes, unfortunately." Cass expelled a gusty sigh. "That's why I asked her to bring me home. I felt totally out of place. Janette and I used to make fun of the kids who were into the party scene. We'd talk about how stupid it was to get drunk every weekend then show up at school on Monday and brag about it. Now here she is doing exactly that."

"Perhaps you helped to keep her on the straight and narrow," suggested Papaw. He turned off the flame and carried the skillet to the table, setting it on the placemat Cass had laid out. "With you gone, she didn't know how to tell her friends no when they began inviting her to these parties."

Cass sat down and divided up the eggs while Papaw fetched a basket of Mamaw's corn muffins from the refrigerator. "Oh, come on," she scoffed. "Surely she has more backbone than that."

"Not everybody does." Papaw took his seat, said the blessing, and picked up his fork. "Some people need others around them to remind them what's right and what's wrong."

Cass' mouth turned down at the corners. "So you're saying it's my fault Jan's into the things she's into?"

Papaw shot her a chiding look. "You know I hold folks responsible for their own actions. What I mean is, it's likely Janette's convictions didn't go as deep as you thought. Without you around to be accountable to, she didn't see any reason to stay on the path." He chewed thoughtfully on a forkful of eggs, swallowed, and asked, "Do you reckon her mother suspects anything?"

"Janette said her mom didn't know about the party," Cass reluctantly replied. "She thought we went to the mall and a movie."

"I don't like to hear she's lying to her mother." Papaw slowly sipped his juice. "I'm trying to decide what my Christian duty is," he explained after a while. "If my child was running wild, would I want someone to inform me?"

Cass' heart sank. She knew the answer to that one, as well as what it would mean to her and Jan's friendship. *If Papaw talks to her mother, it's all over for her and me.*

Isn't it over anyway? inquired another voice.

Yes, but—

But nothing, interrupted the voice. *Face it—you're nothing to Janette now.*

So I'm supposed to encourage Papaw to rat on her as a way to get back at her? demanded Cass.

I'll admit it's one of the reasons, the voice conceded, *but it's not the only one. How would you feel if you heard Jan was involved in a drunk driving accident, and you hadn't done anything to try and stop her?*

That's it! Cass realized with a surge of optimism. *I need to talk to Jan before Papaw says anything to her mother. I'm sure if it's just the two of us, she'll listen to me. She's a great person—she's just gotten turned around, that's all. I'll call her the second she gets in from school and set up a time for us to get together. And I won't take no for an answer,* she vowed.

Aloud, she said, "Papaw, I know you feel obligated to talk to Mrs. Foster. But give me a chance to talk to Jan first. We've been friends forever. I'm sure she'll hear me out. Once she does, I know she'll change her ways. She's a smart girl. She'll listen to reason."

Papaw studied her for awhile. "All right. You talk to Jan, and depending on how it goes, we'll take it from there."

"Thank you. I'll call her this afternoon." Relieved, Cass started eating with renewed gusto. "Are there any more muffins? I don't believe one is going to do me."

CHAPTER 28

After showering and dressing, Cass found it impossible to stay cooped up in the house. Despite temperatures that refused to rise above the thirty-degree mark, she announced to her grandparents she was taking a walk.

Mamaw glanced up from the breakfast of scrambled eggs and muffins Papaw had fixed for her. "Good. A brisk walk should put the color back in your cheeks."

Cass paused in the middle of zipping up her coat to scowl at her. "I have color in my cheeks."

Mamaw dismissed her objection with a wave. "I'm not referring to that tan of yours. The fact of the matter is you're looking peaked, and I reckon I know why. You and your friend are on the outs, and it's eating at you."

Cass glanced at Papaw out of the corner of her eye, wondering if he'd said something to Mamaw. He lifted his hands in a gesture of innocence.

Catching the exchange, Mamaw wagged her finger at Cass. "Now don't you go thinking your Papaw's been telling on you. I don't need him to fill me in on what's been going on. I have two good eyes and an even better brain."

"Tell me about it." Rolling her eyes, Cass finished zipping her jacket. "I used to think you had ESP or something, the way you always knew what was happening."

Mamaw made a face. "What I have—" she tapped a finger against her temple, "—is good, old-fashioned common sense given to me by the Lord Himself."

Pulling her gloves out of her pockets, Cass came around the table to lean down and hug her grandmother. "You're one in a million." She obligingly kissed the cheek Mamaw tilted toward her. "When I'm old—and I'm talking really ancient now—I want to be just like you."

Mamaw reached up to gently tweak her nose. "Go on with you. Take a long walk so I can have a little peace and quiet for a change. You're almost more trouble than you're worth, child."

Laughing, Cass headed for the door. "Aw, you know you don't mean that. What would your life be like without me?"

"Happier?" growled Mamaw.

"Maybe." Her expression impish, Cass stuck out her tongue. "And definitely a lot more boring."

She danced out of the house to the music of her grandparents' laughter. Since their house was a block off Main Street, she automatically turned left, taking the route that would bring her to downtown Jonesborough. The combination of the crystal clear day and her destination instantly buoyed Cass' spirits.

Main Street was as familiar to her as if she'd last walked it yesterday, instead of seven months ago. The brick sidewalk felt comfortable under her feet, and she checked each store she passed to make sure it hadn't changed hands. Cass figured as long as things stayed the same on Main Street in Jonesborough, all was right with the world.

There were some stores that didn't interest her, but others required that she at least stop in. The Cherry Tree, with its quilts and homemade crafts, was where she lingered to chat with the owner, a longtime friend of her grandparents. As usual, the shop smelled of cinnamon and pine, and she inhaled deeply as she came through the door.

"Well, as I live and breathe!" exclaimed Molly, the shop owner, when she spied Cass. "Look what the wind blew in."

"Hey, Molly." Cass lifted a gloved hand in greeting. "Long time, no see."

"Let me feast my eyes on you." Molly bustled out from behind the counter and, walking over to Cass, placed her hands on her shoulders. "Mercy, child, you're brown as a berry."

Cass laughed. "That's what Mamaw always says."

"That's because she's from good country stock." Molly brushed a tendril off Cass' cheek. "Look at your hair. It's more blonde than red. You must be out in the sun from dawn to dusk on that island of yours."

"Just about." Cass glanced around the shop. "It's nice to see some things don't change."

Molly released her and moved back to the counter. "Of course not. Why mess with success? So," she said as she eased herself onto the stool behind the cash register, "how long are you in town for?"

"Two weeks." Cass fingered an afghan draped over a handmade chair.

"Are you having a good time?"

Cass shrugged. "It's okay, I guess. It's great to see my grandparents again. Some other parts of the visit aren't going the way I hoped they would."

Molly nodded sagely. "Sometimes it's hard to come back to a place. In your mind, everything's frozen in time and has stayed the same. Then you return, and you find out just how wrong you were."

"That's exactly what's happened. Oh, well." With a last look around, Cass headed for the door. "I'll survive."

"Would you like a cup of hot chocolate to take with you?" offered Molly.

Cass shook her head. "No, thanks. I'm planning on

stopping in at the cafe for a snack."

"Have fun," called Molly. "Come back to see me before you leave." She pretended to shiver. "I envy you living on a tropical island, especially now. This winter's the coldest one in years. It's almost enough to make me pack my bags and head south. Florida's sounding better and better."

Laughing to herself, Cass exited The Cherry Tree. Molly talked a good game, but her roots ran deep in this part of the country. She'd probably die sitting on her stool behind the counter.

Once outside, Cass turned right. The Main Street Cafe was a block down in that direction, as well as her all-time favorite store, Mauk's Pharmacy. When she was little, it was the highlight of her week when she and Papaw walked to Mauk's, where she was allowed to choose a dollar's worth of candy from the jars lining the shelves. The candy had to last her a week, so she took her time deciding while Papaw patiently waited.

Reaching the pharmacy, she stepped inside to the jingle of the bells hanging above the door. Her eyes misted with tears as the memories of the time spent here with Papaw washed over her. She suddenly wished Tabitha were standing beside her so she could share her recollections with her stepsister.

After a quick tour of the shop, Cass concluded her tour of downtown Jonesborough with a visit to the Main Street Cafe. She loved the old-fashioned atmosphere of the restaurant with its high ceilings, plank floor, and wooden booths. She placed her order at the counter then settled into one of the booths.

The next time Tabitha's in town, I'm bringing her here, she vowed. *If I know her as well as I think I do, she'll love this place. I wish we hadn't disliked each other so much last summer when we had the opportunity to do stuff like this together.*

As Cass savored her cocoa and coffee cake, she thought

about how much she missed Tabitha. She hadn't spoken with her stepsister since they parted company at the Honolulu airport. According to her parents, Tabitha was doing fine, although Cass thought their responses to her inquiries were rather vague. She wished she could talk at length with Tabitha, to hear for herself how things were going, and she regretted not getting Beth's phone number.

As the afternoon wore on, Cass decided being at Janette's house when she got in from school was a better idea than calling. That way, Janette couldn't put her off until another time. Since her grandparents didn't object to her using their car, she left the house at two-thirty and was waiting in Jan's driveway when another friend, Lauren, dropped her off.

After waving goodbye to Lauren, Janette walked over to Cass, who'd gotten out of the car to greet her. "Hey. What are you doing here?"

"Hey, yourself." Cass found it encouraging that Jan didn't seem upset to see her. "I decided to give you a thrill and be here when you got home. So—" she grinned, "—are you thrilled?"

"More than words can say," drawled Jan.

Cass' spirits soared. *Now this is more like it*, she exulted. *This is the way it used to be between us, with the teasing and the not having to watch your every step.*

Aloud, she said, "Does that mean I can come inside or are you planning to leave me out here in the freezing cold?"

"You consider this cold?" Janette scoffed, shaking her head. "Man, you've been on that island too long. This is downright balmy compared to how cold it was around Christmas. You'd have been whining within five minutes of stepping outside."

For some reason, her remark annoyed Cass. She felt like Janette was criticizing her. Rather than saying anything, however, she did her best to shrug off the comment and accompanied her friend into the house.

"Hey! The living room's a different color," observed Cass as she came in the front door. "And the carpet's new."

Jan barely glanced at the room. "Yeah, now that Mom's changed jobs and is making a ton more money, she's determined to give the house a face lift. As soon as she saves enough money, she's going to start on the kitchen."

"Wow." Cass followed Jan into the kitchen. "Do you like the changes?"

Janette shrugged. "They're okay. I hardly notice them anymore. Fixing up the house is Mom's thing. I'm busy with other stuff." She dropped her backpack in the corner and moved to the refrigerator. "Are you hungry?"

"Not really." Sitting down, Cass patted her stomach. "I've eaten more since I've been here than I usually do in a month."

With her head buried in the refrigerator, Janette didn't bother to respond. She emerged after a short while with a plate of leftover fried chicken and carried it to the table.

"Are you sure you don't want some?" she asked, going to the cabinet to get a plate.

Cass shook her head. "I'd better not. I still want to fit into my swimsuits when I get home."

Janette returned to the table and set the plate down with a thud. "You're always doing that," she said suddenly.

Cass' eyes widened in confusion. "What?"

"Throwing Kwajalein up in my face. Maybe I don't want to hear about your perfect life in paradise." With a disgruntled expression, Jan selected a drumstick and bit into it. She continued to scowl at Cass as she chewed.

"You call mentioning Kwaj in passing throwing it up in your face? Please!" Folding her arms, Cass scowled right back at Janette.

"You do more than just mention the place," Jan retorted, waving the drumstick as she spoke. "Does the phrase 'go on and on' mean anything to you? Lauren and I have talked about it. If just half of what you say is true, that stupid island is heaven on earth. It has the best weather, the best beaches, the cutest boys, the nicest people. Honestly! You almost make me want to pack up and move down there myself."

"You've been talking to Lauren about me?" she asked stiffly.

"Duh. We've pretty much become best friends since you left. Of course I talk to her." Janette began gnawing on the chicken again.

"Best friends or not," Cass said in a tight voice, "you should have come to me with whatever complaints you had. After all our years of friendship, you owed me at least that much."

"I don't owe you diddly." Janette got up and stalked to the counter for a napkin to wipe her hands. "You showed up here, full of yourself. You couldn't wait to show off your tan and your sun-streaked hair. Then there were the pictures you forced me to look at. Shots of Logan, shots of you and Logan, shots of you and Logan and Tabitha and her boyfriend, shots of the ocean, shots of the sky. Do you ever do anything other than take pictures?"

Cass couldn't believe her ears. She'd been so eager to show Jan what her life was like on Kwaj, and all along her friend had been bored silly. Her cheeks burned with embarrassment, particularly when she imagined what Jan probably said to Lauren afterward.

Tossing the napkin in the trash, Janette marched back to the table. "Unfortunately, the pictures aren't the worst part."

"There's more?" Cass steeled herself for what was coming.

"You want to know the reason I've been avoiding you like the plague?" At Cass' hesitant nod, Janette went on,

"Because your holier-than-thou attitude makes me sick. You think you're so much better than Lauren and me because you don't go to parties and you don't drink. Well, excuse us for having fun. Maybe if we lived where we could go swimming in the Pacific Ocean everyday, we might not feel the need to party. You've obviously forgotten what life is like in this hick town. There's nothing—I repeat, nothing—to do except party. And if we drink a few beers over the weekend, so what? Does that make us bad people?"

The longer Jan talked, the angrier Cass got. She was tired of being attacked by someone she considered a friend. Jan was making it sound like life had been one long holiday for her since she left Tennessee, and nothing could be further from the truth.

"Are you done?" she asked coldly when Janette grew silent.

"For the moment." Hooking an arm over the back of her chair, Janette met and held Cass' gaze.

"Good. I have a few things I'd like to say." Buying time to organize her thoughts, Cass shifted in her seat and folded her hands atop the table. "First of all, I don't get what the big deal is about me being tanned and stuff. I can't help the way I look. That's what happens when you spend seven months on an island in the middle of the ocean. Why does it bug you and Lauren so much?"

When Jan opened her mouth to answer, Cass raised her hand to stop her. "Let me finish. Secondly, about the pictures. Stupid me, I assumed you'd like seeing some of the people and places I've written to you about. I'm sorry you found it so dull.

"And last, but not least, I don't think I'm better than you, not in any way, shape, or form. I am worried about your partying and especially about the drinking. I know what it's like to have nothing to do. Even being a beach bum gets old after a while. But I've found ways to keep myself occupied without resorting to partying, and so can you."

"Whatever." Janette snorted. "Like Jonesborough is teeming with surfer dudes to keep Lauren and me busy. Face it, that's how you fill up your spare time, hanging out with Logan."

"That's not all I do," asserted Cass. "There's also the youth group and after-school clubs. Speaking of which, are you still involved in the youth group here?"

Janette squirmed and looked away. "Every now and then."

"Which, translated, means hardly ever." Cass frowned at her. "What's going on? You used to love going to youth group."

Jan frowned. "It got old, okay? It was the same old thing week after week. I'm not the only one who doesn't go any-more," she defended herself. "Lots of kids got tired of it."

"I don't care about anybody else. I care about you."

"Well, don't care about me," Janette ordered irritably. "I'm doing fine on my own. So I'm doing some things you wouldn't do. That happens. People develop their own interests."

"You call drinking an interest?" Cass' tone dripped with sarcasm.

"Quit making it sound like I'm an alcoholic. I have five, maybe six, beers a week. That hardly qualifies me for detox."

"Yeah, but you have those five or six beers in one night," Cass pointed out. "What's next? Pot? Crack?"

"Honestly, will you give it a rest? Who do you think you are? My mother?" Janette threw her hands up in exaspera-tion.

"No, but I wish I were," Cass shot back. "I'd ground you so fast your head would spin."

Breathing hard, Jan stood to glower down at her. "Why

don't you go back to paradise where you belong? It's obvious you can't hack it in the real world. I'd like to see how you'd handle not being able to pick and choose whatever guy you wanted. You have no idea what it's like having to settle for whoever shows the slightest bit of interest in you."

"What are you talking about?" blazed Cass. "I know as well as you do what it's like."

"Not anymore."

Jan's quiet retort stunned Cass into momentary silence. When she finally replied, it was with a note of understanding in her voice. "So that's it. You're jealous. You're not happy about me and Logan at all. It's tearing you up, isn't it?"

"So what if it is?" Unable to look at Cass, Janette stared down at her hands as they gripped the back of the chair. "You were supposed to be miserable when you moved to Kwajalein. Instead, it's turned out to be the best thing that ever happened to you. You're crazy about Steve and Tabitha. You've found a whole new set of friends. And the boy you're dating is a prince. Meanwhile, I'm stuck here in one gigantic rut. Can you blame me for wanting to add a little spice to my life? Okay, maybe I overdid it, but Lauren likes to walk on the wild side."

"Nobody's making you walk with her."

Jan rolled her eyes. "What choice do I have? I'm not going to sit home every Saturday."

"What about Carly?"

Releasing her grip on the chair, Jan walked around it and sat down. "We don't see much of Carly anymore. She's all wrapped up in this boy she met in the fall. Lauren and I think she might be sleeping with him."

"Oh, great. What is it with you people?" Cass joked sadly. "I leave town, and y'all fall apart."

"It does seem that way, doesn't it?" Janette was quiet for

several seconds. "I missed you so much when you first left. The only thing that helped was when I started going to the parties and getting in with the social crowd at school. I know you don't like what I'm doing, but I'm not going to stop. Face it, we don't have much in common anymore. You have your life on Kwajalein, and I have mine here."

A lump formed in Cass' throat, and she willed herself not to cry. "I honestly thought we'd beat the odds and stay friends."

"So did I." Janette's heavy sigh was the only sound in the room. After a few moments, she brightened. "You know, we don't have to let our differences keep us from having fun together the rest of the time you're here."

"That's true." Cass forced herself to match her upbeat tone. "What do you say we drive over to Johnson City and get something to eat at Joe's Crab Shack? If I remember correctly, that was always your favorite place."

"You're sure you want seafood?" teased Jan. "Aren't you tired of eating it all the time?"

Cass decided it wasn't worth the effort to explain that she could count on one hand the number of times she'd eaten fish in the past seven months. Instead, she merely shrugged. "There's nothing like the popcorn shrimp at Joe's. Let me call my grandparents and see if I'm allowed to take the car over there."

Even though she kept a smile pasted on her face as she walked to the phone, Cass' heart was a leaden weight in her chest. It was clear that the rift between her and Janette was permanent. Because it was what Janette wanted, she'd spend the rest of the afternoon with her friend. After that, she'd be free to go back to Mamaw and Papaw's and grieve in private for what they'd lost.

Picking up the receiver, Cass once again found herself aching to talk to Tabitha. She knew her stepsister was the one person who could help ease the pain she felt.

CHAPTER 29

Although Cass and Janette spent most of her free time together over the next couple of days, they grew increasingly awkward with each other. Since Cass didn't care to hear about Jan's partying, and Jan wasn't interested in anything having to do with life on Kwaj, they were left with precious little to talk about.

Lauren joined them one afternoon, but her presence only made the situation worse. She and Janette constantly started but didn't finish sentences, then exchanged meaningful looks after glancing pointedly at Cass. As far as Cass was concerned, the get-together was a complete disaster. Other than her first few weeks on Kwaj, she'd never felt more like an outsider.

As if that weren't bad enough, something strange was going on back home. When she called to talk to Mom and Dad, they hardly spent five minutes on the phone before announcing they needed to go. Her questions about Tabitha went unanswered beyond vague reassurances that she was fine and having a good time.

Even worse, Cass hadn't yet spoken with Logan. He wasn't home either time when she called, and despite his mother's promise to deliver Cass' messages, she didn't hear from him. She didn't want to think he was avoiding her, but as each day passed without a phone call, it seemed the likeliest conclusion.

All in all, Cass mused as she lay in bed Thursday night, *this isn't the best vacation I've ever had. Especially now that I have to figure out what to do about tomorrow night. Jan and Lauren swear there won't be any drinking at the party they want me to go to, but I think I'd rather have a root canal than go. Of course, the alternative is to stay home with Papaw and Mamaw or go see Uncle Larry and Aunt Linda, and since I've had my fill of quality time with the family— Why in the world did I ever think this trip was a good idea? If I thought they'd do it, I'd be on the phone to Dad and Mom in a heartbeat, asking them to change my ticket so I could fly home over the weekend. The thought of eight more days here is almost more than I can stand.* She sighed. *I'll give it till Sunday. If things don't improve, I'll take the chance and call Mom and Dad. Anything's got to be better than this.*

Cass felt asleep to thoughts of Kwaj. She imagined her homecoming, concentrating on Logan's delight at seeing her again. In all the mental images she created, Tabitha was with her. There was no way she'd entertain the possibility of Tabitha staying in Oregon with Beth. Her stepsister was returning to Kwaj where she belonged, if Cass had anything to say about it.

Having finally adjusted to Tennessee time, Cass didn't put in an appearance the next morning until nearly nine-thirty. She found her grandparents in the kitchen, chatting as they lingered over cups of coffee. They looked up when Cass entered the room.

"Here's the sleepyhead now," Papaw announced, a smile twitching at the corners of his mouth. "Mamaw and I were just discussing how much longer we should let you stay in bed."

"I voted to wake you an hour ago, but Papaw wouldn't

hear of it." Mamaw's disapproving tone told the others what she thought of her husband's opinion. "He said, seeing as how you're on vacation, we should cut you some slack." She snorted. "Huh! I told him the problem with the world today is that too many young'uns are cut too much slack."

Cass retrieved a glass from the cupboard, then shuffled to the refrigerator to pour herself juice. "I'm glad you won that round, Papaw. Way to stick up for me."

"You're welcome, Sassafras. By the way—" Papaw shared a quick grin with Mamaw, "what are your plans for the day?"

Catching the exchange, Cass frowned, but didn't comment on it. She slipped into a chair and propped her chin on her fist. "You're pretty much looking at my plans. I thought I'd sit around in my robe for a while, eat, shower, sit around some more, eat again. You know, the usual."

"Will you be seeing Janette after she gets home from school?" Mamaw asked.

Cass hesitated then shook her head. "I doubt it. She … well … there's a party tonight, and I'm not the least bit interested in going."

Papaw dropped his secret smile and looked stern. "I reckon your talk with her didn't do much good."

"Not really," admitted Cass. "She and Lauren say there won't be any drinking tonight, but I don't know if I believe them."

"You realize I'm going to have to talk to her mother."

Although she wasn't happy about his decision, she nodded. "I know. Could you wait until after I leave though? Things between us are shaky enough as it is. You talking to her mother will be the final nail in the coffin."

"I'll wait. No sense in making life more difficult for you than it needs to be."

Mamaw stood and began preparing breakfast for Cass. Cass cast a curious eye at Papaw. "Okay, what's up with you two this morning?"

Papaw smiled innocently. "Why, whatever do you mean?"

Cass fixed him with a stern stare. "You know exactly what I mean. Ever since I walked in here, you and Mamaw have been acting like a couple of kids with a secret. What's going on?"

"That's for us to know and for you to find out," trilled Mamaw.

With a sigh of annoyance, Cass retorted, "Which is precisely what I'm trying to do. Now, are you going to tell me what you're up to or not?"

"Not." Mamaw turned to smile briefly at Cass before resuming cooking.

"Oh, brother." Cass briefly hid her face in her hands. When she looked up, she zeroed in on Papaw, seeing him as the weak link in the chain. "Papaw," she wheedled, "you'll tell me what's going on, won't you?"

"I'd like to," at a warning glance from Mamaw, he shook his head, "but someone, and I won't name any names, would do me serious bodily harm if I did."

Cass refused to give up. "Can't you at least give me a hint?" she coaxed.

After silently consulting Mamaw, Papaw nodded. "It's a surprise for you, and it'll be here around noon."

Cass' eyes lit up. "Really?" She gave an impatient flounce. "Give me another hint."

"That's enough hints," ordered Mamaw. She punctuated her command with a steely stare at Papaw.

He shrugged an apology to Cass. "My lips are sealed."

"A surprise for me that will be here around noon," she mused out loud, drumming her fingers on the tabletop. After several seconds of pondering the possibilities, she gave up. "I have no idea. It's a good thing I don't have to wait long. I hate not knowing."

Following breakfast, Cass quickly showered and dressed, on the slight chance the surprise might arrive early. She was back downstairs and restlessly prowling the living room by 10:30.

Mamaw looked up from her knitting as Cass crossed the floor for the dozenth time. "For pity's sake, child. Find something to do."

"Like what?"

"Go for a walk. Read a book. Listen to music. Watch television."

"It's sleeting outside. I finished the book I brought with me. I don't have any of my tapes or CDs. And there's nothing on television that interests me," Cass successfully countered every one of her suggestions.

"John," Mamaw called for Papaw. "Take Cass to the library. She doesn't have anything to read."

"Maybe I don't want to go to the library." Cass defiantly faced her grandmother.

"Maybe you don't have a choice in the matter." Mamaw stared her down.

"I'll get my coat." Cass meekly left the room.

Cass took her time at the library, wanting to eat up as many minutes as she could in the seemingly endless wait until noon. It helped that she ran into the mother of a girl she knew, especially when the mother wanted to hear all about life on a tropical island. It was after eleven when she and Papaw made a mad dash through the sleet to the car.

"Whew!" Cass slid back the hood of her jacket and brushed ice pellets from her shoulders. "It's a mess out there."

Papaw looked worried. "I hope this weather isn't causing traffic problems."

Cass wiped the condensation from her window to peer outside. "I don't see any cars slipping and sliding. But maybe we'd better get home before it starts getting icy."

"Would you consider throwing caution to the winds and stopping at the cafe for a hot chocolate and a brownie?" Papaw had taken off his glasses to wipe them, and the eyes he turned to Cass sparkled with anticipation.

"You know I'd never turn down a chance to go to the cafe with you." Cass made a flourishing gesture toward the road. "Let's boldly go where few men," she paused and laughed, "or women would go in weather like this."

Even with their stop at the Main Street Cafe, they made it back to the house well before noon. As Papaw drove up the driveway, Cass checked the porch for interesting packages, but there was none to be seen.

That's okay, she assured herself. *It's only a quarter to twelve.*

Coming into the house through the back door, Cass thought she heard voices in the living room. She hung up her jacket on a peg beside the door and turned to Papaw to take his.

"Sounds like Mamaw has a visitor."

Papaw cocked his head and listened. "I don't hear anything. It was probably the television. Sometimes your Mamaw likes to watch one of those talk shows when she thinks I won't catch her."

Cass headed toward the living room, laughing to herself at the image of her grandmother doing something on the sly. The moment she crossed the threshold, she came to an immediate and complete standstill. Her jaw dropped, and her eyes grew as round as saucers.

"Hey, Sis," Tabitha greeted her as calmly as if she'd last seen Cass a few minutes ago.

"You're ... what ... how ..." Cass glanced wildly between her grandparents, then looked back at Tabitha who beamed at her from her place next to Mamaw.

"Gotcha!" Mamaw grinned. "Here's your surprise."

Cass couldn't help herself. She started to cry. With one

hand pressed to her mouth, she extended the other one to Tabitha. Her stepsister instantly leaped off the couch and ran to her, and they met in a minute-long, dancing-up-and-down hug.

"What are you doing here?" Cass finally managed to gasp. Although she and Tabitha had pulled back, they continued to hold hands.

Tabitha shrugged. "Things didn't work out with my mother. I'll fill you in on all the gory details later. The folks and I decided I should spend a few days with my grandmother before they flew me out here."

"They never said a word to me about it." Cass shook her head, still not believing Tabitha was really there.

"Of course! It was meant to be a surprise." Her expression turned smug. "And I'd say it worked big time. I've never seen anybody look as stunned as you did when you walked in here and saw me."

Cass started to laugh. "I'll say. In my wildest dreams, I never imagined you showing up here. The best I was hoping for was that you wouldn't want to stay in Oregon with Beth."

A shadow passed across Tabitha's face, but was immediately replaced with a brilliant smile. "You don't have to worry about that anymore."

"Ever again?"

Tabitha nodded firmly. "Ever again."

Linking arms with her, Cass turned to face Mamaw. "How long have you known she was coming?"

"Your Mom called us Tuesday morning." Mamaw looked quite pleased with herself. "Steve had already made arrangements with his parents the night before for them to pick Tabitha up in Knoxville and drive her straight here."

"So everybody knew about this but me?" Cass gave a self-mocking laugh. "Wow, and I always pride myself on being on top of things."

Tabitha elbowed her in the ribs. "Definitely not this time, Sis."

Cass suddenly let out a joyous whoop. "This is so great! Think of the all the stuff we can do. There's the mall. And a place called the Princeton Arts Center that I know you'll like. Oh, and The Dawg House, which serves the absolutely best hot dogs you've ever eaten. And—"

"Don't forget the Main Street Cafe," Papaw put in quietly. "Now I have two girls to take there, so you'd better save a couple of afternoons for me."

Cass felt like she would burst with happiness. Instead of jealously guarding the cafe as her and Papaw's special place, she couldn't wait to share it with Tabitha.

"It's number one on our list," she assured him. Reaching for Tabitha's hand, she gave it a heartfelt squeeze and predicted, "You're going to love being here almost as much as I love having you."

Laughing, Tabitha returned her squeeze. "I wouldn't be so sure about that if I were you. I have a sneaking suspicion it's going to wind up in a tie."

CHAPTER 30

"I feel like there should be fireworks or maybe a brass band," Tabitha said, gazing out the plane window at the Knoxville airport runway. "Something to celebrate the fact that we're on our way home."

"Home." Cass rolled the word on her tongue, savoring the sound of it. "I think back to July and how depressed I was about leaving Tennessee. Now Kwaj is home, and Jonesborough is a place I visit."

"It's weird how things turn out." Tabitha turned to grin at Cass. "How much do you want to bet our grandparents are standing at the window of the terminal, waving madly because they're convinced we can see them?"

"Everybody but Mamaw. She's probably looking at her watch, wondering how long it's going to be before we take off." Cass shook her head. "She and Papaw and your grandparents have a five-thirty dinner reservation, and she's not about to miss it on account of us."

Tabitha laughed. "Mamaw is a hoot. No wonder you're the way you are, growing up around her. She's tough as nails on the outside and squishy soft on the inside."

"Then underneath the squishy layer there are more nails." Cass leaned around Tabitha to look out the window, on the off-chance she might catch one last glimpse of her grandparents. "Papaw, on the other hand, is squishy through and through."

Tabitha vigorously nodded her agreement. "I adore him. The times he took us to the Main Street Cafe are my two favorite memories of my stay here." She grinned. "Thanks for sharing him with me."

Their conversation subsided as the plane lurched into motion to taxi from the terminal and line up for takeoff. Cass kept her gaze riveted to the window.

So far, so good, she thought when the plane lifted off and all she felt was relief that they were airborne. *Goodbye, Tennessee. I'll see you soon. In the meantime, I'm going back to my little island in the middle of the ocean.*

"I'm really worried about Logan," Cass confided once they were well on their way to Los Angeles. "I can't believe he wasn't home one single time I called. But what really gets me is he never called back. The last thing he said to me before I left was that he'd call. He'd cleared it with his parents and everything."

Tabitha frowned. "I know. It's strange. When I talked to Micah the other night, he said he hadn't seen much of Logan. Kwaj isn't that big. It's not like he could hide out."

"He didn't say anything about seeing Logan with another girl, did he?" Cass asked softly.

"Not a word. Neither did Kira when I talked to her, and if anyone would know about something like that, she would." Tabitha jostled Cass' arm. "I don't know what's going on, but I do know it's not another girl. That's not Logan's style. If he wanted to dump you, he'd do it. He wouldn't wait until you left on vacation then sneak around with somebody else."

"That's what I think too." She frowned. "Unless it's the middle of the night, and I'm up to all hours wondering what's going on. Then anything seems possible."

"Actually, I know what you mean." Tabitha propped her chin on her fist. "I've been wondering what's up with Kira. She was really short with me when we talked. I expected her to go on and on about their stay in Hono, but she never said a word. When I asked her how it went, all she said was that it was fun. Normally, you can't shut her up."

"Hmm." Frustrated, Cass couldn't think of anything more to add.

Changing the subject, Tabitha asked, "How do you think Janette will react to Papaw talking to her mother?"

Although she knew Tabitha could probably read her grimace, Cass replied, "Let's just say I'm glad I'll be several thousand miles away when the discussion takes place. If our friendship weren't already over, this would definitely kill it."

"And you're really okay with the way things stand between you and Jan?"

After a brief hesitation, Cass nodded. "I guess I'll always wonder how things would've turned out if I hadn't moved. But I did, so that's what I have to deal with. Mostly, I hope she wakes up before it's too late. I have a bad feeling about the path she's on. I'd hate for anything to happen to her."

The rest of the flight passed uneventfully, as did the journey from Los Angeles to Honolulu. By the time they arrived by taxi at Hickam Air Force Base at three in the morning, Cass was exhausted and not looking forward to boarding the plane to Kwaj in another three hours.

"Let's call our parents and tell them we're renting a room and staying here for a couple of days," Tabitha suggested around a jaw-breaking yawn.

Cass' sour expression matched her bloodshot eyes. "Don't tempt me. The thought of another five hours in a plane makes me want to run screaming from the terminal."

"The only good thing about the next flight is that it ends up back home." Tabitha stretched. "Let's walk around awhile. I'm afraid if we sit too long, we'll fall asleep. Then, with our luck, all our stuff will be stolen and we'll miss our flight."

Cass managed to summon up a bit of humor. "Are you always this cheerful at three in the morning?" she teased.

"How should I know?" grumbled Tabitha. "I'm never up."

"You have a point." Hoisting her carry-on bag onto her shoulder, Cass halfheartedly gestured to her right. "After you. Maybe a couple of laps around the place will wake us up."

Somehow they managed to stay awake until their flight was called. Once they boarded, they collapsed in their seats and were sound asleep before the plane took off.

Cass was the first one to emerge from exhausted slumber. Blinking and running her tongue over her teeth, she stretched and rubbed her eyes. Being in the middle seat of three, she turned to the person on her right.

"Could you tell me what time it is?" she asked in a raspy voice.

The man obligingly glanced at his watch. "7:15, Kwaj time."

"That means we have—" Cass did some calculations in her head, "only 45 minutes before we land."

The man nodded. "Give or take a few minutes."

"Thanks." Shifting her attention to her left, Cass nudged her stepsister. "Hey, Tabitha, wake up. We're almost home."

Tabitha responded by groaning and pulling the blanket over her head. Cass jostled her with more force.

"Rise and shine, sleepyhead. We only have 45 minutes to make ourselves presentable for Logan and Micah."

Groaning, Tabitha followed Cass down the aisle to the bathroom. It didn't take them nearly as long as they thought it would to clean up, so they were settled in their seats and eagerly awaiting touchdown with 15 minutes to spare. Tabitha fidgeted constantly.

"Cut it out. You're acting like a 2-year-old on Christmas morning, and it's driving me nuts," complained Cass.

"Sorry." Tabitha didn't sound the least bit apologetic. "I can't help it." She made an effort to sit still, but gave up after less than a minute. "What can I say? This is the first time I'm coming home with Micah as my boyfriend, not just a friend. It changes everything."

Cass gave her a teasing look. "Maybe not everything. For example, I'd advise you not to run into his arms and smother him with kisses in front of Mom and Dad."

Tabitha burst into laughter. "You're probably right."

Cass gasped and gripped the seat's armrests when the plane dipped and arced to the left. "I hope that means we're coming in for a landing."

Tabitha nodded. "It usually does this. We should be touching down any minute now."

Ten more minutes passed before the plane finally came to a stop and an attendant opened the door. Brilliant sunlight streamed into the aircraft, bringing with it heat and island smells. The girls inhaled deeply then grinned at each other.

"Like Dorothy said in the *Wizard of Oz*, there's no place like home," declared Tabitha.

"Forget Dorothy." Cass grabbed her bag and stood up. "What I say is, I can't wait to see Logan."

As they crossed the tarmac, the first people Cass saw were Mom and Dad, waving madly from behind the concrete wall.

"I'm so glad you're home!" Dad said, hugging Tabitha but also looking at Cass as they came up to where their parents stood. "You wouldn't believe how much I missed you."

Mom grabbed Cass before Dad could say anymore. Alternately laughing and crying, they talked over each other as they tried to catch up on two weeks' worth of news.

"You two have all day to talk," Dad broke in. Taking Mom by the shoulders, he switched places with her. "It's my turn to say hello to Cass, and Tabitha's waiting to hug you."

Another minute passed before the four of them headed for the door into the terminal. The moment she stepped inside, Cass scanned the building, looking for Logan. She immediately spotted Rianne, who jumped up and down at seeing her. After another pass, Cass finally located Logan lounging by the front door. He lifted two fingers in response to her wave and pushed off from the wall to cross the floor to greet her. Rianne reached Cass first.

"Hello!" Rianne flung her arms around Cass and danced her up and down several times. "I'm so glad you're back. Life was unbelievably dull without you."

"After the emotional roller coaster I've been on the past couple of weeks, dull sounds good." With a final squeeze, Cass released Rianne. "I brought back loads of pictures. As soon as I can escape from my parents, I'll bring them over to show you."

"Hey!" protested Mom. "I heard that. You're not back five minutes, and you're already talking about escaping. You sure know how to hurt a mother's feelings."

"I didn't mean escape," Cass hastily corrected herself, a smile tugging at her lips. "I meant break free. No, that sounds just as bad, doesn't it? How about dump?" She broke into laughter. "All right, I meant escape."

Mom laughed, hugging her. "I don't know why I missed you so much."

Logan came up in the midst of their teasing but hung back a little ways out of the circle until they finished. When Cass turned to him, his face momentarily lit up before a shadow settled upon his features.

"Hello, Cass," he said quietly, avoiding her eyes.

Her stomach lurched. *Something's definitely not right*, she thought. *But what?*

Aloud, she replied, less enthusiastically than she'd originally planned, "Hey, Logan. Long time, no see."

"Yeah." Logan didn't volunteer any more than that, asking, instead, "How was your trip?"

Okay, Cass decided, *two can play at this game*.

"Long," she replied tersely, wearily pushing the hair back from her face. "And tiring."

"Ah." Logan nodded.

"Yup." Cass mimicked his nod.

To keep him from seeing the tears that she suddenly felt in her eyes, Cass turned to watch Micah greet Tabitha. Even with Dad watching, he seized Tabitha and spun her around, letting out a whoop of delight. Coming to a stop, he continued to hold her hand as Kira sidled up to say hello.

"I hope you're not expecting me to act as worked up as my brother," she warned Tabitha. "You won't catch me twirling you around and yelling at the top of my lungs, making a fool out of myself."

"A simple hello is fine," Tabitha assured her.

"In that case—" Kira raised her hand in a halfhearted wave, "hello."

"Same to you."

Cass frowned. Although Kira appeared to be kidding, even Cass knew her well enough to know something was up. She caught the hurt look in Tabitha's eyes and knew her stepsister was worried too. *Something is just definitely not right around here.*

CHAPTER 31

Tabitha and Cass remained quiet the whole way home, but on the pretext of bringing their suitcases to their rooms, they ducked into Cass' bedroom as soon as they could and shut the door.

"Is it just me or were Kira and Logan acting weird?" Tabitha demanded.

"It's not just you." Cass hesitated. "You don't think something's going on between them, do you? They seemed guilty about something."

Tabitha held up a restraining hand. "Don't even go there. That's the most ridiculous thing I've ever heard. Kira wouldn't be interested in Logan if he were the last boy on earth and vice versa."

"But why were they both being so strange? Do you really think it was a coincidence they both showed up in peculiar moods?"

Tabitha didn't hesitate. "I really do. Don't forget I've known them longer than you have. Something would have to go very wrong in the universe for Logan and Kira to wind up together."

Cass flashed her a small smile. "Okay, you've sort of convinced me. But if that's not the problem, what is?"

"Beats me." Tabitha sank down on Cass' bed and peered up at her. "I've never known Kira to hold back when something's bothering her. It must be really bad if she doesn't want to talk about it."

Cass sat down beside her. "I'm totally clueless when it comes to Logan. I—"

Mom knocked at the door, then opened it to peek her head around. "What are you ladies doing hiding out in here? Didn't you get enough bonding time in Tennessee? Come on out and join Dad and me. You can talk later."

Placing her hands on her knees, Cass reluctantly pushed herself to her feet. "We'll be right there."

Although Mom left, she didn't close the door behind her. Tabitha took that as a hint for them not to linger in the room. While she appreciated the fact that Dad and Mom were glad to have them home, she would've preferred to keep talking to Cass until they came up with some ideas about what was going on. Sighing, she held out her hand to her stepsister to tug her up.

"Let's go. The parents want to hear all about our trip, every last, gory detail."

"When I have kids, remind me to give them space," Cass said darkly, following Tabitha to the door.

Tabitha flashed her a wry glance over her shoulder. "We've been gone two weeks. How much more space do you want?"

Cass poked her in the back. "Look, I'm being crabby here. Don't confuse me by being logical."

They sat down at the table to eat the breakfast Mom had already made for them. After Dad asked the blessing, Mom propped her chin on her fist and ordered, "All right, now tell me everything. I've been dying to hear a full account of your trips."

Tabitha grinned at Cass, and they begin to alternately relate the details of the last few weeks.

"I wish I'd been there to comfort you after she left," Mom said after Tabitha finished her story of her stay in Oregon. "I can imagine how difficult a discussion like that was."

Tabitha reached over to pat her arm. "That would have been nice, but it wasn't necessary. Mostly I was relieved. I could finally lay to rest my feelings for Beth. I kicked myself for a while for even remotely considering staying with her. Once I got over that, I haven't given her a second thought. Before I went to see her, I used to think about her every day. The visit was a good thing because it made me see, once and for all, the kind of person she is." She smiled in turn at Mom and Dad. "It also made me realize how blessed I am to be in this family. Dad, I appreciate more than you'll ever know the fact that you hung in there after Beth left. And, Mom, thank you for accepting me as one of your own and for showing me what a real mother is like. I love you both with all my heart."

Dad gazed down at his hands clenched tightly on the table while Mom tried to say something, cleared her throat, and unsuccessfully tried again.

"Way to go, Sis!" cheered Cass. "You've actually rendered them speechless. It's not often one of us manages to do that."

Tabitha grinned and winked. "I'll fill you in on my secret of success later."

"Well, I'm pretty glad I went too," Cass said. She looked shyly at Mom and Dad. "I've been wondering if I would be into the same things Janette and Lauren are if I had stayed in Tennessee. Seeing how much better life is here, having fun the way I have it—well, I'm really glad things have turned out the way they have."

"It is amazing how God works, isn't it?" Mom finally said, tears bright in her eyes.

"Yeah," Cass said. "I guess you guys were right. God really is working good—even though we can't always see it."

After a few more minutes of catching up, Tabitha excused herself, rinsed her dishes, and headed to the phone. The sooner she talked to Kira, the better she'd feel. She didn't want whatever was going on hanging over her head one second longer than was necessary.

Kira answered the phone on the first ring. "Hello?"

"Hi, it's me." To her surprise, Tabitha realized her heart was pounding.

This is your best friend, she sternly reminded herself. *There's no reason to be nervous.*

Kira's less-than-enthusiastic response didn't help, however. "Oh … hi."

Determined to forge ahead, Tabitha forced herself to sound more cheerful than she felt. "What are you doing today?"

"I don't know." There was a long pause. "Why?"

Nearing the end of her patience, Tabitha clenched her teeth. "Because I want to see you, silly."

"I don't have any plans. I assume you'll be getting together with Micah." Kira's tone was ice cold. "I'll be here when you come over to see him."

The last thread of Tabitha's patience snapped. "I don't know what's going on with you, but I'm going to make you talk to me if it's the last thing I do. Seeing Micah can wait. Right now, nothing's more important to me than getting this situation—whatever it is—worked out with you."

"Oh." Kira was silent for several seconds before haltingly suggesting, "Would you like to meet at Eamon so we can talk?"

Tabitha expelled a whoosh of air she wasn't aware she'd been holding. "That sounds great. I'll be there in 45 minutes. I need to take a shower first. Oh, and Kira?"

"Yes?"

"Tell Micah not to go anywhere, that I'll be coming to

your house as soon as you and I are done talking."

"Consider it done."

Tabitha hung up and slumped against the counter. Now that she and Kira were set to talk, she didn't have the first idea how to prepare herself for the conversation. She remained completely in the dark as to what Kira's problem was.

Oh, well. Tabitha mentally shrugged and glanced quickly up to heaven on her way to her room. *I may not know what's going on, but You do, Lord. Help me to respond the way You'd have me respond to whatever Kira says.*

Tabitha was waiting at Eamon when Kira arrived, late as usual.

"If it isn't the late, great Kira Alexander," Tabitha greeted her.

Kira responded with a scowl. "Don't try to be funny. I'm mad at you, and I'm going to stay mad until we get this thing settled."

Tabitha raised her hands in a gesture of surrender. "Well, okay—you don't have to jump down my throat." She dropped her hands and slipped them into her shorts pockets. "What's bugging you?"

"You're what's bugging me." Too agitated to sit, Kira began pacing the length of the pavilion. "I can't believe that when you left two weeks ago, you actually considered for one second staying with your mother. How could our friendship mean so little to you?"

Taken aback by her question, Tabitha blinked. Of all the possible gripes Kira could have thrown at her, this one hadn't even entered her mind.

"Well?" Kira demanded when Tabitha remained silent. "I'm waiting."

"I ... I don't see the connection between me staying on with Beth and ... our friendship," Tabitha finally stammered.

Kira snorted. "Let me spell it out for you. We've been best friends for eight years. We share everything. You're the sister I never had and, until Cass came along, I was the same thing to you. But you were willing to throw it all away the minute a woman who hasn't seen fit to have anything to do with you for years snapped her fingers. I'm not embarrassed to admit I was hurt. No," she corrected herself, "I was more than hurt. I was devastated. When you boarded that plane two weeks ago, I watched you leave without knowing if you'd be back. Do you have any idea how painful that was?"

Tabitha sank onto the nearest picnic bench and stared at Kira, her mouth agape with astonishment. "I had no idea you felt that way."

"Of course you didn't," blazed Kira. "You never asked. You were so caught up in the drama of your own life that you never stopped to consider anybody else."

Unable to defend herself, Tabitha lowered her head in shame. "What can I say?" she asked in a small voice. "I don't deserve to live."

Kira's scornful sniff brought Tabitha's head back up. "Don't think for one second that acting all sorry is going to let you off the hook. You behaved like a selfish brat in the weeks before your trip. All you thought about was yourself. Nobody else mattered. Micah and I talked about it while we were in Hawaii. He felt as left out as I did."

Tabitha was dismayed to realize she'd upset both of the Alexanders. "Is he still mad at me?"

Irritated, Kira stamped her foot. "We're not talking about you and Micah. We're discussing you and me. Would you please explain to me why you were so willing to chuck your life here to go live with Beth? I mean, if she hadn't turned out to be such a loser, you probably wouldn't be sitting here right now. You'd still be in Oregon with her. And, excuse me for saying so, but I take that personally. You should have had a ton more loyalty to your friends and family, especially your Dad."

Again, Tabitha hung her head. "I know. The only thing I can say in my defense is that I was living in some kind of dream world. It took meeting my mother to bring me to my senses. But I really believe in my heart that I would have come home even if she'd been the most wonderful person in the universe."

"Yeah, right," scoffed Kira.

"No, I mean it." Tabitha tilted her head to peer up at her. "It was one thing to talk about staying in Oregon while I was still here. It was a whole different matter once I was there. By the first night, I was seriously homesick. I missed being warm. I missed Dad and Mom. I missed being able to pick up the phone and talk to you." She shrugged. "Basically, I missed my life."

"You're not just saying that?" Kira eyed her with a mixture of skepticism and hope.

Tabitha nodded. "Cross my heart. I wouldn't have stayed with my mother even I'd wanted to. Everyone and everything I care about is here." She smiled tentatively at Kira. "And you're right at the top of the list."

"The very top?" Kira tried to look stern, but her eyes danced.

"No, Mom and Dad occupy first place, of course." Tabitha's smile widened. "But you're right after them."

Kira stopped pacing and sat down beside her. "Where do Cass and Micah fit in?"

"Well," Tabitha squinted as she thought about it. "I lump Cass in with the folks and Micah in with you."

"Uh-uh, girl." Kira shook her head. "I want my own slot. I don't want to share with my brother." She gave Tabitha a stern look. "And, if you know what's good for you, you'll place me higher than him."

Taking her teasing as a sign that all was right between

them, Tabitha instantly relaxed. "All right, if you insist. You're second." She waited until Kira nodded with satisfaction then added impishly, "But Micah's a close third. A very close third."

"I don't care." Kira gave a breezy wave. "The important thing is he's behind me."

Tabitha waited a few seconds before asking, "So are we okay now? There's nothing else we need to talk about?"

"Are you kidding?" Kira scoffed good-naturedly. "We haven't even gotten around to my trip to Hawaii."

"Can we head back to your house before you start in on that?" There was a pleading note to Tabitha's question. "I'm dying to at least be in the same vicinity as Micah. You have no idea how much I missed him."

Kira made a face. "Oh, yes, I do. You're forgetting I had to put up with two weeks of him moaning and groaning about missing you."

"He moaned and groaned? Really?" Tabitha's expression was pleased. "I like the sound of that."

"Man, the two of you have it bad." Standing, Kira reached down to pull Tabitha to her feet. "Let's go. The last thing I want is for anybody to accuse me of keeping you two lovebirds apart."

CHAPTER 32

A little after Tabitha left to talk to Kira, Cass worked up enough courage to call Logan. To her relief, he was home when she called. He hastily declined her offer to ride over to his house and proposed that they meet at the high school instead. Glad he hadn't flatly refused to see her, Cass instantly agreed. After hanging up, she went out to the porch to tell her parents the plans.

"Why don't you invite him to eat dinner with us?" suggested Mom after giving Cass permission to go. "Dad and I were just saying how much we miss Logan. We didn't see nearly as much of him as we expected while you were gone."

Cass nodded. "I'll do that. Tell Tabitha to ask Micah, and we can turn the evening into a real homecoming celebration."

"I will. Would you like to include Rianne and Kira too?"

"Sounds good to me. I'll talk to Rianne as soon as I can." Cass headed for the back door. "See you later."

Biking to the school, Cass forced herself to think about anything but her upcoming talk with Logan. She savored the warmth of the sun and the sound of the palm fronds clacking in the breeze. She waved to friends and craned her neck to catch glimpses of the ocean between the houses and foliage. Arriving at the school, she congratulated herself for doing a fine job of distracting herself. Unfortunately, all it took was one look at Logan and her hard work immediately went down the drain. Her stomach knotted and her throat tightened, making her wonder if she'd be able to squeeze out a single word.

"Hi," she squeaked, coming to a stop beside Logan.

He reached out to steady Cass' bike and held it as she climbed off. "Hi, yourself." Wheeling the bike to a nearby rack, he parked it next to his. "How are you?"

"Tired," Cass admitted. She brushed back several strands of hair that the wind had pulled loose from her braid. "I'm running on fumes, and I expect to crash any time now."

"Try to warn me so I can catch you. We wouldn't want you hurting yourself."

Heartened by Logan's teasing, Cass moved closer to him. She removed her sunglasses so he could see her eyes as she murmured, "I really missed you."

Logan's expression was a jumble of longing and what looked to Cass like regret. "I missed you too," he finally confessed.

Cass realized it was now or never so she took a deep breath and blurted, "Then why didn't you call me? I waited every day for you to call, but you never did."

"I … I …" A flush worked its way up Logan's neck to stain his cheeks, and he swallowed hard. "It just didn't work out. Sorry."

"You don't have to apologize. I mean—you wanted to call, didn't you?" Cass gazed anxiously at him.

Logan responded immediately with a vigorous nod. "More than you'll ever know."

"Did your parents decide you couldn't after all?" asked Cass.

Logan stiffened. "Something like that."

Cass wasn't about to let him get away with such a vague reply. "What does that mean? Either they changed their minds or you did. Which is it?"

Logan's jaw clenched a few times before he finally spoke. "I wanted more than anything to call you so let's just leave it at that, okay?"

"No, it's not okay." Her chin thrust forward, Cass propped her hands on her hips. "Did I do something to make your parents stop liking me? Is your family having money problems? What?"

Logan was quiet for so long that Cass began to think he wasn't going to answer her. When he did, she strained to hear him.

"As far as I know, my parents' feelings for you haven't changed. They never told me not to call you. I just … didn't."

Cass threw her hands up in the air. "Then what in the world is going on? You won't give me a straight answer about not calling. At the airport this morning, you acted like you'd rather be anywhere but there. Is this your way of telling me you want to break up?"

Her heart dropped to her feet when he didn't say anything for several seconds. *So this is how it ends,* she thought sadly.

Logan suddenly reached out and took Cass' hands in his. Peering intently into her eyes, he replied, "You're going to have to trust me. I don't want to break up, but it might be best if we didn't see each other for a while. I need time to sort through some things. There's a—" he hesitated for a few seconds, "—situation in my family, and I don't want to drag you into it."

"Can't you even tell me what it is?" Cass clutched Logan's hands, her whole body suddenly numb.

"No. I'm sorry." Logan looked as anguished as Cass felt.

"This is it then?" A tremendous weight seemed to be crushing Cass' chest, and she found it difficult to breathe. "We don't ... talk ... or call or ... anything?"

"It won't be forever." Logan's attempt at reassurance was less than convincing. "Just until I get things figured out at home."

Confused, hurt, and angry, Cass snatched her hands out of his. "You know what I think?" she demanded, willing herself not to cry in front of him. "This is a brush off. There's no situation in your family. You want out of our relationship, and you've come up with this story about a problem that you conveniently can't talk about as your excuse to call it quits. So, fine. You don't want us to see each other for a while? Great. I won't have any problem finding lots of other ways to occupy my time."

"Cass—"

Logan extended his hand to her, but she moved out of reach. "Don't touch me. I'm leaving. You want me to trust you, but you don't trust me enough to level with me. Until you're ready to tell me the truth, I don't have anything to say to you."

Stalking to the rack, she jerked her bike out of its slot and prepared to get on. Logan appeared in front of her, blocking her way.

"Cass," he tried again.

"Move," she ordered tersely.

When he stood his ground, Cass wrenched the handlebars to the right, hopped on the bike, and took off at breakneck speed.

She met Tabitha and Kira as they were coming out of the Alexander's driveway. She would have passed them by with only a wave, but Tabitha flagged her down.

"What are you doing? Why aren't you with Logan?"

Cass' face hardened at the mention of his name. Knowing it would soon be all over the island, she took a deep breath and replied in a rush, "I'm not with Logan because he decided we shouldn't see each other for a while."

"What? Why?" Tabitha and Kira cried in unison.

Shrugging, Cass smiled bitterly. "I don't know. You'll have to ask him. He never gave me a reason that made sense."

"I don't believe this." Kira covered her mouth and gazed at Cass, her expression brimming with sympathy.

"That makes two of us."

"Three," Tabitha chimed in. "Do you want us to talk to him?"

Cass hesitated before shaking her head. "I doubt it would do any good. He's in a weird mood. He said something's going on with his family, but he can't tell me what it is." She snorted, the sound more sad than scornful. "I'm pretty sure I know, though. He's tired of me, but he doesn't have the nerve to tell me to my face. So he's letting me down easy. Only—" her voice faltered, so she cleared her throat to try again. "It's not easy. It really hurts."

"I'm going straight home and telling Micah to talk to him. He'll get to the bottom of this." Kira raised her hand when Cass started to protest. "I don't care what you say. I'm doing it, and that's that."

"Good idea," Tabitha said. "You talk to Micah while I ride home with Cass. Call us after Micah's had a chance to talk to Logan, and we'll figure out what to do next."

"But you had plans," Cass objected, although weakly. "I don't want to ruin your afternoon."

Tabitha dismissed her concern with a flap of her hand. "Our plans can wait. This is more important. Come on." She motioned in the general vicinity of their house. "Let's get you home so we can put our heads together and come up with a strategy for how to deal with this."

"What kind of strategy?" Cass asked, confused.

"A strategy for how to get away with the perfect murder if Micah isn't able to talk some sense into Logan," Kira answered grimly for Tabitha.

Cass figured she was joking, but she wasn't sure. "Let's hope it doesn't come to that." She nodded to Tabitha. "All right, let's go. I need to call Rianne anyway."

After promising to call as soon as she knew something, Kira took off in one direction while Cass and Tabitha headed in the other. They pedaled in silence for several seconds, then Tabitha glanced over at her stepsister.

"How are you doing?"

Cass shook her head in bewilderment. "I don't know. Part of me wants to scream. Another part wants to cry. Still another part would like to smash something. All I know for sure is that it's the worst feeling I've ever had."

"Oh, Cass," Tabitha said, then stopped. "Look, I don't know what to tell you, but I'm sure God has a plan for bringing some kind of good out of this. Even though I don't have the foggiest idea of what that might be," she admitted.

Cass managed a wan smile. "Thanks. I'll try to remember that." She sighed. "This is one rotten homecoming."

"Yeah," agreed Tabitha, adding, "But it could be worse. It could be happening while we were still halfway around the world. At least we're home."

"And together," Cass put in. "I appreciate you giving up your afternoon to be with me."

"I wouldn't have it any other way," Tabitha declared stoutly. "In case you haven't figured it out yet, we're in this together. And I don't just mean the situation with Logan. I mean life. We're a team, Sis. Till death do us part."

"The sister team of Devane and Spencer." Cass nodded with satisfaction. "I like it."

"Hey!" protested Tabitha. "Shouldn't that be Spencer and Devane?"

"Whatever." For the first time since her talk with Logan, Cass laughed. "Maybe we should rename ourselves the battling Devane-Spencer sisters."

"And our motto could be, 'we fight, but we still love each other.' "

Cass' eyes abruptly filled with tears. "Sounds good," she murmured. "Even better, it's true."

"One hundred percent true."

Cass flashed Tabitha a grateful smile. "You know what the past two weeks have taught me? That, along with God and the folks, I couldn't make it without you."

"We've come a long way since last summer, haven't we?" Tabitha let go of the handlebars and flung her arms wide as if to embrace the world. "We still have a long way to go, especially since stuff like this problem with Logan keeps cropping up. But, together, we can handle anything."

"You'd better believe it. I know I do. With all my heart."

Side by side, they made their way home, ready to face head-on whatever life had in store for them.